# Pa... and the Coveters

# II

## LEE M. SAPP

Bishop McKinley & Dr. Dorothy Young

— God's Continued Blessings

*[signature]*

3/31/14

**Pastor June and the Righteous, Book I**

*Christian Fiction for Grown Folk*

"I am still thinking about Pastor June. I am re-reading my book. Hats off to you Rev. Lee!" **Marian Bacon White, Riviera Beach, Florida**

"Awesome book!! I was unable to put it down and was able to complete the book in one day. Looking forward to reading your sequel!"
**Rev. Kathryn E. Brown-Davis, Dayton, Ohio**

"It is so good to read a great story so centered on God, I can't say enough about Pastor June & The Righteous! In Christian Love."
**Rev. Jacquie Wilson, Nashville, Tennessee**

"This story had so many elements, romance, family, spirituality, mystery, religion. Your ability to interweave is masterful! Wow, girl! Excellent x2!! Now, when will "The Coveters" be finished?? You have me on the hook!!!"
**Rev. Renita Lamkin, St. Louis, Missouri**

"Recommend this book for an enjoyable read that includes suspense, mystery and romance while the main character still remains a Christian. Really enjoyed it. I give it five stars!!" (Amazon.com Review) **Iris Etheridge, Mangonia Park, Florida**

"In a day when we have so many books of which to choose. It is exciting and rewarding to read one that holds your attention and is rewarding as well. Sapp has done both. This is one to put on your shelf." **Rev. Anne Henning Byfield, Presiding Elder North District Indiana Conference**

# THE COVETERS

ISBN: 0615949002

ISBN-13: 9780615949000

To the people who expressed their enjoyment of the first book in the series, the *Righteous*. To my family and friends who offered countless encouragement and sacrificed time with me for this effort. Last but certainly not least, my God who often strengthened me in my seasons of weakness.

Mary Sapp, Forrest Sapp, the Saplings, Marian Bacon White, Grant Chapel AME Church, Lake Worth, Florida, St. Paul AME Church, West Palm Beach, Florida, the Shepherd's Heart Ministry, Royal Palm Beach, Florida, the Rev. Barbara Baccus, the Rev. Benjamin McKinney.

The author acknowledges the following persons for their contributions to this work via early reviews, advice, inspiration, and encouragement in the valley.

Forrest Sapp, Betty Rose Harvin, Remar Harvin, Marian Bacon White, Sharon Thomas-Ellison, Mr. Oscar Baccus, the Rev. Barbara Baccus, and Lavette Robinson.

# 1

*"Yet your eyes and your heart are for nothing but your **cove**tousness, for shedding innocent blood, and practicing oppression and violence."* ~Jeremiah 22:17

Detective Mario Grimes was enjoying breakfast with his new wife, Bettina, when he was called to go onto a crime scene in the city of Lake Worth, Florida. Grimes was just finishing his meal of smothered chicken livers and grits and had just another bite or two left of his buttermilk biscuit when the text came in.

"You have me so spoiled, Bettina. How can anybody expect me to want to go to work after a meal like this? Now I'm ready to go back to bed," Mario said while smiling at Bettina.

"Well, we promised to share at least three meals a week together and with your hours you never know when that meal's going to be," Bettina said.

It was the second marriage for them both. Bettina was beginning to get used to her new husband leaving her at any time of the day or night. She also got late night work calls but not as often as her husband did. They agreed to share as many alone moments together as they could, whenever they could. Mario had been advised by his good friend, Pastor June, to embrace as many of these small moments as possible and not to allow the business of busyness to interfere with their new marriage.

This morning Mario and Bettina shared the labor of loading the dishwasher and then they both left the house at the same time. They gave each other a final kiss goodbye and departed the house in their individual vehicles.

Mario was the last one on the crime scene. Six months ago he would have been the first one on scene but, since he married Bettina, he decided some things were just more important than being the perfectionist he'd always been.

"Good morning, what we got this time, Detective Wright?" Mario asked.

"Good morning. Nice of you to show up, Grimes. Well, we got something a little different today. Black male, maybe late twenties, early thirties," Wright said.

"That's it? I'm waiting to hear what's different," Mario said.

As Detective Wright was about to answer, Officer Dees met the two detectives and escorted them to the car where the victim's body was.

"Far as we can tell it looks like he was trying to get out of his car for something. Must have been something mighty important because his car was in park but the engine was still running when we got here and the car is in the middle of the street," Dees said.

Mario slowly walked around the victim's car with his left hand in his pants pocket, shaking his loose change as he always did when he assessed a crime scene. He agreed with Dees because the victim had one leg outside of the car. Mario also noticed that both the driver's side and the passenger side doors were left open. The victim's body lay back draped over the center gear shift, leaving his head propped up across the passenger seat and hanging just underneath the glove compartment. Mario could see that the victim bled profusely. There was so much blood; he couldn't tell where the victim's wound was.

"His throat was slit, Mario, that's why there's so much blood. Somebody sliced right through his carotid artery," Cowboy Joe said as he approached Mario.

"That should have taken some time right?" Mario asked.

"Depends on how good the person doing the cutting was. Wouldn't have taken much time if the person had good precision but I'll be able to tell you more once I get him back to the morgue and clean up the wound. Liver temp puts the TOD about five hours ago," Cowboy Joe said.

"Did you find the weapon? Mario asked Dees.

"Not yet. There are at least two storm drains on both sides of the street, the perp could have easily thrown the knife or whatever in either one and there was a big rain last night so it might be on its way to Lake Okeechobee by now. We just don't know, and it looks like the car was wiped clean. Right now we're waiting till Joe moves the body out so we can tow the car in and look for prints on the inside," Dees said loudly so that Cowboy Joe would overhear.

"Well do you have an I.D. for the vic yet, did you run the plate?" Mario asked.

"We're working on it. The car came back registered

to a Randy Thomas but when we contacted him he said he sold the car to a lady several months ago. She paid him in cash and he signed over the title but the new owner never registered the title with the State, it's still in the original owner's name," Dees replied.

"Does the vic have any ID on him?" Mario asked.

"There was no wallet, nothing at all on him when Cowboy Joe checked his pants pocket. We weren't able to get into the glove compartment because his head landed so close to it. We're waiting for Cowboy Joe to finish up and remove the vic so we can continue to search the car," Wright said, again loudly for Cowboy Joe to hear.

"All right, all right we're moving him now. Just wanted to make sure I got as many pictures of his position as possible," Cowboy Joe said.

As Cowboy Joe's staff began loading the victim into the morgue's van, Mario's cell began to vibrate.

"This is Grimes."

"Hi honey. Listen where are you? You forgot your lunch," Bettina said.

"Really? I could have sworn I picked it up. I'm in Lake Worth by the cemetery on 12th."

"Wonderful, I'm on my way to the Lantana office; I can be there in five minutes to drop it off."

Mario smiled to himself as he thought about his wife dropping off his lunch. Before they were married, it had been a very long time since he'd had the affectionate care of a woman. He spotted her car pulling up to the corner just as the tow truck was hooking onto the victim's car.

"Hey what happened to Dale's car, is he all right?" Bettina asked.

"Dale? Who's Dale?" Mario asked.

"You know Dale, he goes to our church. That's his car," she said.

"This is Dale's car? Are you sure?" he asked.

"Yes, because Toni bought it for him a couple of months ago and she showed it to me. I remember because of that bumper sticker under the driver's door handle. It's in such an odd place so we peeled it back because it's just tacky and we discovered that it was there to cover up a hole. It's his work vehicle. Where is he? Did he have to go to the hospital?" Bettina asked.

Bettina peeked inside the car as it was being lifted onto the tow truck and she saw the blood. Mario lowered his head and reached out for his wife.

"No, Mario, no. Are you sure it was him?" she asked.

"No, I'm not. I mean we found a dead man in this car but I didn't recognize him. I guess his face could have been distorted or something. But look are you certain that this is his car?" Mario said.

"Yes I'm sure of it. You don't remember him at all do you? He's married to Toni."

"Toni?" Mario asked.

"May Bell's daughter, Toni," Bettina said

"May Bell? My old housekeeper?"

"Yes. I've got to call Toni." She took out her cell phone and dialed the number.

"My God, I didn't realize she was -- I guess I should have, she is around the same age as Cady," Mario said.

After a couple of seconds Mario began shushing everyone.

"Hey everybody quiet, turn that off. Listen," he said.

The sound of a cell phone's factory ringtone could

be heard. Everyone stopped moving and making noise as they turned towards the tow truck which at the direction of Mario had stopped pulling the victim's car. Mario and Wright both moved towards the victim's vehicle but the ringing stopped.

Wright looked back at Bettina and said, "Call it again," and she did.

They spotted the cell phone sticking out about an inch under the passenger seat of the victim's car.

Wright reached in the car with a gloved hand and bagged it. "So we need to look for both Dale and his wife Toni Jacobs."

Bettina placed her hand to her mouth and slowly walked up to her husband laying her head against his chest.

"I'm sorry, sweetie. Are you going to be alright? Maybe you should call in today," Mario said.

"No I'll be all right. Sitting at home would be worse," Bettina said.

"Maybe you'd better get going to work then and please try not to be too upset. And don't say anything to anybody until we've confirmed his I.D. okay?"

Bettina nodded as Mario walked her back to her car. "Are you going to call her mother?" Bettina asked.

"Not until I can positively ID the victim. For all we know he had already dropped Toni off somewhere and she forgot her phone," Mario said.

He knew that the scenario he gave to Bettina was highly unlikely. Mario knew in his gut that based on how the victim was positioned and the fact that the passenger door was also left open, coupled with the enormous amount of blood loss, that it was definitely not an accident. It all indicated to him that he was dealing with somebody who had an emotional connection and that was very different than a random killing and much more dangerous.

Mario tried to remember Toni. Her mother, May Bell became his housekeeper after his first wife finally lost her battle with a terminal illness and died. May Bell became more than a housekeeper; she was a surrogate mother to his daughters. She was really the one who raised them. They went to her whenever they were hurt or needed something for school.

Detective Grimes remembered very little about May Bell's daughter Toni except that she always seemed very angry. He remembered when May Bell asked if she could use his home address to ensure that Toni went to the better of the public schools located within his school district. He didn't see the harm as long as May Bell was going to be responsible for getting her to and from school. But, there were a few occasions where she had to ride the school bus home with Cady and Crystal because there was no cab fare to get her back across town. At those times, Toni would help her mother clean Mario's house and then go home with her mother on the city bus.

As Mario watched his new wife drive off, he thought about her big heart and decided he would need to brace her for the bad news that he knew would be coming. As Bettina headed to work, she couldn't help but be worried for Toni. She didn't really know Toni's husband Dale very well but she had been mentoring Toni for the last two years, ever since she joined the church. Toni's mother had been a long time member of New Hope and, although Toni grew up there, she had never officially joined the church. After she graduated from high school, she stopped coming to church altogether. But what disturbed Bettina most was that Toni and Dale recently had their first child, a daughter they named Daleena, after Dale. Bettina was greatly saddened that Toni was now a widow and that her baby girl would grow up fatherless. Bettina got so upset she pulled off to the shoulder of the road so she could pray.

# 2

*I have **covet**ed no one's silver or gold or apparel.* ~Acts 21:33

"Mommy! MOM-MY!" June could hear Rosie yelling for her from downstairs. A four month pregnant June rolled out of bed to descend the staircase.

June had always dreamed that she would be like Pricilla Presley, conceiving on her wedding night but that didn't happen. She did conceive on her honeymoon which took place several months after her wedding night.

Pastor June Harris was the pastor of St. Mark Church and had been married for a year to the newly appointed Supervising Elder, the Reverend Dr. Brice Howard. They discovered that because of her age, conception would require scientific help and after two rounds of drugs to stimulate her ovaries, she became pregnant. When she finally saw the positive pregnancy test, it was the happiest day of her life second to her wedding day. Her husband Brice treated her like porcelain from the very moment they learned about the pregnancy. He wouldn't let her do anything. It was frustrating for someone like June who was very independent. And, although she was madly in love with her new husband and Rosie, she frequently found herself missing her solitude. Being an only child she soon realized after her wedding and welcoming Rosie into their home, that she didn't really share well.

Prior to the success of her fertility treatments, she met and fell in love with seven year old Rosie. June thought that Rosie was absolutely beautiful. She had a dark complexion and the most beautiful and biggest eyes June had ever seen. Her smile always lit up the room. She was a chunky little girl with a bright spirit and happy disposition.

June had officially requested to be taken off the list of volunteer clergy who rode with the Sherriff's Office to do notifications, but the people in the community continued to request her so she told them to put her back on the rotation.

It was on one such notification nearly a year ago that she met Rosie. She was accompanying the Sherriff's Office to do a notification at Rosie's grandmother's home. Rosie's mother had been found dead of an overdose in a seedy part of town. She had been dead for about a week according to Cowboy Joe, the County Medical Examiner. June stayed in touch with the grandmother and extended services from St. Mark Church to her such as hot meals and regular visitations from the hospitality ministry to help her keep her house in order. Shortly though the grandmother died in her sleep leaving Rosie orphaned.

Bettina Grimes, a close friend of June's and the wife of her ex-detective partner explained the situation to June the day after the notification in her office within the Foster Care Unit. "Until we can locate a relative, June, she'll have to go into foster care," Bettina said.

"Bettina, she can't go with strangers. This was a very traumatic experience for her. I can only imagine what I would be like if I'd lost Momma May at such an early age. I've bonded with her. I've had her over to my home on several occasions so the grandmother could have a break. I truly do love this kid. There must be some other alternative. You know that I know what these kids go through in foster care," June said.

"June, there isn't a person in this department who would question your fitness as a parent, if you're saying that you are interested in fostering Rosie," Bettina said.

"Well, I was actually just trying to get you to light a fire under somebody to find her family," June said with a smile. "But I guess you heard my heart and not my words. Okay let me run it by Brice and I'll get back to you as soon as possible."

Rosie was in June's home by that afternoon and she immediately began calling her "Mommy." They had to wait until the time ran out on finding a family member before June and Brice could officially adopt her.

"Rosie, honey, what did Daddy say about yelling in the house? Brice asked. "That's what we have intercoms for."

"But Daddy, Mommy didn't pack my lunch right. I said I wanted peanut butter and jelly and cookies. She put carrots and tuna fish in here!" Rosie exclaimed.

By that time June had finally made it down the stairs. Her baby bump forced her to wobble as she walked.

"Rosie, we talked about this. Your doctor says we need to watch your weight, darlin'. Mommy wants you to be healthy. Remember how the doctor said you need to eat healthier because you're in danger of developing childhood diabetes. We have to watch your weight."

Rosie began to pout and June simply could not deny her anything.

"Tell you what we'll do. After school we'll go shopping to see if we can find foods that you like that are sugar-free okay?" June asked.

"You promise?" Rosie asked.

"I promise," said June.

"Okay, whose turn is it?" Brice asked.

"It's my turn, Daddy," Rosie said.

June, Rosie and Brice stood in the breakfast area of the kitchen forming a circle and holding hands.

"Okay, honey, go ahead," Brice said.

"Let's pray --" Rosie began to say.

"Let us pray," June corrected.

"Let us pray," Rosie repeated and then continued. "God, thank you for our yesterday. We hope today will be even better. Please bless Mommy and Daddy and Ms. Myrtle and Suzie and me being best friends and Ms. Harvey my teacher to have a great day. Amen."

"Amen," they all said together.

"Mommy, your turn for the scripture," Rosie said.

"Oh yeah, okay. Ummm, 'This is the day that the Lord has made. Let us rejoice and be glad in it," June said.

After June and Brice dropped Rosie off at school, they headed for St. Mark Church. Brice vowed to drive June to work every day now that she was pregnant. And whenever he had to go out of town and June could not accompany him, he sent for someone to drive her around. Her surrogate mother, the Reverend Bella Grant, who everyone called Billie, loved to gloat about the fact that June had to be driven around because Billie was 77-years-old and hadn't been able to drive herself for some time. In the past, June had always teased her about the drivers she chose. Billie would only allow single, good looking young men to drive her around because Billie was a huge flirt.

During the drive to the church June continued feeling that something was not quite right. She decided to share this news with her husband.

"Honey, something bad has happened or is going to happen and I'm worried," June said.

"Are you sure it's not hormones? I know you're concerned about all the warnings and testing we've had to endure because of your age with this pregnancy but I believe God will give us favor like He always has," Brice said.

"No, I don't feel worried about the baby or Rosie or you. It's something else. I can feel it in my soul," June said.

"Well, did you call Billie? You know she has a gift about these sorts of things," Brice said.

"No, I didn't. I think deep down, I don't really want to know," June admitted.

When June finally got to her office, she was met by Myrtle with a hot cup of tea.

"I hate that I can't have coffee," June said.

"Oh it's not for much longer," Myrtle said.

June just glared at her.

"Oh, you're a mean prego for sure," Myrtle teased.

"I'm working on it. What's today look like, Myrtle?" June asked.

"Well, you have a premarital counseling session after lunch, just paper work to sign this morning though. You might be able to leave by 2:00," Myrtle said.

"Now you know I'm not going to do that. What if

somebody comes in for prayer or counseling? We have my office hours posted on everything. I can't do that," June said.

"That's what you got Associate Ministers for," Myrtle said.

June had to acknowledge that she was trying to work on her control issues and delegate more work to her ministerial staff.

"Okay, call Reverend Linda to come in at 2:00," June finally relented.

"Good," Myrtle said.

Just then June's office phone rang. "Junie, what's going on? I feel that your heart is heavy," Billie said on the other end.

"I am always amazed at how you keep doing that. Every single time I'm going through something you know about it," June said.

"Well, tell me what it is and hurry up, I got a new driver I need to take out to lunch and get to know better," Billie said followed by her loud raspy laugh.

"You're still a hot mess," June said.

"I know I am. I hope you're not worried about the baby, because I already know he's going to be all right," Billie said.

"He?" June asked.

"Oops. I didn't mean to let that slip. Yep, Junie, y'all are having a boy I just know it," Billie said.

The Reverend Billie Grant was beyond intuitive she was downright prophetic. And from what June could recall, she had never been wrong.

"Wow, okay. I'm going to keep that bit of news to myself if you don't mind. Brice is always surprising me; I want to surprise him for once," June said.

"Well, Junie, I got to go now but know that you and yours is alright. I'll let you know if I pick up on whatever it is outside of that. Bye now, I got to get to this tall dark and -- well he is kind of short but most definitely handsome," Billie said while laughing her raspy laugh and she hung up the phone.

Pastor June sat back in her chair, amazed at how quickly her feet had become swollen. As she rubbed her baby bump she began to pray, "God, I surely do thank you for putting it in Billie's heart to move over here so she can be close to me and help me with this baby. I know that you know that I'm really missing my Momma May right now."

Momma May was Pastor June's mother. She wasn't her birth mother but she raised her as if she was her very own flesh and blood. She had been the owner of a local bar frequented by prostitutes in a tiny town called Belle Glade in Florida. One of the prostitutes literally gave June to Momma May to raise as her own because she had gotten into the habit of being a maternal figure to them all. Momma May sold the bar the same week and purchased a small house where she raised June. She lived for the joy of mothering right up until the day she died.

Just then Myrtle came through the office door. "Pastor, Bettina called while you were on the phone with Billie. She said you have to get over to their house right away there's some kind of emergency," Myrtle said.

"I knew it. I knew it. I knew something bad was going to happen today. What is it about?" June asked.

"She wouldn't say but she was crying and carrying on something awful. I could hear Detective Grimes yelling at her in the background. He kept saying, 'Call June, call June."

June picked up the phone to call her husband but quickly put the receiver back down. She thought better of it. She knew that he would be upset that she didn't call him but she also knew that whatever was going on, he would be too protective to let her get involved without a fuss.

"Myrtle, is there anyone who can drive me over there?" June asked.

"Bettina said they sending that white girl detective over here to pick you up right now," Myrtle said.

"You mean Detective Wright?" June corrected Myrtle.

"Yeah, her," Myrtle said.

June made her way to the front of the church just as Detective Wright pulled into the parking lot.

"What's going on, Sylvia?" June asked as she got into the car.

"Ma'am, all I know is it's got something to do with Grimes' kids," Wright said.

"Oh no, okay lets go. Hit the sirens and get me there in Star Trek time," June said.

On the ride over, June tried to keep herself calm. Mario and June had been police detectives together in Sarasota County, which is on the opposite side of Florida before June was called by God to serve in the ministry. Mario was also June's first love many years ago and they were meant to be married. But instead of marrying June, Mario succumbed to pressure from his parents who felt that she was beneath him. According to his parents, she was a mutt with no social standing. He left her at the altar without so much as a telephone call and married the woman that his parents approved of. His first wife died ten years later, leaving him alone to raise their two little girls on his own.

June and Mario had since worked out their differences and remained close friends. She was even "Best Woman" at his recent wedding to her good friend Bettina. So if something was hurting him, she knew that it would hurt her too.

Mario met them in the front yard of his home as they were driving up.

"June, somebody took my girls. The sons of --" Mario said.

"What? Who are you talking about?" June asked as she struggled to exit the car.

Bettina, his wife interjected, "We don't know who, June. Something happened this morning and I took off work early. When I came home and checked the answering machine, there was a message from some guy that said they had Cady and Crystal. He wants like six million dollars or he will kill them both. I don't know what would make them think we have that kind of money."

"Are you sure they have them? Did you call the college?" June asked Mario, essentially ignoring Bettina.

"Yes, I called the college. They didn't even know that Cady wasn't there. Her roommate's been off campus since yesterday morning and she said she hasn't heard from Cady either," he said.

"Well then maybe it's a hoax, Mario," June said.

"They're not answering their cell phones, June. I've called them each a dozen times. Even if they don't feel like talking to me they would always text me or something. I'm not getting any response from either of them. This is for real, June!" Mario said.

Detective Mario Grimes was the only child of very wealthy and successful parents. He had access to millions of dollars though his lifestyle certainly did not reflect it. The problem that June was having was that no one, not even his current wife, absolutely no one on this side of the state of Florida knew about his wealth.

They entered the house where Bettina insisted that June sit down and Mario frantically paced the living room floor.

"How could they possibly know about your money?" June asked.

"What money?" Bettina asked.

"I don't know how they know about the money. Nobody really knows except you and my parents, Bettina doesn't even know. My kids don't know. I didn't want them to live like I did; I wanted them to have normal lives. I don't know what to do, June. The college said it's too soon to declare Cady missing and that this whole thing was most likely a prank. I don't know where Crystal is but I've had a bad feeling all day. Now, if I go over to the campus I might miss the next phone call," Mario said.

"Is somebody going to tell me what is really going on here?" Bettina asked angrily.

"Bettina, please give us a minute," June said.

Bettina angrily crossed her arms over her chest but stayed silent.

"First of all, calm down Mario, we're going to figure this out. Now can you play the recording back again? I'd like to hear exactly what the caller said," June said.

# 3

*'You shall not **covet** your neighbor's wife; and you shall not desire your neighbor's house, his field, his male servant, his female servant, his ox, his donkey, or anything that is your neighbor's.*
~Deuteronomy 5:21

## Two Months Earlier

Two months earlier, Jackson Davis Bonnen III sat on the window sill in the attic of his parent's home, blowing smoke through the open window as he attempted to get high from an old joint he found in the sock drawer of his boyhood bedroom. Instead of getting a high, he only got a headache. Jackson stomped the joint out with his foot and threw the remainder of the joint out of the window into his mother's flower bed two stories below. He thought to himself, *Nothing ever goes right for me. I can't even get high without it going wrong.*

Jackson had recently moved back into his parent's home after flunking out of his third attempt at college. His father, Jackson Davis Bonnen II, finally gave up on his son. Jackson's college career consisted of flunking out of most of his classes primarily because of his lack of attendance and spending way too much time frivolously spending his father's money.

Jackson was a spoiled rich kid. His father was a CPA whose office was based in Miami's South Beach, a place where many famous and wealthy people lived. His business catered to South Beach's rich and famous, recording artists, professional athletes, actors and actresses. But Jackson's mother, Nedra, did not want to live in South Beach so they lived in Boca Raton. It was a slower pace and much quieter.

Jackson's father decided to cut him off financially when he all but quit school and was living it up in the condo that he leased on his son's behalf. Jackson the father showed up one day during lunch time last month only to discover that his son was still in bed asleep on a Wednesday afternoon, instead of being in class. The huge condo was trashed. There were holes in the walls, the sink was filled with dishes that looked as though they had been there for weeks, some even had mold growing on them.

His father stood in the midst of his son's messy room and realized that he had never made his son work for anything. He and his wife handed him everything and his son's current lazy, self entitled lifestyle was the consequence of spoiling their only child rotten. Jackson the son, all but told his father that he shouldn't have to work at all. That's when the father knew that he had to cut his son off financially and force him to become a man.

Jackson Davis Bonnen II was a self made man. His own father had been a barber and, even though his father owned his own business, they were still very poor. He thought about his childhood as he stood over his sleeping son in the messy condo, remembering how his father gambled away practically every cent he ever made. His mother would come to the barber shop weekly to collect cash from the cash register that she would then slip into her bra and at night, she literally slept with the cash balled up in her fist in order to keep his father from gambling it away.

Jackson the Father realized that he had managed to raise a son that was even worse than his father. At least his father went to work every day. He quietly left the condo without waking his son. When he returned to his office that afternoon, he contacted the landlord of the condo and canceled the lease on his son's beachfront dwelling. He then had all the utilities turned off; the internet, the electricity, the cable and he also turned off his son's cell phone. By that evening his son discovered from his landlord that he was being cut off financially and that if he wanted to remain living there he would need to come up with fifty five hundred dollars within the next two weeks to make next month's rent plus security. The son made a bee line for his father's office.

"Where will I go? What am I supposed to do now, Dad?" Jackson the son shouted to his father.

"You can move back home but only for thirty days. After that, what you do is up to you. If you were wise you would find a job and save your money," his father said.

"You expect me to move back home like some little kid?"

"I expected a lot from you boy, and you continue to fail. Now I don't have any expectations of you at all but I can tell you one thing, whatever you decide to do with your life from this moment on, will be without my financial support."

Jackson the son punched the wall of his parent's attic as he recalled that conversation with his father almost a month ago. His parents did not know that he also now had a son. He really used most of the money he received from his father to keep his son's momma at bay and happy. Now she was threatening to sue him for child support. Jackson knew that any job he could get would not pay enough to keep her in the ghetto heaven lifestyle that she had become accustomed to with his financial support.

He never visited his baby boy; he just sent his baby's momma money. He didn't see his baby as his son but rather as his problem. He decided to dig around the attic to see what he could pawn in order to keep her from filing the suit. He only had a couple of days left before he had to move out of his parent's home.

"What is that god awful smell, Jackson?" He heard his mother ask as she approached the landing of the stairs into the attic.

"Bug spray, Momma. I saw a lot of silverfish up here," Jackson said.

"Why are you going through my boxes, Son?" she asked.

"I'm just organizing them while I look for some of my old stuff," he said.

"Oh. Okay. Well, what are your plans today? Do you have any interviews lined up? That would make your father very happy," she said.

"Yeah, Momma, sure. I have some things planned," he said.

Jackson thought to himself, *I plan to go over to see Two Touch so I can get high for real, that's the only plan I have for today.*

Nedra knew that her son had no plans. She was in complete denial about her son's character at least out loud. She was ashamed of the way he turned out. Especially since all of her friend's children were off in Ivy league schools preparing to graduate, but not her son. Her son was now living back at home stinking up her attic with marijuana cigarettes. She didn't know what she had to do but she knew something had to be done so that she could appease her husband and get her son back on the right track, even if only for appearance sake.

*He **covets** greedily all day long, But the righteous gives and does not spare.* ~Proverbs 21:26

Two Touch slammed the game controller on the edge of his bed out of frustration. He had to pause the game several times because his little brother and sister continued to argue and fight all afternoon. Babysitting was the agreement he made with his mother. He could continue living with her in her starter home as long as he was home to baby sit for her while she worked. Two Touch, whose given name was Demetrius was nick named Two Touch because his obsessive compulsive disorder dictated that he touch everything twice. Two Touch's mother was exactly 16 years older than he was but 15 years after he was born she met and married her husband, a serviceman currently on tour overseas. They had twins, his little sister, and brother so they were much younger than he was.

His mother was a hard worker and worked three jobs for as many years in order to come up with the down payment for a first time homeowners program and she was very proud of her little house. She looked forward to the weekends just so that she could clean and keep her yard up. Two Touch had issues other than his OCD like chronic asthma, epilepsy, and a weak heart. He was on disability but he didn't make enough to live on his own and his mother didn't believe that he was emotionally capable to live independently. So their arrangement was a win-win for them both.

While Two Touch was busy chastising his siblings, the door bell rang.

"Oh, great. Who is this now?" Two Touch said out loud.

"Hey man, open the damn door!" Jackson shouted from the other side of the door.

Two Touch rolled his eyes and stood still with his hand on his hip. He didn't really care much for Jackson but Jackson paid him well for his dope, at least he used to. Jackson told Two Touch that he was having a cash flow problem and would get him straight later on but now it was going on a month and all Jackson had done was smoke up all of Two Touch's product. Reluctantly, Two Touch opened the door and let Jackson inside.

"Man, what took you so long? Do you know how hot it is out there? It's like 80 degrees!" Jackson said as he threw himself down on the couch.

"I didn't hear you. I'm babysitting, Man. You have no idea how much noise these kids can make," Two Touch said.

Two Touch was okay with hanging out with Jackson every now and then but since Jackson moved back home with his parents he'd constantly been coming over to visit him. Two Touch found Jackson to be a soft bully but he never confused him with being his genuine friend. He knew that he was just somebody that Jackson would use until he no longer needed him. Two Touch was quickly growing tired of their pretend friendship.

"Man, I got to make some quick money. You got any ideas?" Jackson asked.

"You? I thought you was Richie Rich?" Two Touch said.

"Man my dad is tripping. He cut me off, won't give me a dime. And you know I got to keep Lakesha quiet about things. Come on man, I know you got some hustle you can let me in on," Jackson said.

"You looking at my hustle. I keep my mom's kids and she let me stay here rent free. I sell a little weed but that's about it," Two Touch said while instantly thinking *and you've already smoked up most of my product.*

Then he spoke before thinking "Burger King is hiring" and regretted it instantly.

"Burger King? Man please. I ain't working nowhere. I have a trust fund. I just need enough money to hire a lawyer to get my trust money released," Jackson said.

"It's so easy for y'all Richie Rich kids. I can't work but if I could, I would love to work and earn my own way," Two Touch said.

"That's cause you a chump. What other rich kids would you know anyway?" Jackson asked laughing.

"Hey I know plenty. I went to high school with these sisters and their people was loaded. I remember when we went on our senior field trip to Disney World in Orlando. A bunch of us skipped out of the park and went to their grandparent's house. It was the biggest house I ever seen. It was a mansion; it was way bigger than four of your parents house put together," Two Touch said.

"Black girls? I don't remember nobody like that," Jackson said.

"Well you were in that private school by the time they left private school to come to public school. Yeah, I only remember one of them really well. She was the only nice one but they was real fine too, I remember that," Two Touch said.

"You remember their names?" Jackson asked.

"Why? You think you gon marry one of them and fix your financial situation?" Two Touch said laughing.

"No man, I'm just curious. What's their name?" Jackson asked again.

"Let me see, one was Cassy, Cassidy, something like that. Man, I don't remember but the nice one I'll never forget her cause I had a huge crush on her in high school, her name was Cady, Cady Grimes."

# 5

*A ruler who lacks understanding is a great oppressor, But he who hates **covet**ousness will prolong his days.* ~Proverbs 28:16

On the same day two months earlier June and Brice were at the obstetrician's office for a routine checkup.

"Everything looks great Pastor June. Can't tell the sex of the baby yet," Dr. Khan said.

"We don't care what the gender is, just so happy that everything is good," June said.

"When will you be able to tell the sex of the baby?" Brice asked.

"Well, we're only doing the sonogram this early because of your wife's risk factor but by your next appointment we should be able to tell," Dr. Khan said.

"Okay, I guess we can wait two more weeks, Brice," June said.

"Okay, Sweetie," Brice said as he stroked June's hair.

"But remember no lifting, get plenty of rest. Did you guys drive together this morning?" Dr. Khan asked.

"Yes, Brice won't say it but he thinks I drive too fast so he's been driving me everywhere since we found out about the baby," June said while rolling her eyes.

"Well, I need to tell you that because of your short stature, you probably won't be able to drive for much longer," Dr. Khan said.

"What? Why?" asked June.

"Well when your baby bump gets bigger it will interfere with how close you can get to the steering wheel and eventually you won't be able to touch the pedals," Dr. Khan said.

Brice unsuccessfully tried to stifle his laughter. June glared up at him and rolled her eyes.

"I don't know about that. I mean I've been humoring him, but I don't much like the idea of being dependant on people to get me around," June said to Dr. Khan.

When they left the doctor's office June and Brice discussed how they should start to tell people about their pregnancy.

"I want to tell everybody, I want to shout it from the rooftop! I don't understand why you still want to keep it a secret, Sweetheart," Brice said.

"I don't know. I guess I still can't believe it's real and I feel like the minute we tell people I'll be worried about losing it all the time," June said.

"Well soon you won't have a choice; everybody will see you getting bigger," Brice said.

"I know. Let's just play it by ear, honey. When the spirit moves, I'll move," June said.

They exchanged a quick kiss before June exited the car to enter St. Mark Church. June had been appointed as the Pastor of St. Mark Church over six years ago. The congregation never had a female pastor before and they were not very welcoming to the change. Their initial questions seemed to always be, "What is she? Is she Spanish? Mixed? Is that a weave?" many thought she was too fair skinned. She was however a native Floridian and spoke with a thick southern drawl. It took many of the members of St. Mark Church some time but now six years later the majority of the members were proud that she was their pastor because she made many positive changes and improvements both to the congregation and the church.

Located next door was St. Mark Church's commercial business, the Sunday Morning Café. The cuisine was soul food and they were open for business seven days a week. June insisted that the restaurant also provide a service for the less fortunate. The church transported the homeless and hungry to the Sunday Morning café every Sunday morning for a free breakfast. June also created meal vouchers for families who were struggling. She decided to do this when she met a young father who had been unemployed for two years and stated to her that he couldn't treat his kids to a meal at McDonalds.

She invited him to dine at the Sunday Morning Café and she was there on the night that he brought his family in. June told the staff that he was a VIP customer and he got over and above great customer service. Weeks later when June ran into the man again he told her that it had been a long time since he was able to feel good about gifting his children. He said that his experience at the Sunday Morning Café revitalized and inspired him to widen his job search and was now gainfully employed at a private golf club in the maintenance department.

"Just seeing my kids so excited to order and seeing

how they lit up eating their desserts, I knew that I could not give up on them."

"Children deserve to be given special treats for absolutely no reason at all. Childhood is precious and should be cherished because our childhood is the foundation of who we become," June told the young man.

When June finally made it into her office, her church secretary was waiting for her, as usual, with a hot cup of French vanilla flavored coffee.

"Oh, thank you Myrtle, but today I think I'd better have some tea," June said.

"Um-hum," Myrtle replied.

"What is that supposed to mean?" June asked.

"Every single morning for the past six years, I have had a piping hot cup of coffee waiting for you when you arrive. Usually you grab the cup like its liquid gold. But today, you came in late and I can't even remember a day that you have ever been late. Your husband drops you off instead of driving yourself and you don't want any coffee," Myrtle said.

"So?" June replied.

"So, I know pregnant when I see it!" Myrtle said.

All June could do was stare at Myrtle. Six years ago Myrtle was Pastor June's biggest opposition to her pastoral charge at St. Mark Church. For her it wasn't June's gender or her complexion but rather her age. June was also the youngest pastor St. Mark had ever had, but over time she and Myrtle became extremely close.

Myrtle attended June's wedding, she taught her how to style Rosie's hair, and, as her secretary, she scheduled all her appointments for ministry. Myrtle never missed a single thing.

Pastor June now sitting at her desk, exhaled a huge breath and said to Myrtle, "It's true, I'm pregnant."

"I knew it! I knew it! You don't even walk the same! We gon have us a new church baby!" Myrtle said excitedly.

"Now, Myrtle, I really don't want people to know yet. You know I hate to be coddled and don't you start doing it either. People think pregnancy is some kind of disability or something and I would just hate that," June said.

"Oh I do know my pastor. I won't tell nobody but I am very happy for you and Supervising Elder Howard," Myrtle said.

"Thank you. We are overjoyed but -- and I'm only telling you this, Myrtle, because of my age this is considered a high risk pregnancy so I do have to be careful," June said.

"Careful like how?" Myrtle asked.

"Like one cup of coffee a day, I don't know how I'm ever gonna to do that. I have to be off my feet as much as possible and the doctor just said that when I start showing I won't be able to drive myself around anymore," June said.

"Well I'm on it. And I'm so happy."

Myrtle had never had any children of her own, her husband passed away over a decade earlier but she had many nieces and nephews who she absolutely adored and was heavily invested in their lives. She considered June to be family so she was extremely excited. Then Myrtle's expression change dramatically as she said, "Sister Barclay is here."

"Yeah, it's about that time ain't it? The Quarterly Status Meeting is this week," June said as she went through the drawer of her desk.

"I don't understand why you put up with her and I will never understand why you keep appointing her to the Steward Board," Myrtle said.

"I have my reasons, Myrtle, go ahead, and send her in," June said.

The Quarterly Status Meeting is when the Supervising Elder of a district holds a meeting to assess that particular church's status over the previous three months. The Supervising Elder wants to know things like how many people joined the church in the last quarter, how many people got saved, if there were any deaths or baptisms, as well as the financial status of the church.

June's husband Brice was the Supervising Elder of June's district. Normally it would have been considered a conflict to have the Supervising Elder also be the husband of one of the pastors but everyone in the district agreed that it would not be a conflict. To help dissuade even the appearance of any favoritism for June from her husband, she gave her Steward Board much more latitude and authority than most pastor's did. She put them in charge of preparing the Quarterly Status report for the Supervising Elder's Quarterly Status Meeting. Sister Barclay was elected to be the one to review their findings with the pastor prior to the Quarterly Status Meetings.

Sister Barclay was a member of June's Steward Board. And she was also a part of the minority of people who hung on to their bias and did not care for June's leadership at St. Mark Church. Each time, in addition to giving June the facts about the report, Sister Barclay felt it necessary to share her opinions with June about all that she thought was going on wrong at St. Mark Church.

"Good morning, Sister Barclay," June said.

"Morning," Sis. Barclay said as she handed June the report.

"How are we doing this quarter?" June asked.

"Financially we are still doing well. But I want you to know that I was outvoted concerning the approval of funding the youth summer camp," Sis. Barclay said.

"You don't think we should have a camp here at the church this summer?" June said as she surveyed the report.

"No I do not. You're going to invite the wrong kinds of kids and they just gon tear up our church."

"Well Sister Barclay, don't you think we should expose as many people to the gospel as possible, especially when they otherwise would not walk in on a Sunday morning?" June said while peering over her glasses.

"Sunday morning is fine. Monday through Friday is a whole nother thing," Sis. Barclay said.

"Well, the camp is happening. We already have all the volunteers, most of the funding is coming from the county and I'm just excited about it," June said.

"Moving on. Again, since Sister Mattie passed away there has been no Steward's Aid report for the Quarterly Status Report because there still ain't no Steward's Aid Board. We are the only church in this district who don't have a Steward's Aid Board."

"Um hum," June said while continuing to review the report.

"And again I am offering to do all the training and recruiting to build up a new Steward's Aid Board with some of the decent young women in the church," Sis. Barclay said.

"Yes, I am fully aware that you're willing to do that.

At this time, I think the Steward Board is fully capable of absorbing the duties of a Steward's Aid Board," June said.

"Stewards are over the Steward's Aid Board, I don't think that's a decision you should have the power to make," Sister Barclay said rather harshly.

"Sister Barclay, the Steward's Aid Board originated in a time when all Stewards on the Steward Board were males. The Steward's Aides were made up of a group of women who were utilized to do what was then considered women's work. I disagree with that concept in this day and age. Traditionally the Steward's Aid Board prepared the sanctuary for communion, but they didn't just drape white linens over everything they did much, much more than that. Dressing the sanctuary was in and of itself a spiritual ceremony, an actual service filled with prayer and singing because you see they weren't only preparing the physical sanctuary but the spirituality of the atmosphere in the sanctuary.

"Now I left the Steward's Aid Board as I found it when I arrived at St. Mark but after Sister Mattie died, I got all you Stewards in here dressing the sanctuary every month, and we have a hallelujah good time preparing the sanctuary for communion service. It's not women's work, it's God's work and both men and women can and should be doing it."

"What are you saying, you gon keep making us do that every month forever?"

"I believe that you believe it's work that's beneath a Steward and I strongly disagree. Stewards are supposed to be the spiritual leaders in the church. If you're trying to get me to say it out right, here it goes, St. Mark Church will not have a Steward's Aid Board because we have both male and female Stewards. The Steward Board will absorb the traditional duties of the Steward's Aid Board.

"You all need to modify the schedule for who is serving in the chancel area each Sunday and include two different persons to also serve during the invitation. You can also rotate preparing the sanctuary for communion, utilizing both men and women and there should be a minimum of four people."

"I will have to discuss this with the board," Sis. Barclay said.

"You can discuss it all you want but that's my final decision. Now is there anything else we need to address?"

June could feel her patience slowly leaving her and decided to sit back in her chair and secretly do some breathing exercises as Sister Barclay went on and on summarizing each church department's report and freely offering her opinion on how each one needed to improve in this or that area.

"Okay. So that completes the departments. They all submitted final reports but there is one last thing I personally wanted to discuss with you that bothered me."

"Okay."

"Well, last month you had the youth in charge of Sunday School and you let that Tara girl be the Youth Sunday School Principal," Sister Barclay said.

"Yes I did. That 'Tara girl' is very active in Sunday school; she's an avid volunteer with the Girls Club. And she's getting ready to graduate from high school with honors; she's going to Spellman in the fall for God's sake. What problem could you possibly have with Tara?" June asked sharply.

"Did you see what she was wearing last Sunday? She

wasn't dressed appropriate," Sister Barclay said.

"You are kidding right?" June asked in disbelief.

"No I'm not. Too much of her arms was showing and that sundress she had on was too short. I think she even had some kind of tattoo on her ankle. I know the kids don't dress up for church no more but that don't mean that we should be condoning the way they dress by rewarding them. If you're going to lift her up as a role model to the other youth, she need to change the way she dress and --

"Get out!" June said.

"Excuse me?"

"You heard me, get out. I refuse to spend another scintilla of a second on this topic with you. There are girls out there her age right now with multiple children, dropping out of school, girls whose only goal in life is to get a Gucci bag and you have the audacity to waste my time about a young person with promise. Get out of my office and come back when you have something real to discuss with me. I won't allow you or anybody else to cast any aspersions against this young lady," June said angrily as she stood.

"Well, let me ask you this, Pastor. You know I don't like you, and I know you don't like me, why then, do you keep appointing me to the steward board if you ain't interested in my opinions or anything that I have to say?" Sister Barclay asked.

Pastor June was angry and spent a lot of time in prayer asking God about giving her the wisdom to take some time before responding out of anger but decided that she would start doing that on another angry occasion and instead said, "Because you keep me righteous. Every time you open your big mouth with some new ignorant statement it reminds me why I'm here and what God called me to do."

Sister Barclay replied as she also stood, "Did you just call me ignorant? You did, you just called me ignorant. Well that's it, you done did it now. I just wonder how your husband will feel about this at the quarter because I am gon lodge an official complaint! Who do you think you are, talking to me like that? And if he don't do something and I suspect he won't, then the truth will finally be out that he can't be fair when it comes to his own wife's church. And I can tell you right now if he don't do something, I will be passing my complaint right on up to the Bishop!"

Sister Barclay stormed out of Pastor June's office and June noticed that she was practically skipping down the hall like a happy little school girl with an ice cream cone and it infuriated June even more. June closed her eyes and tilted her head back in disbelief.

Pastor June sat back down in her seat, and began thinking about the Apostle Peter. She always identified herself with Peter in temperament. She realized that she didn't feel bad or guilty about how she had just spoken to Sister Barclay. She wondered if it was because of her pregnancy, if maybe her hormones had already changed that greatly.

Then she said out loud, "Well, God you knew I was a Peter when you called me, I have to believe you knew you could utilize my temperament for your glory."

But Pastor June knew she should have felt bad and that she had crossed a line.

"What was that about?" Myrtle asked as she ran into June's office.

"I said something stupid. I can't believe I'm going to put Brice in this situation," June said and then relayed her conversation with Sister Barclay to Myrtle.

"Well, she think she run the church anyway, she needed to be told off," Myrtle said.

"Yeah but I could've waited on some wisdom from God and done it in a way that didn't put her down or call her names."

"Well what can you do about it now?" Myrtle asked.

"I'm gonna to have to apologize. But I'll wait until after the Status Meeting, I don't want her to think I'm apologizing to avoid her complaint. Maybe she'll think Brice is making me apologize, I think that would go a long way with her. She would love to believe that somebody, specifically my husband, has put me in my place."

"Don't you dare give her the satisfaction!" Myrtle exclaimed.

"I'm gonna pray about it. I had no idea my emotions would get this loopy this soon," June said.

"To tell you the truth, Pastor, you were always close to loopy anyway," Myrtle said with a giggle.

"Thanks a lot, Myrtle. What time is the summer camp staffing meeting?" June asked.

"After lunch. Speaking of lunch, what do you want today?"

"I'll go to the café and visit with Wendy," June said.

"Okay, see you after lunch," Myrtle said and exited June's office.

Since Rosie had come into Pastor June's life, she had learned to embrace the few moments of solitude that she received and chose to commune with God. She pulled her lavender thin line bible from her briefcase and turned it to

First Peter. She then began meditating on chapter three verses two through to four. It read:

*"Shepherd the flock of God which is among you, serving as overseers, not by compulsion but willingly, not for dishonest gain but eagerly; nor as being lords over those entrusted to you, but being examples to the flock; and when the Chief Shepherd appears, you will receive the crown of glory that does not fade away."*

Whenever June felt that she crossed the line of her call she meditated on this passage of scripture. It reminded her of her responsibilities to the flock that God had placed in her care.

Her meditation was interrupted by a knock on her door. She closed her bible and sighed as she realized her moment of solitude had passed.

"Come in."

"You haven't left for the café yet? I knew it," Myrtle said as she placed a steaming hot plate of rib tips, steamed cabbage and mac and cheese in front of June.

"Thanks, Myrtle. You're a life saver. Listen, what do you think my chances are of getting Sister Barclay back in here to speak with me?" June asked.

"Your chances are real good cause she never left," Myrtle said.

"Really? Where is she?"

"She's in the computer room, I'm guessing she in there writing up her official complaint against you."

Pastor June got up, left her office, and walked across the sanctuary. She found Sister Barclay seated in front of a computer and she looked sad. No one else was there and Pastor June felt bad that she was the cause of Sister Barclay's sadness.

"Sister Barclay, can I come in and speak with you?"

June asked.

Sister Barclay wiped tears from her eyes and nodded her head, yes.

Pastor June closed the door and sat next to her. "Sister Barclay, I want to apologize for my temperament. There is no excuse for the way that I spoke to you and I am sorry. After you left my office I began communing with God and his word reminded me that you are a part of this flock and it is my responsibility to minister to you. So, although I believe that your motives were wrong instead of reacting in anger, I should have ministered to you instead of raising my voice."

"You called me ignorant. And I'm writing a complaint," Sister Barclay said flatly.

"Well, I think you should. I was wrong to say what I said the way that I said it but you need to understand that I have been given a vision for St. Mark Church and I have to stay focused on that vision. It's the only reason we've made any progress at all.

"Now you asked me earlier why I keep appointing you to the Steward Board and I know my answer was vague. I don't want people who are always going to agree with anything I say but rather people who have an interest in the future of the church. Truly you love your church and I believe you love God and those are certainly apart of the criteria.

"Now I want to ask you a similar question. You said it yourself, you are not happy that I'm here and it occurred to me that I don't really know why. I mean I used to think it was because I'm a woman but as far as I can remember you've been to every one of my bible studies, and you've never missed a Sunday service, not even when your niece passed away. Do you think you're ready to explain to me what exactly it is that you don't like about me being the pastor here?"

Sister Barclay turned away from Pastor June, staring into space and said, "My husband left me several years ago. On the job over the last five years I've had six different shift supervisors learning how to do their job from me but I always got passed over for the position. I've had to move three times also. That meant new neighbors. And the one thing I thought I could count on always being the same was my church.

"It was my family what started this church. I was raised in this church, I raised my children here, and it has always been the same. Then you come along and all of a sudden there are people here who have never even gone to church before. And now the new people outnumber the old people who been here for generations. Nobody asked us if we even wanted to grow. Nothing is the same no more. Nobody ever knows what to expect from you. You cut out a lot of our traditional programs we had since forever and you never asked us what we thought about none of it."

"Sister Barclay, this is a church. It's not a club, our membership is not exclusive. Membership will always increase when the true gospel is preached and lived. You know the scripture where Jesus said, 'If I be lifted up from the earth, I will draw all men unto me.' That scripture is speaking about preaching His true unadulterated gospel and that's what we do here.

"I can see that you yearn for your childhood church but the bait that was used back then to draw people to Christ is not appealing to this current generation. In order to catch this new fish, we have to use new bait.

"But I tell you what, I'm sensitive to how hard change can be. And, I did not know that you felt so strongly about the church of your childhood. I will keep that in mind from now on and I promise that we won't forget about your family's contribution to the journey of St. Mark Church.

"I'm also a little disappointed that you didn't feel comfortable to come to me when you ran into your hardships. I am your pastor and I apologize if I ever gave you the impression that I wasn't concerned or interested about what's going on with you."

Sister Barclay nodded her head in the affirmative then said, "I guess you expect me not to turn this in now?" She held up the typed complaint.

"That's up to you Sister Barclay. I still stand behind what I said, just not the way I said it. I was very wrong and I think you should submit it."

Pastor June took Sister Barclay's hand and said, "Let us pray. Father God, I thank you for revelation. I thank you for Sister Barclay and ask that you temper both of our hearts to continue this journey seeking only to satisfy you and that our actions from this moment on will be to your glory.

"I pray, God, that you will touch both of our hearts to bring to a close any discord between us. And Father, I ask that you intervene in her life, make clear the path that you have set for her which may be narrow but certainly smooth and straight. Bring her comfort in those times when she thinks that she is alone. We love you and pray in your Son's name, Jesus the Christ. Amen."

Pastor June then embraced Sister Barclay. While

they embraced, Sister Barclay began to sob and Pastor June hugged her all the more.

# 6

*"...They have a heart trained in **covet**ous practices, and are accursed children."~* 2 Peter 2:14

Two Touch heard the familiar sound of his mother's little red Toyota pulling up into the drive way.

"Shoot, she home early."

He rushed into the kids rooms. They were still sleeping from their late afternoon nap. He returned to the living room where Jackson was still nursing a beer with his feet up on the coffee table. Two Touch stopped himself from telling him to take his feet off the table just as the front door opened and his mom entered.

"Hello."

"Hey, how you doing today?" Jackson said.

"How am I doing? Apparently not as well as you cause I don't even put my feet up on my furniture and I paid for it," she said with her hand on her hip.

"Oh, sorry about that, Debra," Jackson said.

"It's Mrs. Walters to you boy and the next time I come into my own house and see you looking like you live here I will be expecting a rent check. Now because I know for a fact that you don't live here, it's time for you to go wherever it is you do live, we understand each other, Son?"

"Yeah, whatever. Hit me up later Two," Jackson said as he left.

"Why is he here so much?" Mrs. Walter's asked as she watched Jackson close her front door without using the doorknob, her biggest pet peeve.

"I don't know. He got kicked out of school again and I can't get rid of him," Two Touch answered.

"Well, you won't be here this summer so he'll have to find somewhere else to hang out."

"What? Where I'm going?"

"Right now you need to get ready to go over to the church for summer camp staff meeting."

"What? I'm too old for summer camp, Ma."

"You're going to be a camp counselor. I talked to Pastor June, she knows about your epilepsy and it's only for five hours so you should be fine. And you're real good with kids, Son."

"Oh my God, I can't believe you did this without even talking to me first," Two Touch said.

"What else you got to do? You got some big plans I don't know about?"

"No but... "

"Look, get dressed and head over to the church, end of discussion. The twins are going to camp next week and maybe you'll meet a better class of friends," Mrs. Walters said while she went into her bedroom.

Two Touch was nervous as he drove to St. Mark Church. His epilepsy was severe even with medication and his mother had always been overprotective about where he went and what he was allowed to do. For years he accused her of limiting his activities but now he felt as if she was kicking him out into the world with no net at all. Although he was nervous he had to admit that he was also a little excited. When he pulled into the parking lot he saw Cady Grimes walking into the church. Now his nerves were on hyper-drive but so was his excitement.

He remembered her well and she looked much the same. She was average height and was still very shapely. She wore blue jeans that revealed to him how little her hour glass figure had changed since high school. She was the color of honey, her skin and her hair. Her dark honey colored hair was very curly and just reached the top of her shoulders. When they were in school he had a huge crush on her, but she never did give him the time of day. She was always polite and nice but it was very obvious that she had no romantic interest in him at all.

He entered the church and was directed to the proper classroom. Cady was standing next to Pastor June as they were about to begin the meeting. When Cady saw him, her face lit up and they waved to one another. He was on cloud nine.

After the meeting Cady approached Two Touch, "Hi Demetrius, long time no see," Cady said.

"I know, right?" Two Touch said as they embraced each other.

"How are you? What you been up to? I remember you started taking college courses while we were still in high school," Cady said.

"Yeah, I finished college last year but I'm just staying with my mom now to help her out. She got married and has little twins so you know it's about the fam," Two Touch said.

"Oh, that's so nice of you. I'm still in school in Miami, still got another year to go, just here for summer break. I'm so glad to see you again and so glad you're going to be helping out with camp this summer.

"I started coming to St. Mark Church last year but I don't remember ever seeing you here before," Cady said.

"Yeah, I ain't been up in here for a minute. My mom goes here with the twins when she's off work on Sundays. I'm not really a church person," Two Touch said.

"Well maybe that will change," she said smiling.

He missed seeing that smile and it was infectious because he was now smiling too. "Well I've got to go now, guess I'll see you on Monday for camp," Two Touch said.

"Well hey, I'll be here Sunday for church, why don't you come for the service?" Cady said.

"Oh I don't know about that. I'll think about it," Two Touch said as he got up to leave.

"Okay, I'll be looking out for you just in case," Cady said.

As Two Touch drove home he was feeling good and was seriously considering attending church on Sunday morning. Two Touch had no good memories about church. He always felt left out or pitied and never felt any genuine love from the so called church people but now he was wondering if Cady could be the one to change that for him.

Cady began attending St. Mark Church when her father and Bettina were married. She was happy that her father found love and she really liked Bettina but the pastor of New Hope where Bettina and her father went to church was Bettina's younger brother and being new to

Christ, Cady felt uncomfortable asking him questions about God and salvation or the new dynamics of her family. So with Pastor June being a family friend she opted to go to St. Mark Church instead. And she has since grown really close to Pastor June and considers her to be a mentor. She didn't believe that she had been called into the ministry but she loved to study the bible and was seriously contemplating a career that would benefit the church along the lines of Christian Education. She was seriously considering becoming a college professor at a Christian College.

Cady realized early on in her childhood many of the gifts that God had given to her. She was always the peacemaker and mediator for her family and friends and even complete strangers. She had the ability to make people listen and her spirit always drew people in. In no time at all Pastor June also recognized her gifts and asked her to be the head of the Hospitality Ministry. At St. Mark Church the hospitality ministry did much more than merely greet the congregation as they arrived to church on Sunday mornings, they also stayed in contact with the guests for several weeks after their initial visit.

Cady was also responsible for referring and directing the guests and the members to the appropriate ministry to meet their needs. People would contact the Hospitality Ministry when they didn't know who to call. Cady loved her work at the church. Her latest work involved a family of five. The parents were both unemployed and they were quickly becoming homeless. She directed the family to the benevolent ministry for money to help pay some of their utilities but she didn't stop there. She referred the parents to different employment services as well a lawyer who was also a church member who specialized in foreclosures. That family was currently in the process of a new mortgage modification with their lender.

Cady tried never to miss bible study because many of the needs of the members were stated at the end of bible study. Pastor June ended each community bible study with what she called a Koinonia Conference. In the Koinonia Conference members stated what their needs were in front of each other. Pastor June believed that God used people to execute his blessings and Cady had witnessed countless times at the end of bible study a variety of evidence to support Pastor June's belief.

In one such conference a member stated that her car needed more work done to the engine than the car was worth. She needed transportation back and forth to work. Another member happened to have a car repair shop and gave her a loaner vehicle while he rebuilt her car's engine and only charged her for the parts. Then the entire bible study membership gave an offering to cover his expenses for the parts. Within a few weeks that member was back on the road with a rebuilt engine and it didn't cost her a dime. Cady loved seeing that type of love demonstrated and, most of all she loved being an active part in it.

As Cady drove home she thought about how her gifts were more appreciated at church than at home. She thought about her older sister Crystal. Crystal had been bitter for as long as Cady could remember. Cady was aware that Crystal never got over their mother's death but lately Crystal's meanness seemed to have escalated to a new high. Crystal and her father's new wife did not get along. She made a mental note to pray extra hard for her sister to finally receive peace in her life. Crystal was not interested in church, God or anything spiritual at all.

She no longer lived at home since graduating from college two years earlier. She landed a job with an architectural firm. Everyone thought that Crystal would get into the arts, because she was a very talented artist and loved nothing more than to spend an entire day before a canvas with her oil paints. But Crystal confided to Cady in her senior year of college that even more than painting she loved drawing three dimensional buildings, she loved creating the design and the prospect of seeing it come to life.

Then Cady's thoughts turned to Two Touch. She remembered him fondly from high school. She remembered that he liked her and made it clear that he wanted to be more than friends but Cady was not interested in being in a romantic relationship with anybody at that time. She remembered trying hard to be exceptional and being a huge people pleaser. She realized now that she first started this behavior when her mother died. She had somehow convinced herself that if she was a really good person, God would return her mother to her. By the time she was old enough to realize that was not going to happen, it had already become so much of who she was, people pleasing had become habitual. She had often been too trusting and people disappointed her more often than not but she smiled to herself as she recalled her conversation with Pastor June when she sought her counsel after such a hurt.

June told her, "God's people have always been viewed as foolish to the world. What you have is a gift. Not many people are naturally or spontaneously kind. Don't hide away your gift because whenever you expose it, you expose people to the God in you. And I can assure you that you've affected people in ways you may never learn about."

# 7

*"But now I have written to you not to keep company with anyone named a brother, who is sexually immoral, or **covet**ous, or an idolater, or a reviler, or a drunkard, or an extortioner—not even to eat with such a person."* ~1 Corinthians 5:11

Two Touch met Sunday morning with a strange excited feeling. He decided to go to church with his mom and baby siblings after all. He made this decision the previous night because he was hoping to see Cady again. He got this new strange excitement when he awoke to find that he had received a text from Cady that said,

"Looking forward to seeing you in church" with a smiley face.

While he waited for his mother to finish getting his younger siblings ready for church he saw that his caller I.D. was indicating an incoming call from Jackson. He felt so good this morning that he decided to answer instead of hitting ignore as had become his practice lately. "Yeah?"

"What up? What you gettin into today?" Jackson asked.

"Nuttin but going to church with my moms," he

said.

"Church? Oooh, okay you do that man," Jackson said while laughing.

"Hey, laugh if you want to but you remember that girl I told you about?"

"What girl? Oh the rich girl you made up?" Jackson said and began laughing again.

"Yeah, her. I ran into her Friday and she invited me to church. So that's why I'm going. And she look even better than she did in school," Two Touch replied.

"Are you for real? She rich?" Jackson asked.

"I don't know if she is but her Grandma definitely is. All right man, my mom's ready to go."

"Hey, y'all still go to that church with the restaurant where we ate lunch that one time?" Jackson asked.

"Yeah. I got to go, see you later."

When Two Touch and his family arrived at St. Mark Church his mother instructed him to take the kids to the children's church while she talked to some women she hadn't seen in a while. Two Touch didn't argue about checking in the kids because he wanted to look around for Cady. He noticed at the meeting that she seemed to be assisting Pastor June so he figured that she wouldn't be seated yet but that she would most likely be wherever Pastor June was. When he arrived to check the kids in children's church he recognized that several of the children were classmates of his younger siblings. He thought to himself how he might have enjoyed church growing up if they had children's church back then but instead he had to sit through the service sandwiched between his mom and grandmother.

On his way to the sanctuary he finally saw Cady

coming from the lobby. She recognized him right away and his heart began accelerating. That is until he saw Jackson walking only steps behind her holding her hand and then his heart began to sink.

"Hey, Demetrius, look who I found. He said he was looking for you. How great it is to see you again and then you invited a guest," she said as she leaned in for him to kiss her cheek.

"Good morning. Jackson, this is my classmate Cady Grimes. Cady, this is Jackson Bonnen," Two Touch said trying his best to sound upbeat.

"I think we already met," Jackson said as he laughed and added, "Can you believe this guy?"

"Well I'm happy to formally meet you, Jackson. Why don't I show you guys to the section where I usually sit and I'll meet you there before the service starts?" Cady said.

Jackson and Two Touch were seated in the sanctuary when Two Touch turned to Jackson and said, "Man, why are you here?"

"What do you mean? I came to get my church on. Why are you here?"

But before Two Touch could answer they noticed everyone beginning to stand. Two young boys walked up to the pulpit to light the candles on the altar. Then the choir began singing, *Amazing Grace*. The choir sang the hymn in the traditional way until the last two stanzas and then the tempo quickened and they switched to a contemporary version. Pastor June hired a new musician specifically because of his ability to modernize older songs. From the pulpit, Pastor June stood when the choir began the up-tempo version of Amazing Grace and she gave the musician an approving nod while she clapped her hands and moved to the beat.

Pastor June wore a white robe with a hint of gold piping. She did not like to be flashy but she also didn't like to be plain. She stood just four feet, eleven inches tall and because her feet could not reach the ground when she sat in the pastor's chair on the pulpit the Steward Board commissioned a step with wheels so that she could roll it back and forth under the seat as she needed.

The robe she wore hid her frame but those who looked closely would notice that her pregnancy was beginning to show. Pastor June looked like a plethora of ethnicities but the older women knew that something was happening because they began commenting that her complexion, always described as "high yellow" was different and the grade of her hair also begun to change.

Pastor June always wore her hair in a single braid that ran all the way down her back and rested just at the top of her hip but the older women noticed that her hair had lost some of its thickness and it seemed to be much shinier and finer than usual.

Because styling Pastor June's hair was always her Momma May's favorite thing to do, she decided years ago when Momma May died that she would never cut her hair as a way to honor her late mother. However lately Pastor June was finding it difficult to manage the length. Her hair would often get caught in between the seatbelt when she was in the car or she would sometimes literally be sitting on the end of her braid which didn't allow for her to move her head freely. Today she again wore her hair in a single braid but it was wrapped around itself in sort of a knot so that it didn't hang down at all.

Seated to her right was Pastor Bella Grant or Billie for short. Billie was Pastor June's spiritual mentor and mother in ministry. Pastor June came into the ministry under Billie and June considered her to be family. Outside of her husband and Rosie, Billie was the only family that June still had and the only one living that remembered her childhood.

Billie and June's Momma May were very good friends. Billie retired from pastoring several years ago and recently decided to move to West Palm Beach, Florida from Arcadia so that she could be closer to June and her very first grandbaby.

Seated to Pastor June's left was her Associate Minister, Reverend Danny. Reverend Danny was the lead minister at St. Mark Church South. He and Reverend Deena, who was the lead minister at St. Mark Church East, attended the main St. Mark Church every First Sunday so that they could assist with the communion service and also so that the elements that they used at the satellite churches would be consecrated personally by Pastor June. They could have consecrated the elements themselves but Pastor June wanted to keep the focus on the fact that the satellite churches were only extensions of the main St. Mark Church so that no one would get the impression that they were conducting three separate services for three separate churches. So the main St. Mark Church began at 10:00 a.m. while the satellite churches began at 11:30 a.m. June would often show up at one or both after the main St. Mark Church service.

Rev. Deena was absent this Sunday morning which concerned Pastor June about her loyalty to St. Mark Church. When Myrtle gave her the message that she would not make the main service this Sunday morning but would still conduct the St. Mark Church East worship service, Pastor June made a mental note to call Rev. Deena in for a meeting later in the week.

Finally, when it was time for the opening prayer everyone was directed to sit. Two Touch flopped back down on the pew next to Cady like a little kid while Jackson sat down like a grownup. This did not escape Cady's attention and it made Jackson smile a little to himself. Jackson was determined to win Cady over. He wasn't exactly sure why he felt so strongly about taking her attention away from Two Touch but he was on a mission and it seemed to be working in his favor so far.

Two Touch continuously yawned through the prayer. It had been a long time since he'd been in church and without the usual stimuli of video games and television; he was finding it hard to pay attention or to stay awake. Jackson on the other hand continued shooting him disapproving looks as if he was a parent disciplining a child and this greatly upset Two Touch. Of the three, Cady was the only one who actually kept her eyes closed and her head bowed during the prayer. Jackson and Two Touch could hear her saying, "Yes Lord" and "Thank you, God" under her breath. When the prayer concluded, Cady opened her eyes and gave them each a huge smile.

When it was time for Pastor June to preach the sermon, Cady noticed that Two Touch did not have a bible. Jackson had the foresight to bring his mom's bible. This further embarrassed Two Touch until Cady scooted closer to him so they could share hers. Two Touch decided that if Jackson was going to play keep away with Cady, he would be happy to play too. Two Touch placed his arm around Cady's shoulder in an effort to get closer to her as they read the scripture verse along with June. Two Touch thought to himself how well of a show Jackson was performing. He appeared to have a great reverence and appreciation for the sermon that Pastor June was preaching.

Pastor June began preaching from the book of Acts in chapter three. It was about a lame man by the gate called beautiful and how he was deemed to not be ceremonially clean. That was the reason that no one could bring him inside of the temple.

"Today we live under grace and not under the law, but we are still walking pass lame people and leaving them outside of the church at the gate. When we give donations to the 'least of these' in our society we are merely treating the symptom and not addressing their real problems," Pastor June said.

Jackson was up on his feet with loud "Hallelujahs" and "Preach Preacher." Two Touch could only snicker until he realized that Cady didn't seem at all impressed by Jackson's little show because she was too engrossed in the sermon herself and seemed to be tuning everyone and everything out.

Two Touch on the other hand decided to be a little more honest about his bible knowledge in order to take advantage of Cady's Christian nature so when Pastor June concluded the sermon he leaned over to Cady and whispered in her ear, "After church I'm going to need you to help me understand what she was just talking about. You want to meet next door for dinner?"

# 8

*The wicked **covet** the catch of evil men, But the root of the righteous yields fruit.* ~Proverbs 12:12

There was a line of people waiting to be seated at the Sunday Morning Café. The first Sunday was always their busiest day. There was a table reserved for June after every service because she needed time to change out of her robe and to transition from preaching and worship. She didn't like that they held a table for her but Wendy, the manager of the Sunday Morning Café, insisted. So it became June's practice to invite some of the people waiting in line to dine with her at her table. When she passed by the people waiting in the line she saw Cady, Jackson and Two Touch and she asked them to dine with her and Billie.

When they reached the table, Jackson moved ahead of them all and pulled out the chairs for June and then for Cady and Billie. Two Touch couldn't help but roll his eyes.

"A real gentleman in this day and age is nice to see" June said as she looked over at Billie and Billie smiled but said nothing.

"Good morning, Pastor, I really enjoyed the sermon this morning. I don't know how many times I've read that story but you gave me a whole new perspective," Wendy said.

"God bless you, Wendy. What's looking good today?" Pastor June asked.

"Everything of course," Wendy replied and everyone at the table laughed.

"Well I want my usual," Billie said.

While Wendy took their orders June noticed Billie was not nearly as vocal as she usually was. She leaned in to whisper in Billie's ear, "Are you alright, you're being awfully quiet."

"I'm receiving and it ain't good," Billie whispered back in Pastor June's ear.

Receiving is what Billie called listening to the spirit about something.

"I thought you'd like him being that he's your type and all. He's a little too good to be true but I'll be watching him and Cady," June said.

"Not him, the other one," Billie said indicating Two Touch.

June realized that Billie had been acting strange for some time. She was forgetting more things than usual. She was cranky a lot more than usual and it had been a while since Billie shared with her any new updates about her health. June made a mental note to address these issues with Billie the very next time they were alone together. And then June gave her attention to the young people at the table.

"So, I've met Demetrius, is someone going to

introduce me to this young man with the good manners?" June asked.

"Oh, I am so sorry, Pastor June, this is Jackson, he's a guest of Demetrius," Cady said.

"How nice, it's always good to see young men in church. Tell me, Jackson, do you have a church home?" June asked.

"Well my parents are seasonal church goers, Christmas and Easter," Jackson said as everyone chuckled.

"But I was a regular in college and now that I'm back home I'd like to look around for a new church home," Jackson said.

"Well you're always welcome to come back and worship with us. Today was a very traditional service but Cady can give you information on our different services and bible studies," June said.

"Pastor, Demetrius has questions about the sermon this morning so we decided to discuss it over dinner," Cady said.

"Oh goody, I love questions! Fire away, Son," June said as she sipped her sweet pineapple ice tea.

This caught Two Touch off guard but he quickly recovered. "Well, why is it that Jesus healed the man who had been waiting to be taken into the pool but not this lame man by the gate? I mean, this is the same temple where Jesus used to teach and heal when he was here in the flesh isn't it?" Two Touch asked.

Although Two Touch kept his eyes focused on Pastor June he could see through his peripheral view that Cady was very impressed and Jackson was very disappointed.

"Very good question, Demetrius. You're talking

about the man described in John's gospel, the man with the infirmity for thirty-eight years. He was waiting by that healing pool for someone to help him get into the water," Pastor June said.

"Yes, and Jesus walked up to him and asked him if he wanted to be healed. Why didn't he ask the man at the temple the same thing?" Two Touch asked Pastor June.

"Well, I would say that the motivations of these two physically challenged men were different. See, the man by the gate at the temple wasn't seeking to be healed. And as you said he must have been there and even witnessed Jesus healing people at the temple during His earthly ministry but this man was a beggar and he only wanted to receive money or like I said in the sermon, he only wanted to treat his symptom and not address the deeper issue of his problem. But now the man by the sheep's gate who was trying to get into the healing pool, he had been trying for thirty eight years to be healed and Jesus recognized that.

"Jesus had the power to heal everyone on earth from any affliction but they needed to first have faith that they could be healed. Those that remained in their afflicted state after the resurrection of Christ had the opportunity to benefit from the power of the Holy Ghost in the same way that we have that opportunity today, through witness accounts of what Jesus has done. And that's what the man by the gate at the temple received from Peter and John, they testified about the power of Christ. Without that witness that man wouldn't have known that he could be healed. It's the same with many in our society today, they still don't realize that their real hope, their only hope is in

Christ. So we need to be that witness."

"Wow, that's deep, Pastor June. Now I know what the catch phrase 'Believe and Receive' means" Jackson said.

"Yeah, we have to witness to people about the power of Christ not only to heal physically but also spiritually," Cady said.

"The bible says, 'How then shall they call on Him in whom they have not believed? And how shall they believe in Him of whom they have not heard? And how shall they hear without a preacher? And how shall they preach unless they are sent?" Pastor June said.

"The bible also says, 'So I commended enjoyment, because a man has nothing better under the sun than to eat, drink, and be merry.' Enough shop talk, we out of church, where's my food Sister Wendy?" Billie said with a loud raspy laugh.

"Well, now that's the Billie I know and love, welcome back," June said with a chuckle.

They continued to dine and fellowship with each other, and when they were done with the meal, Two Touch said to Cady, "Well, I guess I'll see you in the morning at camp."

"Definitely, I'm so excited to work with the kids," Cady said.

They agreed that they would continue to meet again at the café for dinner sometime during the week after a day of camp. But when Two Touch got into his mother's car with his siblings he spotted Jackson walking Cady to his sporty Jaguar, the only asset his father allowed him to keep. He then saw them pause and talk for about a full minute, that minute seemed to be forever to Two Touch.

Then his heart sank once again as he witnessed Jackson open his passenger car door and Cady got in. When Jackson walked around to the driver's side door, he looked directly at Two Touch sitting in the passenger seat of his mother's ten year old Toyota and he winked. Two Touch was livid and was dying to know where they were going and what Jackson was going to do.

Over the next several weeks Two Touch and Jackson played this tit-for-tat game with Cady as the pawn. Two Touch would spend the days with Cady at the church's summer camp, sharing late lunches once all the kids had gone home but Jackson took Cady out in the evenings.

On the last day of camp, Two Touch and Cady decided to eat their lunch on a blanket under the shade of a big old oak tree about twenty feet from the camp kids. Once Cady distributed both of their ham and cheese sandwiches, sodas and chips, Two Touch finally gathered his nerve and asked, "So what's going on with you and Jackson?"

"Oh I don't know. He wants a romantic relationship but for now we're just friends. We're not really equally yoked. He's still really seeking to find God, while I'm trying to deepen my relationship with God. You know what I mean?" Cady said.

"Well, I don't mean no harm, but he says y'all are going out and I know the bible says that if you are unequally yoked you should have no fellowship. Doesn't it say something like, what business has darkness with light?" Two Touch asked.

"Well, you know that young adult group I keep inviting you to that Pastor June teaches? She calls it 'Real

Talk." She allows us to pick topics and we learn God's will on the subject. So we discussed dating several months ago. It was very enlightening and we learned about how we're expected to date in this present age. I think she called it Godly Dating for Our Current Culture or something like that. I can share my notes with you if you want. Anyway, we learned all about how dating or courtship changed throughout the biblical times. And the thing she taught us that forever changed the way I view dating is when she stated how that scripture that you're talking about, the 'unequally yoked' scripture, is so often misused for Christians to separate themselves from people for the sole purpose of judging them. She said it's used as an excuse for not witnessing to the lost in ways that they're better able to relate to."

"I don't understand," Two Touch said.

"She said we can have relationships with lost people as long as the relationship is about trying to get them found. In other words, I am spending a lot of time with Jackson and I do enjoy his company but I'm also being a living witness because Pastor June taught me that before Jackson should be allowed to get to know me, I need to recognize that I could be a vehicle for him to get to know Christ," Cady said.

"Are you saying that Pastor June said you have to date people in order to lead them to Christ? Do you know what that sounds like?" Two Touch asked bewildered.

"No, no that's not what I'm saying. I am attracted to Jackson, I mean come on, he is fine and quite charming. But Pastor June said before we automatically discount people as potential romantic interests because they're not saved, I need to give Jackson the opportunity to meet

Christ through me. Having the opportunity to witness my lifestyle might lead to him wanting to be saved. If that doesn't happen, then I shake the dust off like the bible says. And even if we don't get romantically involved, the seeds will have been planted and maybe that's the only role God intended for me to have."

"For how long?"

"What do you mean?"

"I mean how long do you think you can keep on spending time with him before he wants more? And you know what I'm talking about. Despite what you believe the relationship is, he thinks you guys are going out," Two Touch stated.

"I'm letting the Holy Spirit lead me. Besides we have a good time together. I thought he was your friend, it sounds like you're afraid for me to be spending time with Jackson," Cady said.

"He is my friend, sort of. But I do know him well and...," Two Touch's voice trailed off.

"What do you know? What aren't you telling me, Demetrius?"

Two Touch lowered his head and thought about what he was actually doing. This was not the way he wanted to win this game that he and Jackson were playing. He decided this was not an honorable way to win at all. So he responded, "Just be careful. Don't play with his emotions. Be upfront with him. I don't want either one of you to get hurt."

"Well I don't know how much clearer I could be. All we talk about is God or the church usually over a meal. We don't go to the movies or dancing or anything that would promote the idea that we're dating. It never occurred to me that I could be misleading him with my intentions," Cady said as she lowered her head.

Two Touch reached out, grabbed her chin, lifted her head back up and said, "Listen you know I like you, I've always liked you. You're the most kind hearted person I know. And I am telling you upfront that I have feelings for you, that's the only reason I stuck my nose in your business."

"Demetrius..." Cady began to say when Two Touch leaned in to kiss her but she jerked back and then saw that he was obviously very hurt by her reaction. She reached out to grab his hand. "I told you in high school I didn't feel that way about you. That hasn't changed, I care a lot about you, and after all this time we've spent together over the summer I consider you to be one of my closest friends. I value our friendship; I don't want that to ever change," Cady said.

But Two Touch was angry and hurt. He closed his eyes to try to stop his tears from falling. "It's okay, it won't happen again. I receive your message loud and clear. Maybe we better go over and check on the kids now."

# 9

*"And He said to them, "Take heed and beware of **covet**ousness, for one's life does not consist in the abundance of the things he possesses." ~Luke 12:15*

While Cady and Two Touch were eating their lunch on the last day of summer camp, Jackson was standing in a pawn shop trying to pawn his mother's diamond bracelet that he had stolen from her jewelry box the night before.

"Eight hundred dollars? Do you think I'm stupid?" Jackson said to the man behind the counter.

"Well now that's not the real question is it, Son," The man said.

"What?" Jackson asked.

"The real question is what level of stupid you happen to be. I mean it doesn't exactly take a genius to try and pawn a stolen bracelet."

"Look fool, I didn't steal anything. This is my mother's bracelet and I happen to know that my father paid twenty grand for this piece in South Beach because I was standing there when he bought it! Now you're going to do better than eight hundred dollars, do you hear me old man?" Jackson shouted.

"You say that's your momma's jewelry huh? Why don't we give her a call and see how much she think its worth?" the man asked Jackson.

Jackson pushed away from the counter and turned his back to the man in frustration. He knew he couldn't call his mom about the bracelet but he had to get some funds if was going to keep his baby's momma mouth shut and if he was going to keep taking Cady out for nice dinners.

"All right, Man, give me the eight hundred dollars but you're the only crook in here today, you better believe that!" Jackson said.

As Jackson headed over to the housing projects in downtown West Palm Beach he thought about his baby's momma, Lakesha. He really did fall hard for Lakesha at first and he remembered that in the beginning of their relationship they had a really good thing going but he had to stop his love for her from growing because he knew he could never bring her home to his parents. In every other way he thought she was perfect for him. He was extremely physically attracted to her. She always wore her hair in long braids and he liked that. He would even ask her to change the color from time to time. Lakesha was what he described as thick in all the right places. She had a medium dark complexion and her skin was flawless and her lips very full. He loved that she wore lipstick all the time even when she was just hanging around the house. It was the only makeup that she wore.

He also loved that she never gave him any flack about his other women and whenever he would go over to her place, she waited on him hand and foot. She always took really good care of him as if he was her husband. Back then Lakesha lived with her mother in the projects and her mother treated Jackson like a celebrity and often instructed Lakesha on her good treatment of him. He also knew that Lakesha was no dummy. She helped him sort through many of his problems, especially his school work but when she told him that she was pregnant he laughed in her face and he stopped seeing her all together.

When he got a letter from child support demanding that he take a DNA test, he arranged for the testing to be done by a private physician. It was the first time that he ever saw his son who was already six months old by that time. He never even looked at the baby, he just glared at Lakesha. He did notice that the tenderness that had always been in her eyes when she looked at him before had become cold and hard. She didn't really look at him at all but rather through him as if he really wasn't in the room, neither of them said a word to each other.

Weeks later when the DNA test came back saying that Jackson was 99.99 percent likely to be the father of Lakesha's baby boy he begin sending her two thousand dollars a month. This arrangement was preceded with a phone call where he gave her the condition that she was not to continue to pursue her child support case. He explained to her that he was simply a college student with no source of provable income and he informed her that the two thousand dollars a month he would be sending her was three times more than she would get if she sought to go through child support enforcement. Within a week or two, he received a notice from the State of Florida which said that the mother no longer wished to pursue the child support matter.

Now his baby was over a year old and this would be the first time that he'd seen Lakesha in person since that day in the doctor's office. After finding a place to park in the housing projects, he made his way up the stairs to her fifth floor apartment. He had to walk past several young black and Hispanic men hanging out on the stairwell and he tried to be cool by making a motion of quickly lifting up his head as a greeting gesture as if to say, "What's up."

He played the bad boy role among his circle of friends but Jackson knew nothing about ghetto life and though he openly showed contempt towards all housing project residents, whenever he had come to visit Lakesha in the past he always did so with great fear. Finally reaching her door he knocked and tried to sound tough by yelling, "Lakesha, it's me, open the door."

He could see someone peeking through the peephole and then he heard the locks unlock but the door remained closed. He opened the door and entered into Lakesha's well maintained living room. He immediately noticed that she had a 60 inch flat screen television on her wall. Her all black genuine leather furniture looked brand new. There were actual framed prints hanging all around on the walls. He could hear an automatic dishwasher going in the kitchen and he could see the baby standing in his playpen wearing Jordan sneakers. It had been almost two months since he'd given her any money and now he was trying to muster up the courage to hand her less than half of what she usually got once a month to cover her expenses for the past two months. When he handed her the money, he stood there and watched Lakesha as she counted it out.

"Where the rest at?" Lakesha asked.

"That's all I got for right now," he responded.

"That ain't enough. That ain't our deal," she said.

"I know but it's all I can do. I told you that my dad cut me off, you thought I was playing with you?" he asked.

"So now you gon cut your son off too? You think you gon treat him like your daddy treat you?" she said angrily.

Lakesha's angry words hit Jackson in a new place within himself. He walked over to the playpen where Jackie was reaching up with his arms indicating that he wanted to be picked up by his father. Jackson picked up his son and brought him to his chest; he stroked the baby's head as he leaned his face in and kissed the boy's cheek. Jackson felt tears forming in his closed eyes. He heard himself say out loud, "No, I am not my father. I will always be proud of my son."

Behind him Lakesha finally seeing Jackson actually acknowledge his son for the first time in her son's life allowed her tears to flow freely. Jackson then turned around and motioned for her to join their embrace and she did.

That following morning as Lakesha lay sleeping next Jackson, he began reevaluating his life. He admitted to himself as well as to Lakesha the previous night that he loved her and never really stopped. This morning Jackson realized that this admission although true didn't really change anything. He could never marry Lakesha but he could marry Cady. He realized early on that Cady was never going to let him in her pants before marriage and although Lakesha wasn't marriage material, Cady very much was.

He decided that if he could get Cady to marry him, he could then set Lakesha up in a nice apartment or a little house across town. He would spend the better part of his life loving Lakesha on the side. Now he only needed to think of a plan B in the event that he could not get Cady to marry him. That was the one valuable lesson that he did learn from his father, to always have a plan B.

# 10

*"And He said to them, "Take heed and beware of **covet**ousness, for one's life does not consist in the abundance of the things he possesses."* ~Luke 12:15

**Present Day**

"First of all calm down Mario, we're going to figure this out. Now can you play the recording back again? I'd like to hear exactly what the caller said," June said.

"Sure, sure," Mario said.

He went to the answering machine and replayed the message that Bettina discovered when she came home.

"Mario Grimes -- if you want to see your daughters again -- it will cost you six million dollars -- you will be contacted shortly with instructions -- if the police are called -- you will be given directions to the bodies of your daughters."

There was a mechanical voice overlay so the voice on the recording sounded like a machine rather than a person.

June stared at Mario and he shrugged his shoulders to indicate that he didn't know who it was.

"Am I allowed to speak now?" Bettina said angrily.

"Sweetheart, I didn't tell you everything about my parents," Mario said.

Just then Mario's cell phone rang.

"It's Crystal," Mario said then put the call on speaker phone. "Crystal, where are you? How are you?"

"I'm fine, Dad. What's going on? I turned my phone off because I've been in a meeting all morning and then I was busy on a project. Why did you call me like a hundred times, Dad, what's wrong?" Crystal asked.

"When was the last time you spoke to Cady?" Mario said.

"I don't know, yesterday I think. What's going on, Dad?" Crystal asked again.

"I'm sending Detective Wright over to your job right now to pick you up and bring you here. I'll explain when you get here," Mario said.

"Dad, what am I supposed to tell my boss, my dad wants me to come home so I have to leave early? No, Dad, you're going to need to give me an explanation now," Crystal said.

"Your sister's missing," Mario said.

"What? Why do you think that?" Crystal asked.

As Mario and Crystal continued their telephone conversation, something Mario said brought a frightening look to Bettina's face.

"What is it?" June asked her.

"Toni is missing too," Bettina said.

"Who's Toni?" June asked.

"Mario, the caller said daughters plural, but he doesn't have Crystal, do you think they got Toni by mistake?" Bettina asked now ignoring June.

"No, why would they think that Toni is my daughter?" Mario said.

"I don't know but Toni's been missing since this morning and now Cady's missing, that's more than a coincidence."

"Who is Toni?" June asked again.

Bettina explained the morning's events to June. When Mario finished speaking to Crystal he joined their conversation.

"June, if we work Toni's case maybe we'll find something that connects to Cady or that would rule out a connection all together," Mario said.

"Wait a minute, Mario. You need to call this in. You can't work your own daughter's case," Bettina said.

Mario and June exchanged looks.

"What?" Bettina asked.

"Bettina, if we call this in Mario would be excluded from the case all together. And they would hand the case over to the feds and their track record for recovering our people in particular is not good," June said.

Then June looked at Mario and said, "I don't know how much help I can be."

"I need you, June. I don't trust any other cop with this. This is my baby girl, June, you know Cady," Mario said.

"What is she doing here?" Crystal asked as she entered the living room with Detective Wright.

"She's going to help us find Cady, honey," Mario said.

"Dad, call the police, the real police. We don't need her," Crystal said.

"Crystal!" both Mario and Bettina said simultaneously.

"It's okay. I need to pick up Rosie. Mario, let me get things settled at home and then we'll regroup," June said.

"What can I do?" Wright asked.

"Can you give me a ride?" June asked.

"Sure. Did you call it in Detective Grimes? I expected to see police swarming all over by now," Wright said.

"I'll explain everything to you on the way," June said.

Crystal followed Detective Wright and Pastor June out to the car and said to June, "We don't need your help with this. This is our family business, you understand?"

"Look, little girl, I don't know what your problem is with me but get this straight right here and right now, you will not disrespect me. I love your sister and that is my business here, now do you understand that?" June said.

But Crystal rolled her eyes and returned inside the house.

Wright shook her head at June as they entered her car. While they drove to the elementary school to pick up Rosie, June explained to Wright that they didn't want to call the kidnapping threat in yet. She told her about the one kidnapping case she and Mario worked in Sarasota County where the feds took over the case and the victim was killed because they procrastinated in the investigation because in her opinion they lacked a sense of urgency.

June had Wright drive her and Rosie to St. Mark Church and, as they were pulling up into the church parking lot, June noticed her husband's car parked in his reserved parking space. She lowered her head and dreaded the fight that she knew was coming.

"Daddy" Rosie said as she ran to Brice who was sitting in June's office.

Myrtle sensing what was coming said, "Rosie, honey, come with Auntie Myrt and we'll find you some snacks."

June explained everything to Brice and that Mario needed her to help him find his daughter and that time was of the essence. "The first twenty four hours are the most crucial, Brice," June said.

"I don't care. I understand that he's worried about his baby but I'm worried about mine too and right now my baby is in your belly. It's one thing for you to go traipsing around town putting yourself at risk, Junie, but now it's not just you. Do I really have to tell you that we have a high risk pregnancy? You're not even supposed to be on your feet for more than a couple hours at a time," Brice said with a raised voice.

"Brice, I promise I won't be doing anything physical. I need to help him gather evidence that's all. It's like finding puzzle pieces and I'm really good at that. I promise that I'll be careful but this is Cady. I've gotten really close to her in the last year, I can't just sit around. I have to help find her," June said.

"Junie, I cannot give you my permission to do this," Brice said.

"Your permission? I don't remember asking your permission to do anything," June said angrily as she began standing to her feet.

"If you do this we will have a problem, Junie," Brice said sternly.

"If you think I need your permission to do anything, you already have a problem," June quickly said.

"Look, you are my wife and Rosie's mother. You can't go gallivanting around town like you're only responsible for yourself, you understand that? You cannot do this, Junie, absolutely not!" Brice said.

"Excuse me? So now I'm a child and don't know how to be responsible? I was the detective not you, Brice. I know what's dangerous and what's not. And as long as this baby is in my belly, I make the decisions not you. When it comes out, you can have half a say, but until then it's on me," June said.

"I can't believe you could do this for that ex-detective so called friend of yours. You and I both know that he's still in love with you. Now I'm wondering where your heart is?

"What? What did you just say to me?" June said.

"You heard what I said," Brice said.

"So the mighty Brice Howard is a jealous man after all," June said.

"Any man would have a problem with his wife risking her life and the life of their baby, mighty or not!" Brice said.

"Nobody said you couldn't have a problem with it, what you can't do is make decisions about me for me. I didn't just come out of my momma's house, man. I'm a fully grown woman and I don't need your permission or consent to do anything," June said heatedly.

"I'm going to take Rosie home before we say more things we will regret," Brice said. He exhaled and then continued softly, "Myrtle says you have people waiting on you in the lobby but I'm serious about this, Junie, don't do this. You can't risk my baby while you're trying to save somebody else's."

Brice turned and left June's office. June slowly sat back down behind her desk.

Myrtle entered. "Are you all right, Pastor?" Myrtle asked.

"Give me a minute, Myrtle. Then send them in," June replied.

"Are you sure? Maybe we should reschedule," Myrtle said.

"No, we already rescheduled them the last time they came," June said sharper than intended. She leaned back in her chair and closed her eyes. "I'll be okay. Just give me a minute, close the door please."

Myrtle knew what that meant. June was entering into prayer. Myrtle had never heard June and Brice arguing before or even saying a moderately unkind word toward each other. She was worried about this and so she decided that she would go into the sanctuary and do some praying of her own.

June sat in her office realizing that her unpleasant disposition had been building for the last several months. She remembered that just over a year ago she yearned for romantic love and motherhood. Now that she had it, she often caught herself longing for private moments and solitude. She was feeling crowded. She was not accustomed to sharing so much of herself with anyone. She exhaled and began to pray, "Father God, I have no idea what is happening with me. Please help me with my temperament. I don't want to use this baby as an excuse to be mean and unkind or to not be understanding. Please Lord, soften Brice's heart about what you know I have to do. I know he loves me and his baby but Lord, you know I can't sit idly by while Mario's daughter is in trouble and possibly in danger. Help me find the words, Lord. Lay them on my heart, please. And please, Lord, give me the strength to counsel this couple with excitement and not sadness. Let me be a positive encourager in their path to marriage. I love you Lord and care only to do your will, please speak to my heart, Lord."

Her prayer was interrupted by a knock on her office door.

"One moment please."

June reached into her drawer to retrieve some tissue so that she could wipe the tears from her face. She checked in her hand mirror to make sure she didn't look like she had been crying. She pinched her cheeks to give them some color because she thought she looked washed out and bland. Once she had done all she thought she could do to look normal, she invited Mr. Evans and Ms. Santos into her office. "Come in please," June said.

Pastor June motioned for them to sit in the two chairs facing her desk. They were meeting for pre-marital counseling. June had a process for this type of counseling and they had come to share their homework with her. Mr. Evans and Ms. Santos was an older couple, both were widows as well as grandparents. They had been dating for five months and were now planning to be married.

"How are you guys doing today?" Pastor June asked.

"We're good, Pastor," Mr. Evan's said.

"Good, good to know. You have your homework completed?" Pastor June asked.

"Well, almost," Ms. Santos said.

"Almost?" Pastor June asked.

"Yes, everybody didn't make it to the clinic," Ms. Santos said as she turned to look at Mr. Evans.

"Is there a problem, Mr. Evans?" Pastor June asked.

"Well, now this ain't my first run around the track, Pastor June. I don't understand why we have to do all this stuff, it's not like we young people doing this for the first time," Mr. Evans said.

"I explained this to you already, Mr. Evans. If you want me to marry you, or to get married in this church at all, I require that this checklist be completed. It doesn't matter how many times you've been married or how old you are. I feel some sense of responsibility to ensure that you both enter into this marriage with full knowledge of the things on this list, full disclosure. Remember agreeing to that?" Pastor June said.

After a couple of seconds with no response, she continued. "Well, let's go over what you do have okay?"

The couple both nodded in the affirmative.

"Number one, did you each exchange your last two bank statements?"

They both nodded yes.

"And you're each okay with how the other is managing their finances?" Pastor June asked.

"Well, there were some things on there that I questioned but he explained it," Ms. Santos said.

"Okay, good. Remember this is not information I need to know, its information that each of you need to know. So if you're okay with it, I'm okay with it. Okay now you've decided where you're going to live and how the finances will be decided?" Pastor June asked.

Again they both nodded yes.

"And did you each take an HIV test and share the results with the other?" Pastor June asked.

There was silence from them both.

"Is there a problem?" Pastor June asked.

"Well, I went to the clinic and got a result the same day but he haven't gone yet," Ms. Santos said.

"Mr. Evans, I may be able to bend my criteria for any other condition but not with this one. I will not marry you until you've shared your HIV-AIDs status with Ms. Santos. Are you nervous about taking an HIV test? Because if you are, I can tell you that it is very normal."

Mr. Evans did not respond so Pastor June continued,

"You know I took the test a couple of years ago and although I was not at all considered to be high risk, in fact even though I was pretty confident I was negative, I was still really, really nervous. It's very natural to be nervous."

Mr. Evans lowered his head and said, "I love this woman. I would love her no matter what."

This was curious to Pastor June, it sounded like guilt and not just a declaration of love.

"Ms. Santos, can I ask you a favor? Can you ask Myrtle to get in touch with my ride from earlier today? I don't have my car today and I don't want to wait too late to ask her for a ride," Pastor June said.

Ms. Santos took the hint. She knew that her fiancé was really nervous and she was happy that Pastor June was going to try to calm his nerves about taking the test. Little did she know that Pastor June had something totally different in mind.

Once Ms. Santos left the office, she looked at Mr. Evans and said, "You've already been tested haven't you, Mr. Evans?"

He lowered his head while reaching into his jacket pocket and pulling out an envelope that he then handed to June. June could see that the postmark was about a year old. It was from the county health department.

"You haven't opened it, why?" Pastor June asked.

"Don't have to. I already know. It's what my first wife died from," Mr. Evans said.

Pastor June let out a long sigh. She was very glad that she hadn't rescheduled them. "You have to tell her," June said.

"I'm scared to, Pastor. Scared she'll leave me," he said.

"Mr. Evans, first of all HIV or AIDS is no longer a death sentence. People are living long lives with the right medication but you have to get the right medication and that only happens when you get your levels tested. Was your former wife on any meds?" she asked.

"I don't know. We split up about two years before she died. She was on drugs real bad and I couldn't take it no more so I left. I didn't know she had it until after she died," he said.

"Mr. Evans, did it ever occur to you that you could very well be negative?" she asked.

She got no response. "Do you want me to open it?"

He shrugged his shoulders, so Pastor June opened the letter and read it to herself then asked, "Mr. Evans, have you had unprotected relations with anybody in the last year and a half?"

He shook his head, no.

"Any drug use in the last year and a half?"

"No, no way, I would never do drugs, I know too much about what it can do," he said.

"Well, then Mr. Evans I would suggest that you go back to the clinic and get tested just to make sure that this is not a false negative result but this result says that you are negative."

"Really?"

"Yes, Sir."

"Oh my God. Thank you, Jesus," he said.

"Look, take your letter back. Go back to the clinic and take the test, Mr. Evans. Then give the results to Sister Santos with a current date on it. Get it?" she said.

"Yeah, yeah thanks, Pastor June. I will go first thing tomorrow, I promise I will."

Tears of relief poured down Mr. Evans' face so Pastor June handed him some tissues and said, "Mr. Evans, I'm going to excuse myself. Feel free to use my bathroom to wash up before you see Sister Santos."

Then she took his hand smiling and said, "Let us pray. Father God, we thank you. Amen."

Then Pastor June left Mr. Evans in her office. She told Ms. Santos he needed a minute but that everything was perfectly fine. After a couple of minutes Mr. Evans came out of June's office looking very refreshed and displaying a big smile; he met up with Sister Santos and June in the hallway. The couple shook Pastor June's hand and left the church promising to return for their next appointment with all their homework finally completed.

Pastor June found Myrtle in the sanctuary sitting in the front pew staring at the altar. She sat down in the seat beside her.

"You're worried about me and Brice aren't you?" she asked.

"Yeah, I hate to hear y'all fightin," Myrtle said.

"Don't worry. I'm not. I know God's got this. In times like these we have to see how big God is. He's big enough to calm Brice down, to find Cady, and keep my baby safe all at the same time because He's a really big God," Pastor June said.

Myrtle nodded her head and Pastor June put her arm around her shoulders to comfort her. At that point the musicians were entering into the sanctuary for rehearsal and they could see that Myrtle was upset so the music director asked, "Pastor, do you want us to wait outside for a little bit longer?"

"No, no, I want y'all to get up there and start playing, 'My God is Awesome' really loud. That's what we need right now. We need to get caught up in praise, right, Myrtle?"

"Yes, that would be wonderful, Pastor June," Myrtle said.

Pastor June and Myrtle walked all over the sanctuary praising God through song with their hands and voices raised high. When June noticed Detective Wright standing at the entrance of the sanctuary waiting to take her home, June motioned for her to join them. Wright hesitated but didn't want to be rude so she came to Pastor June as she was reaching out for her. She tried to teach her the lyrics and took Wright by the hand and led her around the sanctuary while she and Myrtle continued praising God from way down deep. June called it deep belly praise. After a couple of minutes Detective Wright fell right in line with Pastor June and Myrtle. And then finally after about twenty more minutes Pastor June felt a little light headed so she sat down with Myrtle and Detective Wright following suit.

Detective Wright's face was flushed and flooded with tears and Pastor June asked her, "Is this the first time you've done anything like that?"

Detective Wright nodded her head as she tried catching her breath.

Pastor June smiled and said, "Well let me be the first to tell you, praise looks really, really good on you."

## 11

*"Moreover you shall select from all the people able men, such as fear God, men of truth, hating **cove**tousness; and place such over them to be rulers of thousands, rulers of hundreds, rulers of fifties, and rulers of tens."* ~Exodus 18:21

Detective Wright and Pastor June sat in silence in Wright's car in the middle of June's driveway.

June finally broke the silence. "Why don't you head on back over to Mario's in case he needs something and be sure to call me if he does," and then she got out of the car.

Inside the house, she found her husband cooking dinner. She stopped to watch him without him knowing that she was there. She really truly loved him. She loved most everything about him. She never got tired of watching him. He was tall and dark with the hugest hazel green eyes (that were encased with about a million long eyelashes) that she'd ever seen. She couldn't figure out how the man could see. After they were married, he kept his hair cut really short but on the occasion he allowed it to grow out; they formed little ringlets all over. He also had huge deep set dimples that made an appearance whenever he smiled or laughed. He was strikingly beautiful to June and sometimes she couldn't believe that he was her husband. She knew she wasn't exactly hard on the eye but she never thought somebody that could have easily been a supermodel would be interested in her. And, as she watched him cutting the cabbage to steam, she began to think about Mario, her first love. She remembered that when they used to work together for the Sheriff's office in Sarasota County that it wasn't long before they were in a romantic relationship. He was also very handsome but in a different sort of way. He lived for the job as did June at the time.

She realized how far the Lord had truly brought her from. That was a different life, it was a selfish life, and she had to realize that Brice was not Mario and could not possibly understand the drive for justice that she and Mario still seemed to share. Then the Lord began speaking to her heart about all that happened today, as she knew He would.

"Hi," June said to Brice.

"Hi yourself," he replied as he placed the top on the steamer without turning around to look at her. June could tell he was still very angry.

"Is Rosie's in her room?" June asked.

"Yes," he said still without making any eye contact with her.

"Well, we'd better ask Myrtle if Rosie can come over. We'll probably need her to take Rosie for the next few days," June said.

Then Brice turned to face Pastor June. "Why does Myrtle need to take Rosie?"

"Well, honey, Billie's away and there's an emergency. My good friend needs my help and I have to give it to him. I haven't changed my mind about that. But I realize that although he may need me, I really need you, so I'd like you to join us. You could come and be my help," June said.

"What? You want me to help you with the investigation?" Brice asked surprised.

"Sure, I think you could and if nothing else maybe you'll see why I need to help. Mostly though, I think I need you to help me to remember that I'm no longer in this alone, you were right about that. I do have other people in my life now that care and rely on me," June said.

"Are you just trying to appease me, Junie?" Brice asked.

"What? No, I'm trying to show you another side of me," June said.

"I'm still very angry with you, Junie. I know by now that you're going to do what you want to do no matter what I say or how I feel but I will go along you on this only because I don't trust you to take care of you," Brice said rather flatly looking directly at her.

June got upset again because she felt that he was trying to make her feel guilty. She raised her voice slightly and said, "You know I'm really trying here. I don't know how much this is an adjustment for you but it's a huge adjustment for me. I'm not accustomed to having to tell somebody where I'm going and what I'm doing. I'm putting up a real effort here but I am a fully grown woman perfectly capable of making competent decisions and you need to understand that."

"What I know is that you're a fully grown woman walking around with my baby in your belly and I am going to do all that I can do to make sure that my baby is safe, do you understand that?" Brice asked just as tersely.

At that point, June's cell phone began ringing and she saw that it was Mario so she answered. "Hi, Mario. You got something new?"

"No. I'm just not quite sure how to proceed, June. If we were on an official case I would have Cady's phone logs pulled by now but I can't ask that. I really don't know what else to do, this waiting around is killing me."

"Well what about starting with Toni's logs?"

"Her phone is already in evidence and probably waiting in a long line of other evidence waiting for processing," Mario said.

June began pacing. "I have an idea. See if you can get a hold of Toni's phone and Crystal's phone for that matter and meet me in Lake Park at Eartha's place," June said.

"Eartha? Who in the world is Eartha?" Mario asked.

"Oh, yeah you may know her as Mac," June said.

"Mac the hacker? How do you know Mac?" Mario said.

"Her mom is one of my church members," June said.

When Pastor June hung up the phone with Mario, she looked at Brice with her hands on her hips and said, "Well?"

Brice looked at her and sighed then looking directly at June yelled, "Rosie, you need to pack an overnight bag, you're going to have a sleep over with Auntie Myrt tonight."

"Yaay!" could be heard coming from Rosie upstairs.

Brice and June dropped Rosie off with her Hello Kitty suitcase in tow back at the St. Mark Church with Myrtle. They told Rosie that they were going on an adventure and they would tell her all about it when they came back to pick her up. Myrtle observed June and Brice in the car when she went into the parking lot to get Rosie and she could see that there was still tension between them. This distressed Myrtle greatly because the talk around town was that Pastor June Harris and Supervising Elder Brice Howard's marriage would not last. People just couldn't get past what many deemed a conflict of interest with Brice being in official authority over June in the capacity of ministry. Many of these people had already been victimized by June's wrath and could not see her being tamed by anyone. Myrtle decided that if June and Brice didn't get it together soon, she was going to have to host some kind of marriage intervention.

By the time they reached Mac's house, Mario and Wright were parked out front waiting for June. When Mario saw that Brice was accompanying June a genuine surprised look overcame his face.

"Brice," Mario said flatly as he reached for Brice's hand.

"Mario," Brice said just as flatly as they shook each other's hands coldly.

Their relationship had been a bit strained from the very beginning. Although Mario was happily married to Bettina he couldn't help but feel a twinge of jealousy towards Brice. He often found himself pondering and speculating about whatever it was that June seemed to see in Brice that she did not see in him. Mario could acknowledge that the man looked like he stepped right out of a magazine but he felt that Brice just didn't know June the way that he did.

And Brice hated the idea that Mario was the one person that hurt June the most, and that she still continued to be there for him and now also for his wife and daughter. He found himself frequently agitated when they would call on June any time of the day, or night about this or that and it also greatly frustrated Brice that June seemed all too eager to entertain their chaos.

"I'm happy to help but I'm also here to look out for my wife," Brice said to Mario.

June observing the semi-showdown between Mario and Brice, looked disapprovingly at them and said, "Get over yourselves already, both of you," then she turned to ring Mac's doorbell.

"Who dat?" a voice from inside yelled through the door.

"It's Pastor June, Eartha."

The door was opened by an extremely tall and slender African American woman in her late twenties. She was of medium complexion and had long blondish red dreadlocks that fell down to her waist with sea shells on most of the ends. She had multiple piercings on her face, two in her nose, eyebrows and chin. She also had tattoos everywhere, on her chest, arms, and legs, even along the side of her face.

"Awww man, Pastor June, why you got to call me that name, everybody in the world call me Mac because of my mad computer skills why can't you?" Mac said.

"Well, your momma named you Eartha, so I'm just being respectful," June said.

"Not to me, I hate that name."

Then she saw Brice and Mario just outside of her front door and she attempted to slam it close but Mario put his hand up to the door stopping its momentum.

"Awww man and you bought the police to my house too?" Mac said.

"Listen Eartha -- I mean Mac, we're not here on official business at all. We need a favor," June said.

"Oh why not, I'm already on house arrest, it's not like I can leave is it?" She said lifting up her long African print skirt exposing her court ordered ankle bracelet.

"Thank you Eartha. I promise it's for a good reason," June said.

Eartha reluctantly sat down at her desk. "Who am I hacking for the police today?" Mac asked.

"Wouldn't your probation ban you from having a computer?" Mario asked.

"Yes, but this is not a computer, Mr. Police Man, this is a tablet with a detachable mini keyboard. You guys have yet to catch up with technology, you can't hold it against me, so I am not in violation, officer," Mac said.

Mario explained to Mac what it was that they were looking for and within an hour they were all looking at the call records of Toni, Crystal and Cady's cell phones that Mac printed.

"Look to see if there are any telephone numbers that appear multiple times," June said.

After several minutes Mario said, "I don't see any numbers repeating that aren't familiar except for these two numbers on Cady's phone."

"Let me see. I recognize one of these numbers, its Demetrius. He and Cady were camp counselors together this summer at my church. I thought they were dating but she told me that they were just really good friends. This other number isn't familiar but it's probably the guy she was dating. We talked about him remember?" June said.

"Yeah I know Demetrius too, he's been to the house a couple of times, but I didn't know she was dating anybody," Mario said.

"Is that all the information you wanted, Pastor June?" Mac asked agitated and obviously ready for them to leave.

"Why, is there something else we should know?" June asked reading between the lines.

"Wow, you know me too well. Yeah, now I don't know about the phone that we don't physically have but these other two phones have a tracker on them," Mac said.

"What does that mean?" Mario asked.

"It means that somebody's been able to see where whoever had these phones have been going," Mac said.

"Can you tell for how long?" June asked.

Mac took something out of Crystal's phone and put it into the side of her tablet now turned computer and then she removed it quickly and did the same with Toni's phone.

"Both phones have been tracked for the last thirty days. They both started getting tracked on the same day, minutes apart. But I could only find geographical data on one of the phones," Mac said.

"Which one?" Mario asked.

"This one," Mac said as she held up Toni's phone.

"Why would that be?" June asked.

"I don't know, maybe this one was off. Believe it or not there are people who only turn their phones on for emergencies, my momma for example," Mac said.

"Yes, that makes sense because Crystal always turns her phone off during the day. She probably doesn't even turn it on until she's driving home from work," Mario said.

"That would be the reason then," Mac said.

"So he didn't take Crystal because he didn't know where she was but he took Cady because he did," Mario said.

"I think there's more to it than that. Eartha, I mean Mac, you said the tracking's been going on for the past 30 days?" June asked.

"Yes, somebody downloaded a tracking app on each of these phones."

"Sounds to me like somebody was trying to learn about their routine," Brice said.

"Yeah that's what I think too, somebody who knows the same type of stuff you know, Mac. Anybody like that ring a bell?" June asked Mac.

"Are you kidding? This is just my side gig; any high school kid with a smart phone knows how to do this stuff," Mac said.

"Yeah, June, Mac is a master document forger. A really good one but with too much pride, that's why she keeps getting caught. She can't help putting her distinctive signature on all of her work," Mario said.

"I'm an artist, Man. Is that all? I really need y'all to leave now," Mac said.

Everyone turned towards the door when they heard someone knocking.

"Great, this is just great. Hold on, I'm talking with the police in here," Mac yelled through the door.

"I know. It's Detective Wright," the voice on the other side of the door said.

Mac opened the door and waved Detective Wright in. "Come on in and join the party. Are you expecting anybody else, Pastor June?" Mac asked sarcastically.

"Cowboy Joe called. He wants us to come to his office. He discovered something odd with the body," Wright said.

As they all prepared to leave, Mac said, "Pastor June, tell my momma that I'll call her tomorrow before dinner."

June paused and tilted her head bewildered.

Mac continued. "She wanted me to give her a recipe for Sunday dinner."

June nodded and turned to catch up with everyone else. Wright, Mario, June and Brice all gathered outside in front of Mac's place.

"June, why don't you and Brice go talk to this Demetrius kid and maybe he can give you more information on the new boyfriend. Wright and I will go to the morgue and talk to Cowboy Joe," Mario said.

"Yeah, that's a good idea. I don't think I could handle that morgue smell right now anyway," June said.

On the drive over to Two Touch's house, Brice broke the silence that had continued between he and June. "Junie, what was that bit about a recipe back there?"

"Are you talking to me now?" June said sarcastically.

"Come on, Junie, I'm trying here too you know. What was that business about recipes?" Brice asked.

"She's got some more information on who might be behind this I think and she didn't want to say whatever it is in front of everybody," June said.

"How did you possible get that from what little she said?" Brice asked.

"Well because Eartha is gay and I've been counseling her and her mother about her lifestyle on and off for the last three years. They send messages back and forth through me but they have never actually spoken directly to each other in all that time. Eartha is willing to talk to her mom with me in the room but her mother says she's still not ready, she hasn't spoken directly to Eartha. And Eartha is not willing to contact her mother at all on her own. She came out to her family three years ago when she finished her tour in the army and she's still really hurting over their rejection. So whenever she sees me around she tends to speak in code so no one knows that she really misses her mother. Just now she was speaking in that code type way. She's not calling her mother, she's going to call me with new information."

"Wow, you really are good at this puzzle pieces thing," Brice said.

"I told you it wouldn't be anything dangerous, Brice," June said.

"I wasn't trying to control you, Sweetheart. I was just --" Brice tried to say but June interrupted,

"I know, I know you were scared for me, for us. You're the ying to my yang. I jump in feet first without a thought and you catch me in mid-air. I know I get mad and obstinate but I really love you so much for that," June said smiling as she stroked his cheek. "Now let's go do this thing, Babe."

"Yes, Ma'am, Detective, Ma'am," Brice said and began driving to Two Touch's house.

Once they parked in front of Two Touch's home Brice took June by the chin and pulled her lips to his and they shared a long passionate kiss that was then followed by a long embrace.

When Detective Wright and Detective Grimes arrived at the morgue Cowboy Joe was sitting at his desk in his office.

"Hey, Mario, Sylvia."

"Hey, Joe. You got something for us?" Mario asked.

"Yeah, after I got Dale's body cleaned up, I found an injection mark like a hair above the cut on his throat," Cowboy Joe said.

"So the knife wound didn't kill him?" Wright asked.

"Oh, yes. He was still definitely alive until his throat was slit. I know that because of all the blood, that tells me that his heart was still pumping," Cowboy Joe said.

"So then why was he injected with something and what was he injected with?" Mario asked.

"Well I'm still waiting for the tox screen but if I had to guess I would say he was injected with something to incapacitate him first, he was a big guy," Cowboy Joe said.

Mario started walking around the office then said, "Okay the car was at an intersection with a stop sign, so the car could have already been at a stop. If somebody snatched Toni out of the car and then when the husband attempted to get out of the car to help her, somebody else could have injected him and pushed him back into the car. So that means we might be looking for more than one killer."

"And then because the vic fell across the car with his neck exposed just under the glove compartment, the person already on the passenger side could have quickly slit his throat," Wright said.

"Sounds very plausible. But here's the other thing. I had another victim a couple months ago again with the same type of an injection mark and it was on his neck as well," Cowboy Joe said.

"Was his throat slit too?" asked Detective Grimes.

"No, but he was stabbed in the chest directly into the heart, different blade, different wound type. But the curious thing is that the wounds from both of these murders have a single similar notch," Cowboy Joe said.

"What do you mean, notch?" Wright asked.

"Well if I were to guess again, I'd say that these were homemade knife blades. In other words whoever did both of these murders made the blades themselves. And either on purpose or because of the mold he used to make the blades there is a small distinctive notch shaped sort of like the top of a skinny clover leaf," Cowboy Joe said.

"Do you have any information on that victim?" Mario asked.

"Yes, I had his file pulled. His name was Harry Franks," Cowboy Joe said as he handed the file to Mario.

"No convictions but several accusations of child molestation, his step daughter," Mario said reading through the file.

"Was there an investigation?" Wright asked.

"Looks like there were several anonymous calls about the molestation but when the detectives didn't get anything from the wife or the step daughter it was dropped. His murder case is still open," Mario said.

"We need to talk to those detectives," Wright said.

"Well first we need to head over to May Bell's house and make the notification. Dale had no other next of kin. I'm not looking forward to this but she might let us into

Toni's house and maybe we'll find out more there," Mario said.

"Do you know if Cady and Toni kept in touch?" Wright asked.

Mario looked at Wright in disbelief that she would bring up Cady in front of Cowboy Joe. Cowboy Joe and Mario had become good friends in the past year. They went fishing several times a month and Cowboy Joe's wife Wendy was the person who initially introduced Mario to Christ. But Mario knew that Cowboy Joe was a by-the-book kind of guy and Mario didn't want to put him in a compromising position.

"What's Cady got to do with this, Mario?" Cowboy Joe asked.

Detective Wright held her head down from the embarrassment of her slip up.

"I can't tell you anything right now Joe, but when and if I need to I will," Mario said.

# 12

*"Because from the least of them even to the greatest of them, Everyone is given to **covet**ousness; And from the prophet even to the priest, Everyone deals falsely." ~*Jeremiah 6:13

Two Touch invited June and Brice inside. The twins ran up to June and she hugged them both really tight.

"Come see our room, Pastor June," they both shouted at the same time pulling her down the hallway. This left Brice in the living room alone with Two Touch.

"Hi, I'm Reverend Brice Howard, Pastor June's husband."

"Oh, yeah. How you doing? You want something to drink?" Two Touch asked.

"No thank you, I'm fine. June just needs to ask you some questions," Brice said.

June came back down the hallway smiling. "My God they're getting so big. I asked them to draw me a picture so we could talk, Demetrius," June said.

June sat down on the couch next to her husband and pulled a notebook out of her purse.

"Okay. What's going on?" Two Touch asked.

"When was the last time you spoke to Cady?" June asked.

"Last night. I'm waiting on her to call me right now. We're supposed to meet up at the library this afternoon. I was just about to call her when you knocked," Two Touch said.

"So you haven't heard from her since then?" June asked.

"No. She texted me this morning saying she was on her way down from Miami and that she would call me when she was ready to meet," Two Touch said.

"What time was that text?" June asked.

Two Touch pulled out his phone and searched for the text. "It was 9:38 this morning. What's going on? Did something happen to her?" Two Touch asked, standing up.

"We're not sure, Demetrius. She never made it to the house this morning and nobody else has heard from her. Her father is very concerned because that's not like her at all," June said as she watched for Two Touch's reaction.

"Oh my God. You think maybe she got in a car wreck or something?" Two Touch asked.

June noticed his breathing had become labored. She remembered the list of aliments Two Touch's mother had given to her for his summer camp job at St. Mark Church and she realized he was having an asthma attack.

"Where's your inhaler, Demetrius?" June asked.

He pointed to a drawer in the kitchen. Brice got up and fished through the drawer until he located the inhaler and handed it to Two Touch. After using the inhaler his breathing soon began returning to normal.

"Demetrius, Cady has spoken to me about your friendship with her. I know that you care a great deal for each other. We're afraid for her right now. What can you tell me about this Jackson guy that she's dating?" June asked.

Both June and Brice noticed the hurt look on Two Touch's face when June mentioned Jackson's name. Two Touch sat back down on the couch and June and Brice returned to the couch as well.

"He's a friend of mine. I introduced them. I had no idea that they would start dating," Two Touch said sadly.

"What kind of guy is he? Do you think he could hurt her, physically I mean?" June asked.

"No, no way. He's all talk. He's a rich kid from Boca Raton. He don't have no street cred at all but he try to fake like he do. He's going through a rough time right now with his old man but he's not a scary dude, I don't believe he could hurt nobody," Two Touch said.

"What kind of problem, with his dad?" Brice asked.

June looked at Brice pleasantly surprised at his question and interest. Now smiling she then turned to Two Touch, waiting for an answer to the question.

"Well the kid is a bum. I mean his daddy got money, lots of money but he been flunking out of colleges for the last couple of years. His daddy finally got fed up and cut him off. He was hanging around here with me everyday till my momma put a stop to it," Two Touch said.

"Yeah I can totally see Debra doing that," June said.

"You know my momma don't play," Two Touch said with a chuckle.

"What's Jackson's number?" June asked.

Two Touch gave her Jackson's cell number. She took Cady's cell records from her husband and found Jackson's number listed several times over the last month. There were many late night calls especially once she left West Palm Beach and went back to school in Miami. June texted Jackson's cell number to Mac and asked her to pull the activity on his cell phone. After several minutes Mac responded with, "Will do."

At that point June's cell began vibrating, it was the church. "Hello, this is Pastor June."

"Hi, Pastor, is everything okay?" Myrtle asked.

"Yes, is Rosie okay?" June asked.

"Oh yeah, she's bossing everybody around as usual," Myrtle said laughing. "Did you intend for me to reschedule your meeting with Reverend Deena?" Myrtle asked.

"Oh I completely forgot. No, I'll be there in fifteen minutes, tell her to wait. We're almost done here."

She went into the twin's room to retrieve her drawings and to say goodbye. Two Touch walked them to the door. "Please keep me in the loop about Cady, she's my best friend," he said with tears welling in his eyes.

"We will. Don't worry, Demetrius. For all we know her car stalled somewhere but you know how daddies are about their daughters," June said.

She didn't want to let on to anybody that Cady was kidnapped because she had no idea who was involved. She doubted very seriously that Two Touch had any part in it but he might do something stupid like try to investigate Cady's disappearance on his own.

When May Bell opened the screen door and saw Detective Wright and Detective Grimes she smiled a huge smile.

"Mr. Grimes, so good of you to come by to see about me. I told Pastor Brown I was all right, just ain't been able to get to church in a while."

She moved to the side of the doorway, inviting them to come inside. Mario noticed that May Bell was limping as she walked. Her little wood framed house was unkempt. He noticed stacks and piles of newspapers and magazines and he realized that May Bell was on the verge of being a hoarder.

"Get down Peanut," May Bell said to her tom cat as he jumped on the arm of the chair Mario was seated in.

"How are you May Bell?" Mario asked.

"Between fair and middlin' I reckon," May Bell said.

"Have you heard from Toni or her husband Dale today?" Mario asked.

"Yes," she said as she reached into her housecoat pocket and pulled out her cell phone. "Dale just sent me a text saying that Toni left her phone in the car and that she had to work late and could I keep the baby overnight," May Bell said.

Detective Wright reached for May Bell's cell phone while making eye contact with Mario. Mario motioned his head and she responded by going outside with May Bell's cell phone.

"I have some bad news, May Bell. This morning we found Dale's body in his car by the cemetery in Lake Worth," Mario said.

"What? But no, he just sent me that text ten minutes ago. That can't be. You sure it was him?" May Bell asked.

"Yes, we have a positive I.D," Mario said.

"Oh, no. Then who sent the text?" May Bell asked.

"I don't know but it wasn't him. There's something else, May Bell. Toni never made it to the Laundromat this morning for work. Nobody knows where she is," Mario said.

May Bell just stared at Mario then after several seconds she pleaded, "You looking for her ain't you? You not gon let nothing happen to my baby are you?"

"We're doing everything we know how to do, May Bell. Do you know if there was anybody who had something against Toni or Dale?"

"No, nobody. He's a good man, a good husband, and a hard worker. And Toni was going to church regular and making new friends there. Nobody had nothing against them, nobody. What about Daleena, the baby? They dropped her off to me last night so they could get some sleep," May Bell said.

"The baby can stay with you, May Bell until we find Toni," Mario said.

Relieved by that, May Bell then went into the back room where Toni's baby lay sleeping in a bassinette.

Outside on the porch, Detective Wright had Officer Dees on the phone.

"Did you locate Dale's cell phone in the car?" she asked.

"No, nothing other than a packed lunch in the back seat. Why?" Officer Dees asked.

"Because somebody recently used his phone to send his mother-in-law a text," she said.

"This is becoming weirder and weirder. You want me to pull the logs on his phone?" he asked.

"I'll get back to you," Detective Wright said and hung up.

She was growing tired of trying to remember what she should and should not say to people about this case. Detective Wright had been Mario's partner for just a little over a year. She looked up to him but was now being bothered by all this sneaking around. They were considered the odd couple on the force. A rather tall, white, blond woman from Oklahoma partnered with a veteran African American cop who never let anybody in. They were the butt of many jokes at the station.

No one knew that she had taken Toni's cell phone and she didn't want that information found out. She understood that this was about Mario's daughter but she wished that he would report the threat so she could investigate Cady's disappearance above board.

Just then Mario came through the door saying his goodbye and condolences to May Bell.

Back at St. Mark Church, Pastor June was sitting in her office with Brice seated in one of the chairs across from her desk when Reverend Deena came in.

"Hi, Pastor, Supervising Elder Howard, how y'all doing?" Reverend Deena asked.

"Good," Brice answered and then excused himself leaving Reverend Deena alone with June.

"Have a seat Deena," June said.

"Is there something wrong, Pastor?" Reverend Deena asked as she sat down.

"Yes, there is but before I get to that, did you bring your quarterly status report like I asked for St. Mark Church East?"

Reverend Deena handed her the report. Pastor June took several minutes to review the report.

"Pastor, did I do something wrong?" Reverend Deena asked.

"Well, Deena, this report is a little thin. According to the report from the Missions Board and the Finance Board, you've under reported both finances and outreach activity," June said.

"Well, you know I don't have the help over there that you do over here. I might have made some mistakes here and there," Deena said.

"When you didn't show up for service last Sunday, I put in a call to some of your stewards and I was surprised to learn that you've been having in-home bible studies and outreach ministries under another name," June said.

"Well is that illegal or something?" Deena said defensively.

"It is very suspicious. If you want to start your own ministry it is a conflict for you to do it while you are the lead minister over there because you're utilizing my people to do it. So while it might not be illegal, it's not very ethical is it?" June said.

"I just don't agree with some of the things you want me to do that's all. I don't like having to tell you every little thing that I do. I don't think I should have to do all that," Deena said.

"Your problem is not with me. These are not things I'm asking you to do. This is according to the bylaws of the church where we agreed to serve. You knew this coming in. Why didn't you just talk to me about it instead of going your own way and confusing the congregation over there?" June said.

Deena was silent but her face was tense. June picked up her office phone and told Myrtle to send Mr. Davis in.

Mr. Davis was June's head steward. He came and stood inside June's office door.

"Reverend Deena, you need to hand Mr. Davis your keys to St. Mark East. Make an appointment with him to meet you at St. Mark East so that you can retrieve any personal items you have there. As of this moment you are officially relieved as the lead minister of St. Mark East," June said.

"What? Are you for real? Nobody complained about anything over there, you don't have any cause to do that! You better check the bylaws," Deena said.

"What I cannot seem to get you to realize is that that location is an extension of this church. It is not a separate church. That means it is under my governance. It's no different than if you were an associate minister right here and so my authority extends there. You are being duplicitous in the focus of your ministry there. You're trying to steal my St. Mark East members and that I cannot allow. You're more than welcome to come back here, I won't be taking you off the ministerial staff unless you officially request that I do so as the bylaws state but your duties are whatever I say they are within this ministry. And, if you stay, you can consider yourself on probation," June said.

"So it's your way or no way, is that it?" Deena said.

"I am the only one who was appointed to pastor this church, Deena. If you can't follow my vision for the ministry of this congregation, then you are working against me. Look, there's nothing wrong with pursuing your own vision but there is a proper way to do that. You know all you need to do is to petition the Supervising Elder that you want to pastor a church and they will consider you for a pastorate appointment.

"But, you didn't want to go through the proper procedure. You wanted to highjack my people and that's just plain wrong. I don't mind telling you that I'm very disappointed. I considered you to be one of my daughters in ministry. Now you seem to be turning into David's son Absalom but unlike David, I ain't running from you. I'm nipping this mess in the bud right now, today. Now is there anything else you want to say?" June asked.

"No," Deena said while rolling her eyes.

"Have a blessed rest of the day and I hope I see you in the pulpit at this location Sunday morning. If not, I will begin the process of removing you from the ministerial staff," June said.

Two Touch ran up to Pastor June's outer office door just as Reverend Deena was removing her church keys from her key ring to hand over to Brother Davis.

"Pastor June, Pastor June, I just got a text from Cady. She's all right," Two Touch said excitedly.

"Let me see," June said.

He handed her the cell phone and Pastor June read the text which said, "Hi, sorry couldn't call. At a friend's house in Hollywood. She needed to talk. Can we reschedule the library? ~ Cady"

# 13

*"But now I have written to you not to keep company with anyone named a brother, who is sexually immoral, or **covet**ous, or an idolater, or a reviler, or a drunkard, or an extortioner—not even to eat with such a person."* ~1Corinthians 5:11

Later that night, Cady began to regain consciousness. She realized that she was lying on her side and she discovered that something was preventing her from opening her eyes. Her mouth was also covered with something so that she was unable to part her lips. Her hands were behind her back, and both her hands and feet were bound rather tightly. She felt as if the room was moving but not moving at the same time. Something also kept hitting up against her lower back. Then she heard a clicking sound, followed by a voice.

"You should be awake now. I'm going to untie you and take off your blindfold and gag so that you can eat. If you scream or make any noise I will put them back on and I will not take them off again. Nod your head if you understand. Now nod your head if you agree to these terms."

Cady nodded her head. The voice Cady heard sounded mechanical like a robot. She could hear someone moving around and then she heard a sigh. Someone peeled the tape from over her mouth and then untied whatever was around her eyes. She opened her eyes but the room was blurry and dark. She then felt whatever was binding her hands and feet being cut loose. She sat up and her eyes began to focus. A man stood in front of her. He was huge, tall, and wide. She suddenly remembered the remembering games her dad played with her and Crystal when they were little girls. It was a game to help them remember things. Often when they would take trips, usually to grandma's house, he would ask them to close their eyes and recall what they had just seen like the details of a gas station or a particular vehicle. She used word association. So she tried to recite in her mind, puffy coat, shiny pants, doorframe, ski mask, no skin, black Nikes. She noticed that the man's head almost reached the top of the door frame; he wore a black puffy coat with shiny black sweat pants. None of the man's skin showed. He wore a black ski mask that covered his entire head and it went down into his neck underneath the collar of his coat. The man also wore sunglasses under the ski mask so that his eyes were also not visible, and he wore black gloves. She had no idea of his race or complexion.

The man turned to leave the room, but he paused and clicked a button on a small digital recorder, "Remember if you scream or make any loud noises you will be gagged again. If you cooperate no one will get hurt, your father will come through soon so just relax, and this should all be over soon."

And then the man clicked the button to stop the digital player from speaking and he left the room. Cady's eyes began to regain their focus and she noticed that she was not alone in the room. Another woman was seated about two feet away from her. The walls in the room where she was being held were covered with what looked like hefty bags. No windows were visible, no openings at all except the door that the man appeared and disappeared through. She focused her attention on the woman. In front of the woman was a white box. Cady looked down in front of herself and saw another white box. It was a snack box from the Chicken Shack. Suddenly she was famished. Then she heard the woman say something.

"What?" Cady asked.

"You."

"Do I know you?" Cady asked.

"No, you never did."

"Oh my God, Toni, is that you?" Cady asked.

After Cady left home for college she had often wondered what happened to her. Toni was incredibly tiny, short, and skinny. In high school she always wore her hair in a short Jeri curl. Cady noticed that now her hair though still very short, was natural. Toni had a dark complexion and her face had beautiful bone structure. She could have easily been a model, if she was taller.

"I should have known that you were involved in this. Everything bad that has ever happened to me was because of your family," Toni said.

"What are you talking about? I have no idea what's going on. I was hoping you knew," Cady said.

In a low, angry voice Toni replied, "What I know is that man out there killed my husband for absolutely no reason," she said as a tear began running down her cheek.

"Killed? Are you sure? Did you see the man's face? Do you know who he is?" Cady asked. "Toni? Toni?" Cady repeated but Toni lay backwards, rolled onto her side, and remained silent.

Cady's mind was reeling. She couldn't think of anything to do. Although the ropes were removed she discovered that one of her ankles was chained to the center of the room on the floor with the same anchor as Toni's chains were. She noticed she had about two feet of chain. After trying to figure out where she was she realized that the movement she'd felt earlier was not moving but rather swaying. She deduced that they must be on the water in a boat. Once she examined the room where they were several more times, she realized that the best thing she could do at this point was to pray. She looked over at Toni curled up in a fetal position on the floor about four feet away from her and she got up to sit on her knees, placing her hands in a prayer position she began to pray.

"The Lord is my Shepherd. I shall not want. He makes me to lie down in green pastures --

"Stop," Toni said.

"Excuse me?"

"Stop. Don't do that," Toni said.

"Don't do what? I'm praying," Cady said.

"Stop talking to the air, there ain't no God. No good God would have ever allowed me to have this life. There ain't no God and all you doing is making noise, so stop it," Toni said.

"Toni, I know you're upset but when I take time to talk to God, He takes time to talk back to me. I believe in God and I have to pray to Him in this moment or I will go crazy. Now I won't pray out loud but I am going to pray," Cady said.

"If I had your life, it would be easy for me to believe in a God too. If you want to waste your time and energy go right ahead but I don't want to hear it, you understand me?" Toni said.

Cady closed her eyes and began reciting the Lord's prayer in her head. *Our Father who art in heaven, hallowed be thy name. Thy kingdom come, Thy will be done on earth as it is in heaven. Give us this day our daily bread and forgive us our trespasses as we forgive those who trespass against us. Lead us not into temptation but deliver us from evil.* She stopped short of ending the prayer as she went back over those last two verses: *Forgive us our trespasses as we forgive those who trespass against us and lead us not into temptation but deliver us from evil.*

Suddenly Cady felt as though God reached down and was comforting her with his righteous right hand. A calming peace fell over her as she visualized the words in her mind. Her heart rate went from beating extremely fast to almost normal. All of the anxiousness she felt due to her captor and then being insulted by Toni seemed to simply evaporate. She turned to look at Toni and realized that God was expecting her to take charge of this situation in a loving but stern way.

"I'm sorry for however you feel that my family has wronged you but fighting with me now won't help our situation. We have to work together if we want to get out of here. All I remember is walking out to my car this morning. Now I need you to tell me everything that you remember about getting here."

Toni slowly sat up and said, "Who do you think you are? You ain't running nothing here, not with me," Toni said.

"Okay, fine if you can't let it go, then you need to let it out. What exactly is your problem with me?" Cady asked.

"Everything. I can't stand you, never have and don't let me get started on your sister," Toni said with a raised voice.

"You're not here with my sister you're stuck here with me. I can't speak for her but I can speak for myself. What have I ever done to you?" Cady asked.

"You always thought you were better than me. Whenever I came to your house you would…"

"I would what? Be nice to you? Because that's all I ever tried to do, Toni," Cady said.

"You always thought you were so much with your designer clothes, your high yella skin, and curly hair. I never could stand you," Toni said angrily.

Cady looked at Toni with a confused expression on her face and said, "So it really isn't anything that I did, you just don't like me because I'm me? What was I supposed to do? Run up to my room before you came over and put on rags and a hat and give myself a spray tan? Let me tell you what I remember, Toni. It's not that you didn't like me; your problem is that you never liked you. You have an issue with the way you look. You allowed the world -- and let's be real, your mother, to convince you that because your skin is darker than mine, because your hair is kinkier than mine, that you were…"

Toni interrupted. "My momma thought the sun rose and set on you and your sister. She thought I should have been more like you guys. She even moved me to your stupid school; she tried to make me dress like you guys…"

Then Cady interrupted. "Then you should be mad at her and not at me. I never told you that you needed to be like me. I always tried to compliment you and I was being genuine, Toni. I never had a problem with you but you made it clear from day one that you didn't want anything to do with my friendship."

"You expect me to believe that you don't know what your sister did to me?" Toni said.

"Crystal? What did Crystal do to you?" Cady asked.

"You're going to sit there and act like you don't know?" Toni said angrily.

"I don't. I have no idea what you're talking about."

"Raymond Dover. Does that name ring a bell?" Toni asked.

"Dover? Wait a minute…wait, wasn't that Crystal's boyfriend when she was in high school?"

"Yeah, he was Crystal's boyfriend alright. I caught him pushing her around one time when my momma cooked a dinner for your grandparents while they visited."

"Crystal's boyfriend? Why didn't I ever hear about that?" Cady asked.

Toni put her head down. And after several minutes she looked up at Cady and said, "I really thought you knew. I thought she would have told you."

"I promise you Crystal never told me anything. What happened?" Cady asked.

Toni sat with her arms wrapped around her knees resting her chin on her folded arms; she looked only straight ahead and blankly stared at the wall on the opposite side of the room and said, "While I waited for my momma to finish serving your family their dinner she asked me to take the garbage outside. When I did, I could hear some noise around the corner of the house, it was like muffled, but I could tell it was somebody talking or at least trying to. When I peeked around the corner I saw this Raymond guy pinning Crystal to the side of the house. He had one hand around her neck and with his other hand he kept trying to unfasten her pants. She kept saying, 'Stop and no' in a scruffily voice. So I ran over to where they were and I pushed him, I didn't even think about it first, I just did it. When I pushed him, he lost his balance and fell to the ground. Crystal kicked him in the face but when he got up, she ran into the house, or at least I thought she did. I tried to run but he caught me, then he pinned me up against the house."

Toni was silent for several minutes as tears began forming in her eyes and then she continued, "He was so strong. He was able to pin me with one hand and pull down my underwear with the other hand. Then he pinned my head against the house with his hand over my mouth."

"Oh no, Toni, he raped you? I swear I didn't know. I don't think anybody knew that."

"Your sister knew all about it," Toni said softly.

"But you said she ran back into the house, didn't she go to get you help?" Cady asked.

Toni continued to stare at the wall across the room and after several more minutes while her tears began racing down her face she said softly, "I've thought about this a million times. I've played it over and over again in my mind every single day since it happened. That night when Crystal ran around the corner, I thought she went in the house to get help too but I never heard the door open or close. What I do remember is that when he finished and loosened his grip so that I could turn my head I finally opened my eyes and when I did, I saw your sister standing exactly where I was standing when he had her pinned up against the house. She was just standing there. She didn't say nothing; she didn't do nothing, at least not until after he was finished with me. When he was done with me, he threw me down on the ground like a piece of tissue paper he just blew his nose on. And just before he turned around to where he would see her, I sat up. I saw Crystal run around the corner of the house and that was the only time I heard the door to the house open and close."

"Crystal saw him rape you? Why didn't you say anything?"

"She told me not to. I was only sixteen years old and I already felt like…"

"Like what?" Cady said.

"Like I wasn't as good as you two," Toni said.

"Toni, what Crystal did was horrible but I always thought you were great. You were so strong and brave. You were never afraid to tell people just what was on your mind," Cady said.

"I wasn't brave, Cady. I was angry and by the time I was a senior in high school I just stopped caring about anything including myself. I did a lot of drugs just so that I wouldn't feel anything at all. There were many days when I didn't care if I lived or died but for Momma, I think I would have killed myself but I'm all that momma has."

For the first time, Toni smiled as she said, "And then I met Dale. He said I was the most beautiful woman he ever saw."

"Dale is your husband?"

"He was my husband. That bastard out there killed him this morning. He came up to our car when we were at the stop sign and shot Dale with a needle. Then he -- then he cut him with a knife across his throat. When I reached over to Dale, that man came around to my side of the car and injected me with something. I started passing out, but not before I watched my husband gasping for breath and then he just died. The next thing I know I was waking up here with you," Toni said and then she began to openly sob.

Cady pulled the chains that were attached to her ankle and stretched them for as far as they could go. Sitting directly in front of Toni, she reached out and put her arm around the small of Toni's back. Toni tried to pull away but Cady pulled her back into her embrace until Toni's head finally relaxed onto Cady's shoulder. With her other hand, she stroked Toni's hair as she laid her head on her shoulder then she began humming in Toni's ear and after a while when Toni's sobs quieted down, Cady begin softly singing,

> "When peace, like a river, attendeth my way,
> When sorrows like sea billows roll;
> Whatever my lot, thou hast taught me to say,
> It is well; it is well with my soul."

Cady's song was interrupted by a noise coming from the other side of the door. They both abruptly lifted up their heads and sat up. They saw the door knob begin to turn and the man entered the room. It seemed to Toni and Cady that he stood there forever watching them. Then he placed a box next to his Adam's Apple and began to speak. The box changed his voice and made him sound like a robot.

"I see you didn't eat nothing," the man said.

Then the man walked over to the other side of the room and pulled down the plastic covering that covered another side of the wall revealing another door.

"Do you have to go to the bathroom?" he asked.

Cady, still with her arm around Toni in comfort whispered to her, "You go first; you may feel a little better after you wash up."

Toni nodded her head and stood up. The sound of the chain attached to her ankle reminded her that she was limited in how far she could walk. The man reached into his pocket and pulled out a single key. He walked over to where the girls were and when he bent down to unlock Toni's chains; she made eye contact with Cady who nodded her head once. She held up her hand over the man's head as he was kneeling down below her and lifted one finger, then another, then a third finger. Both she and Cady suddenly pushed the man down. The three of them struggled over the key as it slid back and forth across the floor. The man grabbed the key and both Toni and Cady tried to unclasp the man's grip on the key but the man was able to pull away from them and go beyond the length of the chains that still had them bound. The man looked around the room for his voice box but Toni spotted it first next to where she was laying on the floor. Just when the man made a step towards it, Toni snatched it up and threw it against the wall, shattering it in pieces.

The man said, "What the hell is wrong with you?"

He instantly noticed the change in Cady's facial expression. She recognized his voice. He quickly left the room, locking the door from the other side.

"What was that all about?" Toni asked.

"I know who he is, and he knows that I know," Cady said softly.

"Well don't you dare tell me who he is. I know why you're here but I don't have a clue what he could want with me. My people don't have nothing. I don't know why he brought me here."

"I heard him say earlier when he brought the food, 'when your father comes through it'll all be over.' I think he either thinks you're Crystal or that I have two sisters. Either way, we can't let on that you're not my sister at all because then he for sure won't need you."

"Oh my God," Toni said.

The next morning when the girls awakened, they heard a series of footsteps and then they heard him talking. Cady, who was closest to the door tried to get as close to the door as possible but the chains kept her from getting more than midway.

"Can you hear him?" Toni asked.

"I can but it's too muffled, I don't understand anything he's saying. I think he's on the phone with somebody."

Then Cady couldn't hear anything for what seemed like a very long time when suddenly the door to the room where they were being kept flew open and all hell broke loose.

# 14

*"By **cove**tousness they will exploit you with deceptive words; for a long time their judgment has not been idle, and their destruction does not slumber."* ~2 Peter 2:3

Mario played the voicemail for the sixteenth time. The call came about three O'clock that morning. The voice simply said, "If you want to see your daughters alive, spread the deposits of the money in any amount among these three international bank accounts within the next twelve hours…"

The voice was mechanical again, like it was the first time. Mario was truly stumped. The caller kept referring to his daughters, plural but Crystal was asleep in Cady's room. Mario realized that the kidnapper, whoever he was, was a pro. He never spoke to Mario directly but only left messages. Mario knew that was intentional because it left no room for negotiation at all. What was most perplexing to Mario was that the kidnapper seemed to know that Mario had the money that he was demanding but he didn't seem to know that Toni was not one of his daughters. He decided to call June and strategize their next move because he knew that Cady was running out of time.

"June, I got the ransom demand and I need to go see my accountant. I really need you to come. We can't include this on Toni's case and I'm so upset I'm afraid I might let too much slip."

"Sure, Mario, let me call in one of my associates to take some of my appointments today. What time's your appointment?"

"I'm not making one. I'm just going to flash my badge."

"Okay, all right. I get it; this is officially an unofficial visit," June said.

"Exactly, what time can you be free?" Mario asked.

"Pick me up at 10:30," June said.

"Is Brice going to need to come too?" Mario asked and then instantly regretted it.

"He's just concerned about the baby, Mario. I think meeting with an accountant would be safe enough, I'm sure he'll be fine with it," June said.

"Did I mention that my accountant is in South Beach?" Mario said.

"Are you kidding? Two hours away in Miami? That means we'll be gone most of the day, Mario. I don't know if I can be gone all day I have to pick up Rosie."

"Please, June. I only have twelve hours before they expect the wire transfers."

"Are you sure your accountant doesn't have a closer office?" June said.

"Well, I can check. I'll call you back," Mario said.

By 11:30 a.m. Mario and June pulled up to the beautiful home of Jackson Bonnen the II. Mario rang the doorbell and a housekeeper answered the door. They were escorted to the center of the foyer where they were asked to wait for Mr. Bonnen.

"Mr. Grimes, it's been a long time," Mr. Bonnen said extending his hand.

"Yes, it sure has," Mario replied as they shook hands.

"I just saw your parents at a charity ball in Orlando last week," Mr. Bonnen said.

"Oh, excuse me. This is Detective -- I mean Reverend June Harris. She's an old friend," Mario said.

"Wonderful to meet you. I don't think I've ever seen a woman priest before."

June was used to this. Society had become accustomed to only seeing male priests in clergy collars from the movies and television.

"I'm not a priest, Sir. Many denominations wear clergy collars," June said.

"Oh, I didn't realize that. Won't you come into my office and we can talk in there," Mr. Bonnen said.

June couldn't help herself, although she hadn't been an official detective for a long time she always continued to detect wherever she went. She thought Mr. Bonnen's house reminded her of Mario's parent's house, though half the size, it seemed just as cold and impersonal. When she entered Mr. Bonnen's office, finally there was some personality. June thought that his office was as big as her first condo. His desk was made of glass and so the things on the desk had the appearance that they were floating. The credenza behind the glass desk was also topped with glass shelves all of which contained personal photos. As she got closer to the desk she began to recognize someone in the photo. She realized Mario never gave her the name of his accountant.

"And your name, Sir?" June asked.

"Oh how rude of me I'm so sorry, June. This is Jackson Bonnen. He's been my family's accountant for -- well, for as long as I can remember," Mario said.

"And that's your son, Jackson Junior?" June asked while pointing to one of the photos.

"Actually he's Jackson Bonnen the III. Do you know Jackson?" Mr. Bonnen asked.

"Yeah, actually I do. He came to my church at the beginning of the summer. He spent the summer dating one of my bible study students."

Pastor June studied for Mr. Bonnen's reaction; there was none, at least nothing positive.

"Well, Ma'am, my son, and I are estranged now. I haven't seen much of him since about that time. I guess if he's going to church that's something," Mr. Bonnen said.

"Well, he only came the one time. I haven't really seen him since then either," June said.

"Mario, what can I do for you today?" Mr. Bonnen asked, abruptly changing the subject.

Mario explained to Mr. Bonnen that he needed funds transferred. He gave him the account numbers for the transfers then he said, "Now this may sound very strange to you, Mr. Bonnen, but I'll need to have access to you so that I can tell you when to make the transfer."

"Why not just give me the date and time now?" Mr. Bonnen asked.

"I don't know them yet but when it needs to be done, I will need it to be done immediately," Mario said.

"Is that why you insisted on handling this in person? Mario, my clients are rap stars, T.V. and movie stars, politicians, this is the most normal request I've had in a while," Mr. Bonnen said while he chuckled.

June and Mario looked at each other but June said,

"Well we need to get going, Mr. Bonnen, I have an appointment with a Mr. Heathcliff."

When June and Mario were detectives in Sarasota County they had several code words and any reference to Heathcliff meant things seem normal, but they are not as they appear. It was a reference to the Cosby show. Mario picked up the clue right away. Mr. Bonnen gave Mario his personal cell number and assured Mario that his request was not unusual and that it would not be a problem. He then walked them to the front door.

They got into Mario's car and he said, "Well, I guess I really didn't need you after all. I thought he'd ask a lot of questions and I would blow it. What makes this a Heathcliff, June?"

"First, promise me that you won't overreact," June said.

"What is it, June?" Mario said concerned.

"Your accountant's son is the guy who's been dating Cady," June said.

Instinctively Mario reached for the door handle to exit the car and go back inside the house to confront Jackson Bonnen II.

"Mario, no. It's obvious that he doesn't know anything and you still need his cooperation with the money," June said.

Mario closed the car door and put his hands over his eyes in frustration.

June continued, "We need to find the boyfriend."

"How do we do that? The father said they were estranged," Mario said.

"We need to go back and talk with Eartha," June said.

"Who?" Mario asked.

"Mac," June said.

"Well I guess we can get the logs from his phone from her," Mario said.

"Oh she can do much, much more than that," June said.

When they arrived at Mac's apartment, Mario stayed behind in the car talking on the phone with his wife, Bettina.

June walked up to Mac's front door, anxious to utilize Mac's restroom. She didn't have the heart to ask Mario to stop while they were on the road but her pregnancy caused her to make many a restroom her second home.

"Eartha?" June said as she knocked frantically because her bladder began begging for relief.

Mac opened the door.

"Pastor June, you didn't get that I was trying to say that I would get back with you on Sunday?"

"Yeah, 1 got that. Hold on, can I use the bathroom?" June asked as she ran past Mac to the bathroom through the narrow hallway of Mac's apartment.

"But I don't have it ready yet," Mac said while June ran around her.

"Have what ready?" June asked from behind the bathroom door.

"I'll wait till you come out," Mac said.

When June finally came out she said, "Thanks so much, Eartha. What did you have for me?"

"Okay, Pastor June, if you call me that name one more time I'm not going to share anything with you," Mac said.

"Okay, okay, Mac, what do you have for me?" June said.

"Well, when you had me to run the search on that girl's cell phone one of the numbers that came up several times, I recognized it."

"Who is it?" June asked.

"Well, if you had waited till Sunday like I wanted you to I would have that information. Right now all I have is an alias, Richie Rich."

"Well, how do you recognize it?" June asked.

"Um now, Pastor June, you know I don't exactly make my living legal," Mac said.

"Just tell me what you have, Mac, it's really important," June said.

"Well it didn't really hit me until your cop friend mentioned the girl's name right before you guys left but I was hired to do a financial trace on that girl's family," Mac said.

"A what?"

"A financial trace. Whoever this Richie Rich is, he hired me to find that girl's family's financial worth," Mac said.

"How did you -- never mind. How did 'Richie Rich' contact you?" June asked.

"That part's not important, but that girl is loaded. I was able to trace her finances to her grandparents. These are some very rich black people let me tell you. And as far as I can tell all their money is legit, I mean for real," Mac said.

June began to ask another question when there was a knock on Mac's door. June told Mac that it was Detective Grimes. After Mack let him in, she said, "I'm not sharing this information with no cop, Pastor June."

"Eartha -- I mean, Mac, the girl we're talking about, this is her father," June said.

Mac exhaled a deep breath and began to fidget around and June asked, "What is it?"

"Well there's something else you might need to know then," Mac said, staring down at the floor.

"What is it?" June asked.

"Richie Rich also asked for a referral."

"A referral for what?"

"For someone to do a hit," Mac said.

"A hit on who?" June asked.

"On one of those sisters," Mac said.

# 15

*"Therefore put to death your members which are on the earth: fornication, uncleanness, passion, evil desire, and **cove**tousness, which is idolatry.* ~Colossians 3:5

Joseph Addelbury Junior was an Assistant Public Defender. He was also the adopted son of County Medical Examiner, Joseph Addelbury Senior better known as Cowboy Joe. Cowboy Joe and Joseph's biological father were best friends who grew up together in Jacksonville, Florida back in a time when little black boys and little white boys were friends only in childhood. But Cowboy Joe and Derek remained friends through adulthood.

When they were young the two best friends, Cowboy Joe and Derek made a pact to name their first born son's after each other so when Derek's wife gave birth to their oldest son, he was named Joseph Addelbury Junior after Cowboy Joe. And, in turn, many years later when Cowboy Joe's son was born he named him Derek Junior after his best friend.

When his friend Derek and his wife were killed in an automobile accident, Cowboy Joe adopted his three boys.

That was many years ago and now Cowboy Joe had four children, all sons, three black sons, from his best friend Derek; Joe Jr., who became a lawyer like his biological father, and twins Michael and Marcus. Michael was following in Cowboy Joe's footsteps and was in medical school, and Marcus was serving in the military. Cowboy Joe and Wendy had one biological son, Derek Jr. now 17 years old.

Joe Jr. sat in his office at the public defender's office staring at the pile of cases on his desk. He fished through the files until he found Robert Hoshter's file. He was expecting Ms. Hoshter at any moment. She was the mother of the defendant. He flipped through the file and said out loud to himself, "I could so win this."

His hunger for trying cases was growing out of control yet he was very cognizant that actually going to trial was heavily discouraged in the PD's office. This was his fourth year and he'd only been to trial a dozen times but had well over three hundred cases. Joe Jr. became more and more discontented as each new case was piled on. He saw a repetitive pattern.

He looked at his watch and then began dividing his case files. He made one stack for white only defendants, another stack for black only defendants, and one for those defendants who were entering into plea deals. The result was that the white only stack was a third of the black only defendant's stack. And all but one case file of the black defendant's stack simply became the plea deal stack. That was an assault case where the defendant refused to plea so his boss transferred the case to Joe Jr. in the hopes that Joe could get the guy to take the plea offer. Joe was able to add two white only defendant files to the plea deal stack.

Now the pattern was visible. Young black defendants were being arrested and encouraged to plead their cases in order to avoid going to trial three times as much as white defendants. Joe was sure that if he had gone to trial for many of the cases in the plea deal stack, he could have won. He often daydreamed about opening his own law practice but reality would always interrupt his dreams as he was the father of three children himself. He was married to Lillian or Lily for short. And their oldest son was named Joseph Addelbury the III, after his father Cowboy Joe. His next child was a daughter and she was named after his mother, Wendy but his daughter's name was Wind Marie, the way his mother's name was originally spelled when she was born on the Indian reservation outside of Okeechobee, Florida. His other child was really his nephew, the son of his wife's late sister and he was named Tevin. He realized that he could not just pick up and leave the Public Defender's office with so many people depending on him to have a steady paycheck.

His thoughts were interrupted when his assistant stood at the doorway of his office.

"Ms. Hoshter is on her way up, Joe," she said.

Joe Jr. put the files back in alphabetical order and went to the elevator to wait for his client's mother. The elevator was crowded with people but he saw her. He'd never met her before but somehow he knew it was her. She looked to be in her thirties but her face was hard with a story, as his mother would often say. Joe Jr. could see that this lady had been through some things and it showed loudly in her face.

"Ms. Hoshter?" Joe Jr. asked and she nodded yes.

"Please follow me," Joe Jr. said as he escorted her to his office.

"Please have a seat, Ms. Hoshter."

After Joe Jr. offered her coffee and water which she declined, he sat at his desk and pulled out her son's file.

"From what I can see, Ms. Hoshter, your son didn't do anything wrong. Let me see if I have this right. He was standing by his brand new car, a cherry red mustang with expensive rims. You got it for him for his birthday?" Joe Jr. asked.

"Yeah. But it weren't brand new, it was a junk car and my brother had it for months fixin' it up for him," Ms. Hoshter said.

"And the police approached him?"

"Yeah."

"And they frisked him and found $1k in cash in small bills?"

"Yeah my whole family chipped in and gave him some money for his birthday and for graduation. He's the only one in our family who ever graduated school."

"And they arrested him because -- says here for suspicion of distribution and that he assaulted an officer?"

"That's my fault. He didn't know no better. He knew he didn't do nothing wrong and he wanted them to tell him why they threw him on the ground in front of his momma's house."

"Well I think if he goes to trial we could prove that the money wasn't drug money and, if you can produce a title for the car, he might get probation for the assault but …"

"He'll take the plea," Ms. Hoshter said.

"But Ms. Hoshter, I don't think he needs to take a plea because…" Joe tried to explain but she interrupted.

"Look, Mr. Addelbury, I got three boys and Bobby is the only one ain't never been to jail and he ain't going to jail. We'll take the plea," Ms. Hoshter said.

"But I'm telling you I don't think he will have to go to jail," Joe Jr. said.

"Is they offering a plea?"

"Well yes but… "

"Tell the D.A. we gon' take the plea," Ms. Hoshter said as she stood up and then left his office.

Joe Jr. was dumbfounded but certainly understood. He'd seen it too many times to count. He'd seen too many people take pleas because they feared going to jail. Many were not totally innocent but often the cases that the police had were filled with holes and never would have been substantiated in trial. He gathered the case files for his afternoon docket and packed them into his brief case.

He sighed at the thought of taking the plea offer for Robert Hoshter's case. And for the millionth time he began daydreaming about his own practice and how if he had his own practice, he could have taken more time to convince the mother to let her son go to trial. How he would have gone to her house and explained to her how the system worked. Then he closed his office door and returned to his desk and prayed,

*Lord, bless my efforts this day. Please bless the heart of the court and the prosecution. And, Lord, if there isn't any way for me to do what I know I can do for these people please take this desire to have my own firm away from me and return me to my sweet sleep. These blessings I ask in Jesus name. Amen.*

When he finished praying, he thought about his mom. Wendy had been hinting around for the last several weeks at Sunday supper that she knew that something was causing him discontent. He knew his mother was extremely intuitive when it came to her children. Joe Jr. smiled as he recalled when he was in middle school and Wendy was called to come to the school because Joe Jr. had gotten into a fight. Joe Jr. was being bullied because he was a black kid being raised by a big white guy and a little Indian lady. Joe Jr. remembered the bully, Casey Cavanaugh. He called Joe Jr. the U.N. N. which stood for the United Nations Nigga. Casey mistakenly thought that because he didn't pronounce the "er" at the end that it wasn't a racial epithet. Joe Jr. had been the butt of Casey's jokes daily for weeks. Being new to the school and to the city, and having just lost his biological parents in a fatal car accident Joe Jr. just exploded and attacked Casey.

When Wendy came to the school and saw Joe Jr. sitting in the office with his face full of regret, hurt and shame, she sat beside him and whispered in his ear, "Every man has his limits, Son. He pushed you to yours but now it's time to take responsibility for your actions. But next time, and there will be a next time, be wise and not emotional."

Then she kissed his cheek and they went into the principal's office. It was the first time that he'd done something wrong while in Cowboy Joe and Wendy's care. And he remembered the flood of relief that he felt because of what she said. She understood his situation without him having to say a word about what happened. Now he picked up his phone to call her, "Hi, Mom, what you doing?"

"Oh I'm just going over a catering order. How are you doing today, Son?"

Joe Jr. was silent.

"You ready to talk to me about it now?" Wendy asked.

"Yeah," Joe Jr. replied.

"Well, Son, I know you already prayed about it so now it's time for you to let God decide," Wendy said.

"What do you mean let Him decide?" he asked.

"When we make petitions to God He always answers, sometimes the answer is the solution that we offered and sometimes God has a better solution than we can think of and then sometimes His answer is no because it's not to your benefit and therefore not to His glory."

"What do I do in the meantime?" Joe Jr. asked.

"You praise Him for listening."

# 16

*"For neither at any time did we use flattering words, as you know, nor a cloak for **covet**ousness—God is witness.* ~1 Thessalonians 2:5

When Mario and June pulled up into her driveway, she noticed a strange car parked next to Brice's car. She figured it was one of the pastors from the district helping him to prepare for his annual district convention. All the pastors in the district were expected to attend and give status reports. It was also the time of the year when the Supervising Elder appointed ministers to various district appointments.

Since coming into the district June held several district offices. Last year she was on the District Finance Committee, the District Ministerial Supervising Committee and every year since she moved into the district she'd been the president of the Women Clergy Group. This year she would have no office. That was Brice's suggestion in order to avoid the appearance of impropriety or nepotism. He said it was the price they had to pay for being married as he was her supervisor and their marriage could be viewed as a conflict of interest if he gave her appointments. June was upset initially because she was willing to let all the offices go but she loved the Women's Clergy Group. She felt they did a great work nurturing young women who were committing their lives to ministry, but then Brice said to her,

"Junie, leaders are not made, they are born. And it doesn't matter who I appoint to lead the Women's Clergy Group, they're not going to follow somebody just because they're in the position. They're going to follow the person who is doing the leading. So it boils down to whether or not you can be satisfied with the work without getting the credit, which is most important to you?"

June knew intellectually that he was right but she didn't like the fact that it seemed to her that every price being paid for their marriage, every sacrifice was being billed to her. He was able to fully function in his ministry without making any concessions. Eventually June agreed to not have any office this year and then she began to realize that now that she had Rosie and a new baby on the way she could use her new found freedom from the commitments of a district appointment to spend more time preparing Rosie for the new baby.

Then she began thinking about Rosie. Whatever kind of day that June might have, it all got better when she saw Rosie at the end of the day. Whenever June came home at the end of the day Rosie would stop whatever she was doing and run to June with open arms often yelling, "Mommy, you're home!"

She realized that she was still sitting in Mario's car and smiling at the thought of being greeted by Rosie. Then she remembered the hell that Mario was going through and felt guilty. She turned to him and said, "I think we've done all we can do today, Mario. Mac promised to get the information to me as soon as possible. Look, I don't know what this is like for you but now that I have Rosie, I have a very good idea, if you need me or if anything new comes up please don't hesitate to call."

"I know, June. I will," Mario said.

When June walked through the front door of her house she was met with silence. She began calling for Rosie when was met by Brice in the foyer.

"Brice, where's Rosie?"

"I asked Myrtle to pick her up today," he said.

"Why? What's going on and whose car is that outside?" she asked.

Brice leaned down to get closer to June's ear and said in a lowered voice, "There's a man in there who says his name is Kwame Stevens. He says he's Rosie's biological father."

June felt like someone had just sucker punched her in the stomach. She literally reached down with her hand to hold onto her baby bump.

"You don't believe him do you?" June said.

"I don't know what to believe, Junie. I mean he just showed up and when he told me who he was, I invited him in and called Myrtle to pick up Rosie. I was just about to call you when you came in."

At that June grabbed Brice's hand and led him into the living room where the man was.

"Hi, I'm Pastor June Harris. My husband tells me you think you're Rosie's father. How did you even know that she was here?" June asked as she tried to stay calm.

"Ma'am, I didn't come to make no trouble. My momma's neighbors told me the preacher lady was raising Rosie. I haven't seen her since she was about six months old," Kwame Stevens said.

June sat down as she could feel the Holy Spirit calming her. She motioned for Brice to sit down as well. He did so grudgingly.

"So now where have you been all this time, Mr. Stevens?" June asked.

"Well, Ma'am, I've been in prison."

"I see," June said.

"And in prison you can't make phone calls or write letters or email your children?" Brice asked sarcastically.

"Well, Sir, I didn't know how to contact Rosie. I don't mean to speak ill of the dead but it was her momma Leslie's case I caught, not mine," Kwame Stevens said.

"When I got locked up my momma said Leslie took Rosie to her momma's house and she got strung out on crack and that was that. Leslie's momma blamed me for her addiction and she changed her phone number whenever I called. She moved so that I didn't have her address. I never forgot about my baby, Ma'am."

"Well what do you want from us, Son?" Brice asked.

June knew that Brice was now softening his heart a little towards this young man. She smiled at him.

"I don't know, Sir. I just wanted her to know that I never stopped loving her, I never stopped wanting to be a father to her but I also knew her momma, Leslie would never survive prison. That's why I took the fall for her. I thought Rosie needed her momma more than she needed me. Turns out I was wrong."

"Well, Mr. Stevens, we're going to have to look into this. You caught us a little off guard here today. We have a court date for the final adoption hearing scheduled for next month. I mean there was no father on the birth certificate and Rosie's grandmother said she didn't know who her father was. See I knew Rosie's grandmother. I preached her eulogy. I don't know you at all. So you can't expect me to just take your word for it and give you access to Rosie now do you?" June asked.

"And we are going through with the adoption, make no mistake about that," Brice said hardening his heart again.

"Well I would just like to see her, really. I just want her to know that I exist and that I never stopped wanting her," Kwame Stevens said.

"Give us your contact information and we'll contact you, I promise but we need to check with the Foster Care Unit first and see what, if anything, that we are obligated to do in this situation. We're just protecting Rosie, you can understand that can't you?" June said.

"Yes, Ma'am, yes I do. My momma said you were good people and I appreciate that you care about Rosie," Kwame Stevens said while rising to leave.

Brice walked him to the door without saying another word. After he closed the door he came hurriedly back to June.

"What are we going to do, Junie? We can't let him see Rosie; we don't know anything about that man. And Rosie will get all confused. I am her daddy, Junie," Brice said.

"I know babe, I know. Let me call Bettina and see what our rights are," June said.

As she fished her cell phone from her pants pocket it began to vibrate. The caller I.D. said it was Mario.

"Hello, Mario, I was just about to call Bettina," June said.

"June, it might be a stretch but I had Detective Wright do a property search on my accountant's kid. She found out that he's been living in a condo on Singer Island for the past year and I want to go and talk to him right now," Mario said.

"Mario, Mac is going to get the name of the guy to us by tomorrow," she said.

"I can't wait till tomorrow, June. Why should I? We're working off the books anyway and if I can exclude him now that's less we'll have to do tomorrow," Mario said.

June knew that her current potential problem with Rosie paled in comparison to what Mario was going through not knowing where his daughter was or what state she was in. June looked up at her husband and realized that at this moment, he was her biggest problem. He would not be happy about the timing of her leaving to go "detecting" with Mario.

"Okay, let me change my shoes and I'll be ready in about fifteen minutes," she said as she watched Brice's face transform from worry to anger.

"Just come outside whenever you're ready I'm sitting in your driveway," Mario said.

"What?" June said while she looked out of her front window.

"When I dropped you off and got to the end of the block Detective Wright was giving me the information on the phone so I just turned around. By the way, who was that guy that just left?" Mario asked.

"I'll tell you about it in the car," June said and then hung up.

"No," Brice said.

"Brice," June said.

"No, Junie. This isn't fair now. We have a huge problem. Our family is being threatened and you want to just leave me in this situation all by myself. Plus look at you, your feet are so swollen and sore you're limping. No way, no!" Brice said.

"Brice, baby we're just going to do an interview. I will call Bettina on the way. Rosie is fine, she's with Myrtle, but Mario doesn't know where his daughter is. How would you feel about trading places with him right now?" June asked.

"God dammit, June!" Brice said.

June had never heard Brice raise his voice much less curse and it began to anger her.

"I am sick of this. I'm sick of your friendship with your ex-lover, I'm sick of him always needing you, I'm sick of all of it you understand!" Brice shouted.

June just stared at him in disbelief. She was trying not to allow anger to swell up and overtake her. She was wondering when his real feelings would surface about Mario. Before June and Brice were married she told him all about her friendship with Mario, that they would always be friends and Brice told her that he was not a jealous man. She continued staring at him while she picked up her purse. "You know what? I'm sick of it too. I'm sick of always being the one having to compromise who I am. I'm sick of thinking about what you will think about every decision I make about me or for me! I am carrying your child; I am not your child, do you understand that?" June said.

They stood and stared at one another for several seconds and then June said, "I will call Bettina before the end of the day," then she turned away from him and left the house.

The drive from Loxahatchee where Pastor June lived to Singer Island was approximately forty five minutes. June relayed the events that had just occurred to Mario.

"I'm so sorry, June. I appreciate you coming with me after having that news sprung on you," Mario said.

"Yeah well, let's find Cady first and then I can concentrate on Rosie. Right now Cady is the priority and Brice knows it."

The upscale community of Singer Island is actually a peninsula, but in order to get to Singer Island they had to drive across a very long bridge. Singer Island is under the governance of Riviera Beach. The irony is that before they can cross over the bridge into the elite community of Singer Island, they first had to go through the mainland area of Rivera Beach. The mainland is a predominately African American community with a population of approximately twenty thousand residents, an area of modest to dilapidated homes, low rent apartments, public housing and small businesses all crammed within less than a five mile radius.

This area had the reputation in the past of having been plagued with drive by shootings, gang violence, drug deals and homelessness. The last time June was in Riviera Beach it was concerning an alleged theft committed by one of her church youth. Police presence used to be non-existent, but now June subconsciously counted at least a half dozen police cars within the three blocks that they traveled.

Rivera Beach in its prime was filled with prestigious African American residents, including notable civil rights leaders, most of whom have long since moved into the suburbs. Now the city was undergoing regentrification as a new generation of community conscious leaders were taking control. June could see many visible improvements in the city compared to the last time she was there.

Once they crossed over the bridge the environment changed drastically. There were beachfront properties, luxury hotels, and Mercedes Benz everywhere. After another mile they were able to locate Jackson Bonnen III's twenty story condo building complete with a door man and valet parking. Mario and June looked at each other and simultaneously said, "Richie Rich."

"June, you better take this. We don't know what we're going to find in here," Mario said as he held out his spare gun to June.

June stared at the gun. It had been the better part of a decade since she'd touched a firearm. In that instance her mind went to Exodus 20:13, *"Thou shall not kill,"* but Mario interrupted her thoughts.

"I know what you're thinking, but I've been learning more about the word too you know and Exodus 23:7 says, "Keep yourself far from a false matter; do not kill the innocent and righteous. For I will not justify the wicked." After I got saved I had to be able to justify what I did for a living and it involves potentially killing people. We're not here for the innocent, June. I have no problem about carrying a gun and loving God at the same time," Mario said.

"Well, I guess I do. I've never even thought about it before. I haven't touched another gun since I resigned from the Sarasota P.D. and turned all my weapons in. I'm not going to start now. I love Cady and I love my unborn baby but I have to trust that God will protect us. Sorry, you can put that away, Mario," June said.

"Are you kidding me? June, if something happened to you preacher or no preacher, Brice would kill me. Now that's a fact. You're a much better shot them I am. I have to insist that you be armed," Mario said.

"Mario, if you want me to do this with you, this is how it's got to be done. At the end of the day I have to live with the things that I do and if I killed somebody, even if the world thinks it's justified, I don't know that I could ever forgive myself," June said.

"Even in self defense? Mario asked.

"Yeah, even in self-defense. That's where my faith has to come in. Now are we going to do this or what?" June asked.

"I don't know, June. You better let me lead if you insist on being unarmed," Mario said.

"Yeah, of course you lead," June said as she exited the car and headed towards the building ahead of Mario.

She waited for him to catch up as the doorman held open the door for them. When they entered the elevator Mario asked, "How did you get him to open the door for you? I was prepared to show him my badge."

"Like American Express, clergy membership has its privileges," June said with a smile.

"I bet stuff like that happens to you all the time. I know you still can't drive the speed limit. When's the last time you got a speeding ticket?"

June just smiled.

"I knew it. Who's going to give a ticket to a preacher? You gave me all that hoopla that wearing your clergy clothes was all about ministry, you're trying to avoid getting speeding tickets. I bet you don't have to wait for a table in a fancy restaurant either do you? Incredible," Mario said.

"Oh you're making more out of it than there really is. Sure there's some favoritism but there are also a lot of people out there who've been hurt by the church and they are not happy to see me coming at all," June said.

At that point, they reached Jackson's floor. When the elevator doors opened they saw the manager speaking to a custodian. Mario flashed his badge at the manager and asked him about Jackson.

"It's the strangest thing. His dad had been paying for the lease on the condo for the last year then all of a sudden he said he was refusing to support his kid anymore, so I had to evict him. Then about a month later, I got an email from the kid saying that he wanted to renew his lease," the manager said.

"It was still available after a month?" June asked.

"Well, yeah the kid had done so much damage to the place it needed a complete overhaul. Holes in the walls, the wood floors were beyond repair. Don't get me started on the dishwasher. He seemed so desperate to move back in, I was able to make a deal with him to take it as is, but he had to be responsible for all the repairs."

"So when's the last time you've seen him around?" Mario asked.

"Now that's the really strange part. When his dad was paying the bills, the kid was here all the time. And he was never here alone. The kid had like an entourage. For the longest time I thought he was some type of movie star that I'd never heard of or something," the manager said.

Mario and June looked at each other and then back to the manager who suddenly realized he neglected to answer the detective's question.

"Since the lease renewal, I've never seen him here, not once," the manager said.

"What? You mean he's paying the lease every month and he's never actually lived here? Has anybody been living here that you know of?" Mario asked.

"I haven't seen a soul come or go from this place," the manager said.

"Where are your security cameras?" June asked as she looked around.

"We have them all over the place but I'm telling you, he's not been here at all. Never even moved his stuff back in. The place is still empty," the manager said.

"Mind if we took a look around?" Mario asked.

"Sure, I'll let you in with the master key," the manager said.

When they entered Jackson's condo they could see what the manager was talking about, the place was a pigsty. June could see no evidence of anyone having lived there recently. In the rear of the living room the wall was completely glass exposing a spectacular view of the ocean. June could see people water skiing, sailing and surfing in the ocean below.

"I told you he hasn't been here. The place has been left untouched since I gave him back the lease. What is that smell?" the manager asked.

Then June and Mario could smell it too except they knew the only thing that would emit that type of stench was death.

"Sir, I'm going to ask you to step out into the hallway now," Mario said.

"You think he came back in here and died? Oh my God that never occurred to me," the manager said as he exited the condo.

June and Mario slowly followed the odor of rot and decay. They went into the bedroom where the smell seemed to be the strongest but they didn't see anything. Then June began to look up and saw a crawlspace. She then opened the French doors in the bedroom that led out onto a balcony and she could see where the crawlspace also led to the outside. She motioned for Mario. The door that covered the crawlspace opening on the outside had been pulled away. Mario reentered the condo and returned to the balcony with a utility ladder and a flashlight. When he finally got the ladder situated, he climbed up and stood on it and lit up the crawlspace with light.

"It's just a raccoon, June," Mario said.

"Thank God," June said.

June returned to the inside and put on the latex gloves Mario handed her and began riffling through the bedroom drawers. There was no order to anything. It seemed that Jackson had cleared out all of his personal items. As she turned to walk back into the living room area she thought the floor creaked strangely. She positioned her feet so that she could make it repeat the sound again. She reached down and pulled up a wood plank which revealed a customized safe.

"Mario, you better come and take a look at this," June said.

The safe had a combination lock and June went right to work on it. It was hard on her to try to listen for the clicks while laying on her side but her baby bump wouldn't allow her to lay directly over it.

"If your husband could see you know he would kill me for sure," Mario said.

"Shhh," June said.

One of the well hidden talents of June that only Mario knew about was her ability to break into things. It was something she practiced a lot as a child. It just fascinated her to be able to figure out how something worked, to take it apart and then put it back together. She could open all kinds of locks; door locks, car locks, combination locks and the like. Momma May would often lock the keys in the house or in the car and June would pick the locks, she did it often. So it was a skill that June felt she acquired honestly.

Once she was able to open the safe, the inside proved very disappointing but typical. There were pictures of Jackson in compromising positions with many different women.

Mario looked at June and said, "You let this creep date my daughter?"

"I didn't let her do anything, Mario. Cady is grown. I personally liked Demetrius better myself," June said.

"Those are my daughter's choices? The playboy or the half-wit?" Mario said sarcastically.

"Stop it, Mario. You don't know either of them well enough to call them names," June said.

"You just wait until Rosie's old enough to date. I can only imagine the names that will come flying out of your mouth," Mario said.

"I don't like to think about that," June said.

After looking through the items in the safe Pastor June said, "Well I don't really see anything. There's some -- oh wait. Do you happen to have those bank account numbers on you? There are some banks listed here with account numbers. There's a boat title here too," June said.

"A boat? What kind of boat?" Mario asked.

"I don't know what any of these numbers mean but it's registered as -- oh my goodness," June gasped.

"What?"

"It's registered as the Richie Rich," June said.

Then they both ran outside onto the balcony to look around. About a quarter of a mile down the shoreline they spotted a cluster of different types of boats docked at the shore.

"That's a lot of boats; we don't have time to search each and every one of them. There must be an easier way to find out which boat is his?" June said.

"The manager should know or maybe even the doorman," Mario said.

"Mario, his father lives on waterfront property too, that boat may not even be here at all. I don't know if I can spend much more time here. It looks like a dead end to me," June said.

"Just let me ask the manager, June and if he doesn't know then I'll take you home, alright?" Mario said.

"Aright," June replied.

# 17

*"For the iniquity of his **covet**ousness I was angry and struck him; I hid and was angry, and he went on backsliding in the way of his heart".* ~Isaiah 57:17

Detective Grimes and Pastor June were back downstairs in the lobby waiting for the manager to contact one of the tenets who he knew had previously been aboard Jackson's boat. They waited for what seemed like forever to June. She knew that the longer she stayed, the angrier Brice would be when she returned home.

"Please wait, June. I have a feeling about that boat," Mario said.

"Really?" June said looking strangely at Mario.

She had always been the intuitive one when they worked together. He always found it hard to believe in her intuition so his confession to now have a feeling was both surprising and ironic to her. Then she thought about the bond between parent and child. It made her think about Rosie and her new found biological father.

Then she turned to Detective Grimes and said, "Okay, Mario. I trust your fatherly intuition. I'm all in," she knew he would do the same for her.

The manager came back and pulled up a picture on his cell phone. The picture showed Jackson and three young blonde ladies on the deck of a decent sized boat with the name, "Richie Rich" inscribed on it.

"Text that to me will you? Do you know what slip the boat is in?" Mario asked.

"Not really but if you look for the boat called 'Chloe' it's usually next to that one because the guy that owns that boat always complained about all the noise coming from Jackson's boat but that guys out of the country right now," the manager said.

Mario looked at June. He watched as she looked down at her swollen feet.

"Oh my God, June, why didn't you tell me that you were in pain," Mario said.

Mario went into protect mode. He called the manager over once again and arranged for a life guard to be at the beach entrance in the back of the building with a jeep ready to transport him and June down the shoreline to where the boat slips were so June didn't have to walk. June was relieved at the thought of finally getting off her feet. When they arrived there were well over twenty boats docked.

"I don't even know where we should begin, Mario," June said.

Mario gave the life guard instruction to inch his way down the shoreline as Mario got out of the jeep and proceeded to run from boat to boat looking for the Chloe or the Richie Rich insignia. And then June heard a familiar sound.

"Mario, get back in the jeep, shots fired, shots fired!" June yelled.

Mario had heard them too and he made the life guard exit the jeep and he got into the driver's side and proceeded to drive down the shore of the beach. People were exiting their boats and running back up onto the shore and by the time Mario and June arrived a small crowd had formed.

"Where did the shots come from?" Mario asked nobody in particular as he held his badge up in the air.

Everyone started pointing in different directions or shrugging their shoulders. June stayed in the jeep to have a height advantage over the crowd and then she heard more gunshots.

June tapped Mario on the shoulder and said, "Keep going. I think you're right. I'm starting to get a feeling now and it ain't good."

When they got to the end of the line of boats they saw a boat with brown trim and painted on it was 'Chloe'. Mario jumped out to go to the neighboring boat hoping it was Jacksons but to his disappointment June was right behind him and tapping him for his attention. She then pointed to the boat on the other side of the Chloe and whispered to him, "That's the one."

Mario pulled his gun from his waist and then instinctively reached down to grab another gun from his ankle holster and handed it to June. She grabbed the gun without a second thought. Together they slowly approached the boat, crouching down as they boarded. They could hear a commotion coming from inside. Mario helped June aboard the vessel and they signaled to one another with their hands as to the direction each of them would go. When June reached a portal or window she tried to see inside but it was pitch black. She continued around to where the deck led to the sleeping quarters down below. Mario arrived at the same place on the opposite side of the entrance at the same time June had. Mario nodded and began the descent down the stairs with June following closely behind, both had guns drawn.

They entered into a common area and they could hear someone shouting, "Cady, Cady, oh my God."

Mario stood outside a small room where they heard the voice coming from and slowly opened the door. The room was darkened and his eyes had not yet adjusted to the lack of light.

"Police, drop your weapon, come out with your hands up and identify yourself" Mario said.

June had the flashlight directed to the door way of the opened room. As the light from the flashlight captured shapes of people lying on the floor, June now aimed her gun for the door opening.

"I didn't do this. Oh my God, I didn't do this," the voice coming from inside the room said.

June lowered her gun and went to where Mario was standing, she put her hand on his gun pressing down to force him to lower his gun as well.

"Jackson, is that you? This is Pastor June," June said.

"I didn't do this. I don't know what's going on, Pastor June," Jackson said still from inside the room.

"Is there anybody else in there with you, Jackson?" June asked.

"Yeah, but nobody who can move," Jackson said.

"Do you have a gun, Son?" June asked.

"Huh? Oh, yeah but I --" Jackson said but then was interrupted.

"This is Cady's father if you don't slide that gun out through this door within the next ten seconds I swear to God I'm coming in that room to blow your head off, do you get that, Son?" He said angrily looking directly at June.

"Jackson, slide the gun on the floor out to where we are and then slowly, slowly now, walk towards us with your hands on the top of your head. Now your hands must be visible at all times. Do you understand?" June said.

The gun slid out to them. It was a small 22 caliber gun with a unique marble handle.

"Now come out slowly with your hands on your head," June cautioned him again.

Jackson appeared in the doorway, and as the light met his shirt, June and Mario could see that blood stains were visible on his chest and the sleeves of his shirt.

"Pastor June, I..." Jackson attempted to say.

"Keep your hands where I can see them," Mario said while he handed June some zip ties and entered into the darkened room.

June proceeded to tie Jackson's hands behind his back and sit him down in a chair.

Then she could hear Mario yelling, "Send for a bus, June, Now! Everybody in this room has been shot. Cady's breathing but she's not conscious."

June couldn't come in the room and leave Jackson there alone because she didn't want him to run. She couldn't bring him in the room because she was afraid of what Mario would do to him.

"Check the vitals of the other people Mario. How many more people are there?" June yelled while she called 911.

"Looks like that goofy kid, Cady's friend. I can't find a pulse on him. You know the tall lanky kid that said he got a text from Cady."

"Oh no, Demetrius," June said.

"June?" Mario shouted.

"What is it, Mario?" June asked.

"The other person is Toni, she's dead," Mario said.

By that time they could hear the sirens from the ambulance approaching. June put her attention back to Jackson as Mario came out of the room carrying Cady in his arms. He ascended the stairs leading back up to the deck of the boat so he could meet the paramedics as they arrived.

"Jackson, don't say a single word to anybody including me. Not a single word. The only words that should come from your mouth should be, I want a lawyer. Not another single word," June said.

Jackson nodded his head in response to June. She didn't know exactly why she felt the need to protect Jackson but she did. She realized the way things appeared but something seemed really out of order about this whole thing to her. She stroked Jackson's back as she watched him put his head down and sob.

The police begin entering the boat where June and Jackson were. After June watched Jackson being escorted back upstairs she followed Officer Dees and Detective Wright into the darkened room where the other bodies laid lifeless.

"Pastor June, are you sure you want to be in here?" Wright said.

"I've seen more bodies than I care to recall, Detective Wright. I'd just like to pray for them if that's okay," June said.

Detective Wright handed June a pair of gloves and foot booties then she slowly and carefully removed the black plastic that was covering the portal in order to expose the room to light. When the light invaded the darkness of the room June could see that Toni had been shot in the chest and that Two Touch or Demetrius had been shot in the neck. She couldn't help but to assess the scene.

"Detective Wright, these shots look rather random don't they?" June said.

"Yeah I've counted three other bullet holes in the wall here and over there. Looks like somebody was shooting fish in a barrel with no discernible target," Wright said.

Pastor June stooped down over Toni's body which was lying closely to Two Touch's body. She stretched out both of her hands touching them each on the foreheads and prayed,

"Father, I pray for the souls of these young people. I pray that they called out to you, Lord God, realizing they might be facing the end of this life. I pray that their souls are resting with you now, Lord God, in Jesus name, Amen."

When June tried to stand back up after finishing the prayer, she found it quite difficult. She realized that morning that her belly bump seemed to have just popped out over night. She had to wear one of the male clergy shirts she purchased for when she could no longer button her regularly sized ones. Detective Wright saw her struggling to rise to her feet and she took Pastor June by the hand and helped her to stand up. When she stood, she wobbled.

"Whoa there. Let's get you to the other room. Are you feeling okay, Pastor June?" Wright asked.

Detective Wright put her arms around Pastor June's shoulder and helped her into the other room. Once Detective Wright let go, Pastor June suddenly felt the room begin to spin and then the room went black and she collapsed to the floor.

"We need a medic down here right away, Pastor June's fainted," Detective Wright said into her radio.

# 18

*"For this you know, that no fornicator, unclean person, nor **covet**ous man, who is an idolater, has any inheritance in the kingdom of Christ and God."* ~Ephesians 5:5

June awoke to see Brice sitting in his easy chair next to their bed. She rolled over from her side onto her back. She closed her eyes again and began thinking about when she first awakened in the hospital two months earlier after fainting at the crime scene. Her obstetrician, Dr. Khan explained to her and her husband that she had a condition called preeclampsia or toxemia which is caused by high blood pressure. June felt really guilty because she didn't recognize that her frequent swelling was a warning sign that something was very wrong. She read all the pregnancy books and familiarized herself with all the things that could go wrong including preeclampsia.

When she was finally released from the hospital, Dr. Khan mandated her to have total bed rest. She knew that Brice was livid with her about the dangerous situation she allowed herself to get into but he never said so out loud. He watched her like a hawk when they got home and he had been waiting on her hand and foot for the entire time, she absolutely hated every minute of it. She felt that Brice was being extremely overprotective because he would not give her access to her cell phone and he would not allow any visitors with the exception of Bettina and Myrtle, but because she felt so guilty about her condition she didn't bother to argue the issue with him.

Since her husband was the Supervising Elder of her district, she knew that he had the authority and the obligation to pastor her church in her absence and for that she was truly grateful because she felt that no one else in the world knew her vision for ministry as well as he did. But, he wouldn't give her any details about how the church was functioning and that drove her crazy.

Then June opened her eyes again and began smiling as she realized that it was Sunday. This was the day that Dr. Khan said that she could go out and June was ready to go back to church, although only for a couple of hours. She hadn't been to the church since before the day Jackson was arrested and this Sunday morning she had an overwhelming urge to preach. She didn't realize how much the church meant to her until she couldn't go.

She rolled back onto her side to face her husband who was still sitting in his easy chair starring and smiling at her and she said, "I feel like preaching, husband!"

"Promise that you're going to take it easy, wife!" Brice replied.

"Yeah, yeah, I know, I will. I promise," June said as she sat up in the bed.

"Mommy, you're awake!" Rosie said as she ran into the room and jumped into bed with June.

"Good morning sweetheart. Oh, I love your braids. Did you remember to thank Ms. Trunetta for making your hair so pretty?" June asked.

"Uh huh. But it kind of hurt a little bit, Mommy," Rosie said using her fingers to demonstrate what a little bit was.

"You might as well know now my darling, beauty is painful," June said with a chuckle.

The doorbell rang and they all quieted down so they could listen for who was at the door. They then begin to hear footsteps slowly ascending the stairs.

"Junieee!" Billie shouted.

June immediately brought her hands to her face, expressing her surprise. Billie had been in Carolina with her family since the beginning of June's pregnancy. She said before she moved to West Palm Beach to help June with her baby she wanted to tie up some loose ends with her family.

"Oh, Billie, you're here," June said and then she suddenly started to cry.

Billie came and sat down next to June on the bed and said, "Of course I'm here child. I came to the hospital to see you too but you weren't awake yet," Billie said.

"How long are you going to be here?" June asked.

"I'll be here for as long as you need me," Billie said.

"Jon, do you want your breakfast up here or downstairs?" Mila asked as she entered the bedroom.

"I'm getting dressed and coming down stairs, praise the Lord!" June said.

Jon was how Mila's accent forced her to pronounced the name June. Mila had been June's housekeeper since before she and Brice were married. Mila was much more than a housekeeper to June though, she was also her personal assistant, and June considered her a valuable friend.

"Rosie, you come and help me with breakfast so your mommy can get dressed, okay?" Mila said.

"You go on downstairs and help too, Brice. I got this," Billie said.

Brice reluctantly left the room.

"Listen, Junie, you let it go now hear?" Billie said to June.

"I don't know what I was thinking. Billie, he kept telling me to be careful and instead of listening to his heart I felt like he was just trying to boss me around. I haven't spent any real time by myself since we got married. I just didn't know it would be this hard," June said.

"Listen, darlin' I've lived long enough to tell you from experience nothing worth having is ever going to be easy. It's hard because it's real. Now if it was hard and miserable that's a different story," Billie said with a chuckle.

"I'm so glad you're here, Billie. I felt so alone," June said.

"Of course I'm here, where else would I possibly be? But listen, you've got to let that man in because I won't be around forever. You hear me?" Billie said as she held up June's chin.

June nodded her head and said, "I will. I love him so much."

Billie helped June get dressed. June neglected to buy maternity pants so Billie found a couple safety pins and a big rubber band that she rigged onto June's pants so that she could leave the zipper down and not worry about her pants falling down. Then they descended down the stairs and they both clung on to the railing as though their lives depended on it. June held on tightly because her equilibrium was off and Billie because her vision was getting worse. When they reached the bottom of the stairs they looked at each other's tight grip on the railing and begin laughing hysterically. June was also trying to carry a black robe and her bible. She was very eager to get to the church.

"Mommy, I cut your orange into slices and I put your toast in the toaster all by myself," Rosie said excitingly.

"That's wonderful sweetheart," June said.

The last thing June wanted to do was to stop and eat, but she knew she wouldn't make it out of the house if she didn't. After breakfast they all piled into the brand new Suburban that Brice purchased after June got home from the hospital. He told June they needed a bigger vehicle with Rosie, Billie and a new baby. June hated it. She was feeling really crowded and her drives to the church were usually her only alone time. She couldn't wait to give birth.

As had become their custom, before they started the ignition in the car they all bowed their heads and closed their eyes for prayer.

"Dear Lord and our God, we have to give you thanks this morning," Brice said.

"Amen," Billie said.

"We thank you for June's health. And we thank you for the good health of our baby," Brice continued.

"And for me too, Daddy," Rosie chimed in.

"And thank you for our incredible bright light, Rosie, Lord. We also thank you for Billie's arriving safe and sound. Lord we know that you know all things. We know that you are our protector and our provider. We surrender this day to be consumed with our worship of you and to give you praise. Lord, we can't praise you enough for all you've done and we intend to worship you this morning with our whole hearts. We pray for your grace during our travel and safe return. We pray always in your precious Son's name, Jesus the Christ."

And everybody said, "Amen."

June begin to quickly tire of Brice's driving. She always thought he drove like a little old lady. She realized that she was being anxious and secretly prayed for God's forgiveness. During the drive to the Church from Loxahatchee, since June was not driving she surveyed the scenery. Loxahatchee is where Brice surprised her with their dream house when they were married. It was a rural equestrian community. On this Sunday morning drive June could see people riding horses, walking their dogs, jogging and working in gardens on their multiple acre lot properties.

Then something else caught June's eye, she saw a woman riding a sporty supped up motorcycle passing them and June decided in that instant that as soon as she was no longer sharing her body that she was going to go out and get a motorcycle of her own. The thought of riding alone on her very own motorcycle returned her good mood and she began to smile.

When they arrived at St. Mark Church Myrtle was waiting outside with Brother Davis. "My Lord, you got huge," Myrtle said.

"Thanks a lot, Myrtle," June said as she exited the truck with Billie and Rosie following close behind.

"You look beautiful though," Myrtle said.

"Nice try," Pastor June replied.

Pastor June insisted on putting her robe on while they were still outside because she was self conscious about her sudden increased size and found that she really didn't like it when people reached out to touch her belly. When they finally entered the church they were met by many of her church members who approached to welcome her back. Everything was just as Pastor June remembered it. During her bed rest she had a consistent fear that her husband would somehow rearrange everything, she realized now as she stood in the sanctuary how silly that thought was.

Supervising Elder Brice Howard met Pastor June at the entrance of the sanctuary. He held his hand out for Pastor June and she placed her hand in his. They walked hand in hand to the pulpit. Brother Davis had already positioned the step that rolled back and forth under Pastor June's seat on the pulpit so when she stood on it, she was several inches taller and before either of them sat down, her husband leaned in and kissed her fully on the lips.

Brice sat on her left and Billie on her right. When she finally got comfortably seated, she got a little misty eyed as she realize that her entire ministerial staff was there with the exception of Reverend Deena, who had officially left St. Mark to start a church of her own. Those who were already seated got up and came to Pastor June's seat to extend their hand and welcome her back.

Danny handed Pastor June a bouquet of red roses and leaned in to say in her ear, "Me and Reverend Linda decided to bring the satellite church members here this morning. I hope that's okay, Pastor," Reverend Danny said.

"That's perfectly fine, Danny," Pastor June said smiling while trying to hold back her tears.

Pastor June was getting uncomfortable with all the fuss that everyone was going through. And she was trying to convince herself to be patient because all the fussing over her would end soon. When the Minister of Music approached, Pastor June couldn't help herself so she pulled him close so that she could whisper in his ear,

"Please, please start playing something so we can start the service."

He immediately looked at his watch but Pastor June said,

"It's okay. We can start a little early we're not married to time. Go ahead and start the praise music, please. We'll just go a little longer than usual."

He nodded his head and smiled and then proceeded back to the piano. The musicians began playing one of the songs that they knew Pastor June loved. The musician along with the choir began singing a song by Charles Jenkins,

*"My God is awesome, He can move mountains*
*Keep me in the valley, hide me from the rain*
*My God is awesome, heals me when I'm broken*
*Strength where I've been weakened, forever He will reign*
*My God is awesome…*

Pastor June, still seated in her chair, lifted up both of her arms in the posture of surrender and sang along with the musicians and the choir. When they reached the end of the song, Pastor June turned and motioned for them to continue singing by swirling her finger. They repeated the entire song another time. In the midst of the second round of the song Pastor June had her husband help her to stand and she began pacing across the pulpit with her arms raised while shouting, "Hallelujah! Glory! Thank you God, Yes Lord, Yes Lord…"

Intensity was displayed all over her face as she gave praises to God. By the time the musicians finally did end the song Pastor June, Billie, Supervising Elder Howard, all the ministers, the musicians and at least half of the congregation were up on their feet shouting, clapping and jumping up and down in praise.

Flooding through Pastor June's heart, soul, and mind was an overwhelming sense of gratitude to God for all that she had just survived. She felt as if her soul was literally pulling against her body in an effort to get out and get closer to God. This went on for another fifteen minutes without any musical accompaniment before Pastor June finally returned to her seat. After wiping her face with her hand towel she then looked past Billie to catch Danny's eye and nodded her head, signaling to him that it was time to officially start the worship service.

When Pastor June looked through the service program she realized that they preplanned this general assembly of worship because Rev. Danny and Rev. Linda's names were printed in the program along with her main St. Mark Church Ministerial Staff. When every minister took to the podium they each expressed their joy at the return of their pastor. It was like an impromptu Pastor's appreciation worship service.

When the worship service had progressed to the point where the choir would sing their final selection before Pastor June would bring the message, she stood up and took to the podium. She realized that the spirits of the people were in such close communion with the Holy Spirit it would take very little to get them all back on their feet again and she didn't want to risk losing the high level of worship that they had attained.

"I know it's time for the choir to sing but if you've been through anything like I have, it's hard to stay in your seat and follow the preprinted program. If you feel like I feel, you ought to get up on your feet right now and give our big God, some big praise!" Pastor June shouted as she removed the microphone from its stand.

Just as she discerned, everyone on the pulpit and in the congregation were back up on their feet and the mass praise began all over again. This time the musicians just played the standard praise music and the people in St. Mark Church praised the Lord for almost twenty more minutes.

Once everyone regained their composure Pastor June decided it was time to preach God's word. She purposely had nothing prepared. God had been speaking to her through scripture the entire time she was at home on bed rest and the one scripture that God kept giving to her over and over was in Second Samuel chapter six regarding how King David had made an arrogant mistake with the Ark of the Lord and when he realized that he did and that God forgives, he offered praises to God and danced in celebration of God's goodness.

Pastor June began by following the proper protocol of giving honor to her husband, Supervising Elder Howard, the ministers and officers.

Then she said, "Let us pray. Father God, may the words of my mouth and the meditation of my heart be acceptable in your sight. O' Lord, you alone are my strength and my redeemer." Pastor June then opened her bible and said, "Please turn with me to second Samuel, chapter six. And we'll begin at verse twelve. When you have located this passage of scripture let us reverence God's word by standing."

While the majority of the congregation and the ministers slowly rose to their feet, Pastor June continued,

"And thus says the word of God, *'Now it was told King David, saying, 'The LORD has blessed the house of Obed-Edom and all that belongs to him, because of the ark of God.' So David went and brought up the ark of God from the house of Obed-Edom to the City of David with gladness. And so it was, when those bearing the ark of the LORD had gone six paces, that he sacrificed oxen and fatted sheep. Then David danced before the LORD with all his might; and David was wearing a linen ephod. So David and all the house of Israel brought up the ark of the LORD with shouting and with the sound of the trumpet. Now as the ark of the LORD came into the City of David, Michal, Saul's daughter, looked through a window and saw King David leaping and whirling before the LORD; and she despised him in her heart,"* Pastor June then said, "Now let's jump up to verse twenty one where it says, *'So David said to Michal, "It was before the LORD, who chose me instead of your father and all his house, to appoint me ruler over the people of the LORD, over Israel. Therefore I will play music before the LORD. And I will be even more undignified than this, and will be humble in my own sight. But as for the maidservants of whom you have spoken, by them I will be held in honor."*

And Pastor June followed by saying,

"Here Saul's daughter, Michal is accusing King David of worshiping God as a commoner. I know you've probably heard phrases like, David danced out of his clothes, but that's not what happened. David is described as wearing an ephod. An ephod was a priestly garment; it was symbolic of serving before the Lord. All those who served God wore them. And so Michal's accusation was that David reduced himself from a King, to being like everybody else who served God. In essence King David responded back to her by saying, however I decide to worship God is kingly simply because I am the king. He said to her, God saw fit to make me the King instead of your father. In other words, David is saying ain't nobody mad about my praise except the folk who don't know about praise.

"See people who don't have the spirit can't know about the things of the spirit, amen. The bible says spiritual things look foolish to those who don't know. In Mark chapter three at verse twenty one, there we can see that when Jesus was engrossed with ministering to the needy crowd, and neither he nor his disciples themselves took time to eat, the bible says, *But when His own people heard about this, they went out to lay hold of Him, for they said, "He is out of His mind."*

"In the book of Acts in chapter two, on the day of Pentecost, when they were all filled with the Holy Spirit and began to speak with other tongues the folk mocked them and said, *'These men are full of new wine'*. And also in the book of Acts in chapter twenty six at verse twenty four, when Paul spoke so passionately about the Lord before King Agrippa, Festus replied by saying, *'Paul, you are beside yourself!'* See if you don't know what I've been through you cannot possibly understand my praise."

Many "Amen's" were heard all around the church. Pastor June continued preaching about the various reasons we give God praise and she concluded by saying we should give God praise because of the hope that we have in Christ Jesus. Pastor June was animated when she continued,

"When Paul and Silas were locked up in the prison, chained to the floor without any idea as to what their end was gonna be, they just started praising God! And see like we just saw here this morning, genuine praise is infectious, it's contagious, Amen? So then everybody in the prison began to praise God, And then the spirit of the Lord moved through that prison, just like He did this morning and He set all those captives free!! I know somebody got free up in here this morning, hallelujah!"

At this point in the sermon Pastor June came from behind the podium and started walking down the steps to the floor level where the congregation were seated and as she did she said, "I don't know about y'all, but I'm praising God this morning -- because I can remember when I was a prisoner to sin. And like Paul and Silas, when I opened up my mouth -- and offered praise to my God -- my prison floors began to shake -- and God broke every one of my chains, and I began to see His light penetrating through all of my darkness -- Oh you better know I'm gonna praise Him! Is there anybody else here this morning that just has to praise Him? Is there anybody here who's gonna help me Praise Him?"

By this time the congregation were back on their feet, the musicians had began once again playing the praise music.

After several more minutes of praise Pastor June went into the chancel area and said, "I believe in the power of Jesus Christ through the laying on of hands. If you need your chains broken this morning, if you need the doors to your prisons opened, meet me here for prayer and we will call upon the name of the Lord, because Christ came to set all the captives free, Hallelujah somebody!"

Supervising Elder Howard and all the ministers came down from the pulpit and joined Pastor June in the laying on of hands to all that came forward. There were many who came forward. There were also several people who had fallen backwards and fell limply onto the ground or were slain in the spirit as Pastor June and the other ministers laid hands on them. Supervising Elder Howard went out into the pews of the sanctuary to lay hands on those who were unable to make it to the front and often had the same reaction of people falling limply deeper into their seat as if they had fallen asleep. Pastor June could feel her feet beginning to swell again and decided to let the other ministers finish the prayer service without her and she returned to her seat, but she could not hold back her tears or her smile as she continued witnessing the movement of the Holy Spirit all over the room.

After the worship service had ended Supervising Elder Howard insisted that Pastor June return to bed rest and would not permit her to dine with the members at the Sunday Morning Café as had become her custom.

Once back in her bed June began planning how she would spend the three hours a day she was allotted to leave her bed for the next day. She decided that tomorrow she would visit with Mario and Cady in the hospital. Then she rolled over onto her side smiling as she drifted asleep.

# 19

*"For I will cast out the nations before you and enlarge your borders; neither will any man **covet** your land when you go up to appear before the LORD your God three times in the year." ~* Exodus 34:24

The next day was the first time since Cady was hospitalized that Bettina didn't feel guilty about leaving Mario's side. She missed church the day before so she decided to go to the hospital chapel to pray. The result of the shooting that occurred when Cady and Toni were discovered on Jackson's boat was that Cady's gunshot wound to the head left her comatose, and Toni's gunshot wound was fatal. The other victim was *DOA*; Bettina remembered hearing the dispatcher say over the police scanner that Mario kept at the house.

When the shootings first happened Bettina sought counsel from the pastor of New Hope Church, the Reverend Jeremiah Brown who was also her brother. She never experienced such a tragedy before and she wasn't sure how to console her husband nor May Bell, Toni's mother.

Pastor Brown said to her, "The bible says His strength is perfected in our weakness. Stop trying to find the strength or the wisdom on your own power, let God use you to dispense his comfort through you to those who are grieving. He'll show you what to do and He'll tell you what to say. Take the time to listen for his instruction."

So she began praying every day specifically about God using her to bring comfort to those who were suffering because of the shooting on Jackson's boat. Mario was beside himself and he refused to pray with Bettina. He told Bettina he wasn't going to pray to a God that would allow something this awful to happen to someone as good as Cady.

Mario also refused to reach out to June. There was no talking to him Bettina decided. So she just stayed by his side offering him things of comfort like coffee or food and she would sneak down daily to the chapel to commune with God. She felt that her entire life was falling apart but she also knew that if she didn't hold on tightly to her faith, her family could easily unravel, become corrupted and leave the faith altogether.

Bettina was feeling a little ashamed that she'd only been to see June once since she was home on bed rest. She knew that Mario was angry with June but she wasn't sure exactly why. She also prayed for June and her unborn baby. She asked that God protect her friendship with June because she found herself feeling lonely without their daily communications.

Joe Jr. sat alone in the interview room at the county jail remembering how he got this case.

"You want to go to trial, here you go," his boss said as he threw the case file on Joe's desk.

"What's this?" Joe Jr. asked.

"It's a multiple murder case. If you want to go to trial, you won't find a better case, it's a slam dunk. The police caught the guy red handed. He's charged with two counts of first degree murder and one count of attempted murder, and two counts of kidnapping."

"Is one of the victim's named Cady Grimes?" Joe Jr. asked.

"Yeah, you know her?"

"Well no not her but her dad and my dad are good friends. Would that be a conflict?" Joe Jr. asked.

"I don't think so. It's yours now," his boss said.

Joe Jr. knew his boss expected him to be afraid or hesitant but this was what he prayed for. Now he was meeting his client for the first time and he was excited, but he vowed not to let on to his client that this was his first murder trial. He studied the case file all night and felt that he was ready. He definitely had some questions for his client.

Jackson Bonnen III walked slowly into the holding cell with his hands cuffed in front of him. It appeared that he hadn't shaven or groomed himself in weeks. As he came and sat down across from Joe Jr., it became apparent that he hadn't showered either.

"Hi, my name is Joseph Addelbury; I'm with the Public Defender's Office. I'm going to be representing you in this case."

"The PD's Office?" Jackson said. Then he covered his face with his hands in exasperation.

"You were expecting a private attorney?" Joe Jr. asked.

"Well, man, do you know who my father is?"

Jackson asked.

"No I don't. Have you contacted your father? Your file says you were appointed the PD's office at your arraignment."

"My old man just sat there in court and let them give me a welfare lawyer. What the hell is his problem?" Jackson said, really to himself.

"Well, Mr. Bonnen, I need to ask you some questions," Joe Jr. said.

"Wait, Addelbury. Don't I know you?" Jackson asked.

"I don't think so."

"Don't you know Cady?"

"Not really, but her father and my father are good friends. Is that going to be a problem for you?" Joe Jr. asked.

"Oh wait a minute. Your dad is the big white guy right?" Jackson said.

"Yes, he adopted me and my brothers when we were very young," Joe Jr. said.

"Yeah, Cady told me all about it. She and I were out on a date one time and we saw your dad -- oh, so your moms is that Indian lady at the café then right?" Jackson asked.

"Yes. Can we talk about your case now?" Joe Jr. asked.

"Yeah, small world. Cady said y'all were good people so okay I'll give you a shot. Well I didn't do it. I said that to that other welfare lawyer and I'm saying it to you. I didn't do this, none of it," Jackson said.

"Mr. Bonnen, there's a lot of evidence against you. You were found holding the gun that killed those people.

It happened on your boat and you knew the victims."

"Hold on, that's a lie, right there. I only knew Cady; I don't know who that other lady was. Two Touch is the one that killed them ladies. I saw him do it. I tried to wrestle the gun from him and it went off. It could have just as easily been me who got shot, man. Can't you do some kind of trajectory test or something?" Jackson asked.

"Well it's the police's job to gather the evidence. The PD's office just doesn't have funding for that," Joe Jr. said.

"Funding? You just aim a beam of light from where I was standing to where he was laying, how much could that possibly cost? Look, man, I know you just doing your job but I need a real lawyer with some real money to represent me! I ain't like these ghetto boys they got in here. My father is the highest paid accountant in South Beach, you hear me?" Jackson said.

"Well, sir, as far as I know he hasn't tried to contact a private lawyer for you, so I'm all you've got," Joe Jr. said.

"Listen, I'm telling you that fool set me up! I know he did. I need somebody that can get an investigator, do some DNA analysis, all that stuff. You just ain't gonna cut it, Son," Jackson said.

"Okay, this is what I'll do, if your father is who you say he is, you should have a private lawyer because there's a predetermined expense budget set by the PD's office for your case. I'll go and see your father," Joe Jr. said.

"For real? Thanks man," Jackson said, then lowering his head he said, "He's mad at me. Disappointed in me, has been for a long time. He's got to come around though. Hey, can you get my girl in here to see me?"

"Your girl? Cady's in a coma, didn't anybody tell

you?" Joe Jr. asked.

"She is? No, nobody told me that. I'm glad to know that she's not dead, but I didn't mean her. We were really more like friends than anything else. I have another girl. We have a son together. Her name is Lakesha Dames and I love her."

"Okay, I'll see what I can do, but for now I need to know what you were doing on that boat."

"Man, I'm not going through all that again. Get my father down here. I can talk to him. If he won't come you bring my mother, she'll come up with the money. I know she will," Jackson said.

Nedra, Jackson's mother was already three steps ahead of her son. She was walking into the law firm of Weinstein, Rosen and Ross located a mile within her husband's CPA firm in South Beach, an upscale community of Miami Beach. She was met in the waiting area by a slim young white lady with fiery red hair and with what Nedra thought was a skirt that was too short and too tight. Her hair was piled up in a loose bun on the top of her head and as she led Nedra into the conference room, she looked as though she was looking at the ceiling.

Nedra recognized highfaluting racism from the old days. It had been a long time since she conducted business with people who didn't know her standing in the community.

When they reached the conference room instead of the lady offering to serve her coffee or water, she simply motioned towards the back of the room and said, "There's coffee and water there if you'd like some."

Nedra couldn't help herself, "Yes, I would. I'll take my coffee black with a splash of cream please."

The lady just stood there and Nedra stared her down until she went over to where the coffee was and poured Nedra a cup and crossed the room to hand it to her.

Then the lady said, "Someone will be with you in just a minute," and she left the room.

Shortly thereafter a young African American man came into the room. He introduced himself and sat down across the conference table from Nedra.

"What can I do for you today, Ms. Bonnen?" he asked.

"You've got to be kidding me. You can go finish high school and send Weinstein's butt in here right now," Nedra said.

Nedra and Jackson Bonnon the II were from new money as were most of the residents in South Beach but Nedra was an educated woman and she was sharp. When she was earning her MBA she desired to work in a corporate finance office, but then she met Jackson Bonnen II in grad school and fell in love. She gave up her dreams to help him realize his. And now she had this entirely different life than she ever thought she'd have as a young woman. She was a part of high society but she still knew how to get down to business and she also knew how to tell people off, regardless of who they were.

As the young man left the room to get the named partner she thought about her life. She realized that she spent an awful lot of time over the years trying to fit in with her rich socialite friends but as she sat there she couldn't think of a single one that she felt comfortable enough calling on to support her through this mess that Jackson had gotten himself into. She decided at that moment that it was time for her to get real about Jackson as well as her husband and all her snooty friends.

Weinstein finally entered into the conference room. His firm received several referrals from Nedra's husband's business in the past so initially she felt comfortable going to this specific law firm. She also knew that when her husband  found out about it he would hit the roof.

"Mrs. Bonnen, how are you?" Mr. Weinstein said as he shook her hand.

"I don't know how I am, Mr. Weinstein, I'm waiting for you to tell me that," Nedra said.

"Mrs. Bonnen, -- Nedra, I'm not going to waste your time. This isn't a case that we feel comfortable taking on, I'm sorry."

"I'm sorry? You don't feel comfortable? What's that supposed to mean?" Nedra asked.

"Right. We just think that this type of case would be more suited for a different type of law firm," Mr. Weinstein said.

"Right," Nedra said as she stood picking up her purse. "You just want to stick to rap stars with paternity suits, or movie stars who get caught with drugs or firearms. But a non-celebrity case isn't your type of case because my son is not a famous thug, but a decent law abiding young man. There's no press involved, no limelight. I understand perfectly. Have a great day, Mr. Weinstein. I will make certain that my husband, who by the way, referred at least thirty percent of your current clientele, knows that his only child's case is not your firm's type of case. Have a great day."

Nedra was furious. She decided to go speak to Jackson's current Public Defender to see if he could recommend a private attorney who would take the case.

On the drive to the Public Defender's office Nedra thought about her family situation. She was silent when her husband wanted to stop supporting their son financially. When he threw him out of the house, she remained silent because that was one thing, but prison was an entirely different matter. She would not let her only child go to prison, much less rot there. She was willing to accept responsibility for spoiling their son and she agreed he could use some tough love but prison was simply out of the question.

Nedra spent a great deal of time driving around the block of the courthouse downtown where the Public Defender's office was located in search of a parking space. In frustration she illegally parked in a space reserved for police. When she entered the Public Defender's office she found the atmosphere much different than the law firm she had just come from. There was a bustling of people walking all around and no one seemed to notice her entering the elevator in the lobby or exiting the elevator on the floor where Jackson's lawyer was located.

"Excuse me?" Nedra said to at least three different people before someone asked if they could be of help.

"I'm looking for Mr. Addelbury, please," Nedra said.

She was finally escorted down a long hallway, where she noticed that the noise level dropped considerably. She stood at the door as the young lady knocked on the opened door announcing Nedra's arrival.

"Mrs. Bonnen, please come in," Joe Jr. said.

"Pardon my intrusion, Mr. Addelbury. I've run into a little difficulty and I need your help," Nedra said.

"Sure, anything that I can do. I am due in court in

about twenty minutes though," Joe Jr. said looking at his watch.

"First of all, have we met before? I mean, you already knew my name," Nedra asked.

"No, Ma'am we've never met but I spoke with Jackson this morning in holding and he asked that I get in touch with you. I Googled you and saw several pictures of you on the internet."

"Oh okay. Listen, I mean no offense, but I cannot have my son represented by a Public Defender and I was hoping that you could recommend a good private criminal attorney who could represent him in this matter, money is not an issue."

Joe Jr. thought to himself, *Dare I? I may never get this kind of opportunity again. The revenue from this case alone could set up a decent respectable law practice.*

"Mr. Addelbury?" Nedra repeated waking Joe Jr. from his daydream.

"Yes, I'm sorry. Let me make some calls and I will get back to you by this afternoon," Joe Jr. said.

"Thank you so much for your time, Mr. Addelbury. I'll wait to hear from you," Nedra said.

Joe Jr. could hardly contain his excitement at even the thought of being free to practice law as he had always dreamed. He could think of nothing else for the rest of the day. In fact, the Judge had to call him several times to bring his attention back to the plea bargain for the petty theft case he was on.

After the hearing, Joe Jr. went to eat his lunch at his desk instead of the break room because he wanted to be alone and continue his daydream of starting his own law firm. Minutes after he unpacked the lunch that his wife

Lily packed for him, Sandy came rushing in. Sandy was one of the few other African American lawyers in the PD's office who had been there as long as Joe Jr. had.

"Joe, I need a minute," Sandy said.

"What's up?" Joe Jr. asked.

"I don't know how much longer I can do this."

"Do what?"

"Work here. I mean why should we even bother to go to court at all? We can phone this stuff in," Sandy said.

"What happened?"

"I got this girl, young girl, nineteen years old, an assault case. The victim doesn't really have any permanent injuries. My client was really only defending herself. I mean you should see this kid, she's like three feet tall, and the supposed victim is like a sky scrapper. It's ridiculous. But Bob wants me to plead it out," Sandy said.

Joe Jr. sat there smiling at Sandy. He believed that Sandy's frustration was confirmation that he was not losing his mind. He was happy to know that he wasn't the only one who wanted to do legitimate legal work.

"Why are you grinning like that?" Sandy asked.

"I think I can help you out more than you know," Joe Jr. said.

# 20

*"Incline my heart to Your testimonies, And not to **covet**ousness."*
~Psalm 119:36

June met this new Monday morning with great expectations. When Brice and Rosie served her breakfast in bed, she decided to speak to her husband about what she wanted to do in her three hours of non bed rest.

"Mommy, there's no school today," Rosie said.

"Really?" June said while turning to look at her husband.

"Nope, so what are we going to do today?" Rosie asked.

"Well, I planned to go to the -- Rosie, will you please ask Mila to send up a little bit of butter for me please?" June asked.

As Rosie left the room June turned to Brice and said, "I didn't know there was no school today. I had hoped to go see Mario and Cady today. What did you plan to do with Rosie?" she asked.

"I don't know, I thought we could do something around the house. You know you haven't seen her ride her new bike yet. She would really get a kick out of that," he said.

"I don't know. I feel really bad that I haven't being there for Bettina and Mario in all this time. I haven't even spoken to them on the phone," she said.

"I don't feel any condemnation about that, Junie. I do understand how you feel and I love you for being the person you are but I don't want you to have any more stress than is absolutely necessary."

"I understand that you're concerned," she said.

"Junie, Grimes and Bettina are your good friends, I get it. You're feeling guilty that you can't be there right now. If you could, you would have spent this entire time in the hospital right along with them. I understand that's where you're heart is but my heart is with you. My job is to keep you safe, to make sure you're well. And, sweetheart, I know that you're worried so let's do this, I will go on a visitation with them. After all I am their Supervising Elder, and I will come back and report to you all that's going on, within reason," he said.

"Do you promise? I am worried about them," she said.

"Yes I will do that for you and in service to God. But now why don't you plan on spending your non bed rest time as you call it, watching our daughter ride her new bike?" he said.

"I will. I will enjoy that. Honey, when are we going to discuss Kwame?" she asked.

"We're not," he said.

"Brice, come on. I'm serious."

"So am I. I don't think there's anything to discuss. I called the attorney while you were in the hospital because we had to postpone the final hearing until you were better. The lawyer says this guy has a legitimate case. What we have on our side is that if he petitions the court for custody, he would have to prove paternity, and he would have to pay for it. He would also have to pay for an attorney and we both know he can't afford it. So I say we just ignore him and move on with our lives and the adoption."

"That just doesn't sit right with me, Brice. I'm going to let it go for now but I want to talk about it more later," she said.

After a long pause, Brice said, "Okay. But I can't think of anything that would make me change my mind, just so you know."

Brice got dressed for the visitation with Mario and Bettina. He asked Billie if she would keep an eye on June with a wink. Billie picked up on his hint because she knew how stubborn June could be. He left June and Billie sitting on the front porch with a glass of tea and a tray of fruit. They were watching Rosie ride back and forth on the sidewalk in front of the house as he drove away.

He smiled as he looked back at his family in the rearview mirror. He used the solitude of his drive to commune with God.

"Father, I know you know my heart. Help me to conquer my fears, Lord. I fear for Junie and our baby. I fear that we might lose Rosie. I fear that all the things I love about Junie will be the very things that could drive a wedge between us. Help me, Lord. Help me to walk firmly in faith that you will not put more on us than we can bear. Help me, Lord by increasing my wisdom so that I don't get distracted by these things and fail at leading the shepherds of the district that you've appointed me to lead. I love you, Lord. I love you with all my strength and might. In Jesus name I pray, amen."

Brice realized that he had forgotten the task at hand and continued. "And Lord, help me get over my insecurities about Junie and Mario's relationship. I didn't think their friendship would bother me but I admit that it does. Help me, Lord here today as I go to minister to this man. Provide me with the words to show him empathy and comfort. Please take malicious and bitterness towards this man away from me today, O' Lord. Again, I pray in Jesus name, Amen."

Crystal stood just outside the hospital chapel doorway watching Bettina pray. Bettina noticed her there and patted the space next to her on the pew, inviting her to join her in prayer. Crystal reluctantly came in and sat down. They did not exchange any words but just sat still in the quietness of the room.

Bettina began thinking about Toni's funeral the previous month. Bettina drove into the New Hope Church's parking lot and discovered Crystal standing in the parking lot away from all the parked cars smoking a cigarette. She was not dressed for a funeral in her jeans and T-shirt, so Bettina surmised that it was a last minute decision. She walked over to where Crystal was standing and saying nothing simply held out her hand. She was pleasantly surprised when Crystal took her hand. They entered the sanctuary of the church and walked down the center aisle behind a couple of people until they were standing directly in front of the casket where Toni's body laid. Bettina thought that Toni looked at peace. Bettina squeezed Crystal's hand and when Crystal shifted her weight, Bettina took it as a sign that it was time for them to sit down. However, with tears about to escape Crystal's eyes, she leaned into Bettina's ear and said, "I have to go."

"Okay. We'll talk later," Bettina said.

Bettina thought that the attendance at the funeral was extremely low for such a young woman. The church members were there in their prospective places. Her brother, the Reverend Jeremiah Brown led the procession of his Associate Ministers ahead of May Bell, the only family member present to mourn Toni. There were others in attendance from her job at the Laundromat and a few of her classmates. Bettina knew Toni to be a very private person so to that degree the low attendance was understandable.

She was also told by May Bell that when Toni's husband was buried weeks earlier that his extended family blamed Toni for his death and was unsympathetic to May Bell. They also vowed that a custody petition would be filed shortly for Toni and Dale's daughter, Daleena but Bettina reassured her that because they were only third and fourth cousins, that was very unlikely.

Bettina watched as May Bell continued trying to console Daleena, but whenever May Bell cried, so did Daleena. The service was short. Pastor Brown preached a nice eulogy expounding on an unknown tomorrow. Bettina didn't stay for the repast because she was anxious to get back to her husband at Cady's bed side.

In Cady's hospital room, Mario turned when he heard Brice knocking lightly on the open door

. He turned back around to face Cady and said softly, "Did you come by here to beat me up, Preacher?"

"Not today, Mario," Brice said.

Brice went into Cady's room and pulled up a chair and sat down.

Mario said, "I'm sorry, Brice. You were right. I shouldn't have asked June to take such a risk to help me."

"There isn't anything either one of us could've done. She would have helped you anyway," Brice said.

"I have to be honest and tell you though, I am angry with her because if June didn't require special transportation that day on the beach I could have reached Cady sooner, maybe before she was shot."

"What? You're blaming June for what happened?"

"I know. I can't help it though."

"I think you better try. She's the one who sent me here to visit with you and Bettina because she feels bad that she was unable to come. Look, I know we have our issues and if we're both going to be in June's life we're going to have to work them out, but that's not going to happen today. So let's not discuss my wife at all," Brice said.

"Okay," Mario said.

"How's Cady doing?" Brice asked.

"She's not responding. Her hair is growing back in. They cut it all off when they operated to remove the bullet from her skull," Mario said.

"I can't imagine how you feel, Mario. I don't know what I would do if something happened to Rosie."

"Yeah, I guess."

"What does that mean?"

"Brice, you've known Rosie for what, less than a year? Cady is my blood. She's my real daughter," Mario said.

"Wait a minute, man. Are you saying Rosie's not

real? She breathes, she laughs, and she loves. She may not be my blood but she is a huge part of my heart. I can't imagine loving any child more; it would literally hurt if I did. I know you're hurting but that's no reason to be hurtful. God is with you right now hearing your heart, you have to trust Him," Brice said.

Mario turned to face Brice and said sharply, "God? How can I believe in a God who would let this happen to my baby? She never did anything to anybody. I know it might sound like I'm being biased but Cady was a really loving person. Everybody she ever met loved her. Where was God when that fool shot my baby? No real God would have let this happen to her!" Mario said.

Brice hung his head down slightly fighting for patience. Then he said, "Mario, horrible things happen to good people every day. You, of all people should know that. We can't blame God. We have to blame ourselves," Brice said.

"What?" Mario said.

"You asked where God was, this is the same God who watched his own Son being tortured and crucified. He gave us dominion over the earth and I believe every time something horrible happens to His people, especially something that could have been prevented he's asking, where were we," Brice said.

"What could have been done? How could this have been prevented?"

"Look, Mario, I didn't come to argue with you but I can't let you blame God and I hate to see you lose all the ground you've gained in your salvation. As Christians we're supposed to be the optimists. The blessing is that God didn't let Cady die. Three other people did die and I'll bet you their parents think that they were really good people too. Cady, the only one shot in the head is still here. She's not breathing through machines, she's breathing on her own. You've got to see God's hand in that," Brice said.

Mario was silent and then lowered his head and began to sob; Brice placed his hand on Mario's shoulder.

"I just feel so helpless, Brice."

"You're not helpless. You have direct access to God. Why don't we pray?" Brice asked.

Mario nodded his head in agreement while wiping away his tears.

"Heavenly Father, we believe you to be Jehovah Rophe, the ultimate healer. Lord God, we know you are sustaining our Cady with your righteous right hand. We know that you are a God of restoration. We are asking for a miracle today, Lord. We're asking in the name of Jesus Christ of Nazareth that Cady rise up and walk. Let your glory be revealed in her recovery oh, Lord. We will not be detoured by the sight of the machines and her unconsciousness, Lord we will walk by faith and not by sight. And Lord, I pray for this father and his family. I pray that you will give them comfort in this time of sorrow and worry. Remind them that you are near, that nothing is beyond your power. May this be a time that unites them and not divide them. Remind them of those around them who love and care for them in times of loneliness dear, Lord. We ask these and all blessings in the matchless name of your Son, Jesus the Christ. Amen."

Downstairs in the hospital chapel, Crystal broke the silence; she turned to Bettina and said with tears in her eyes, "I think I need to talk to someone."

"You can always talk to me, honey," Bettina said.

"I think I need to talk to Pastor June," Crystal said.

"I don't think she would mind that at all," Bettina said.

"But I've been so angry with her," Crystal said.

"Why is that? I mean did she do something to you?" Bettina asked.

"No, she barely knows me. I've been so dumb. I know she's not well but I feel like if I don't talk to her right now, I never will," Crystal said.

"I know Pastor June really well. She is my very best friend and I would never tell you to go to her if I didn't think she would be willing to help you in any way she could. Go on, I promise she won't hold anything you've said to her against you," Bettina said.

When Crystals single tear fell down over her cheek and landed on her lap, Bettina put her arm around Crystal's shoulder and Crystal rested her head on Bettina's shoulder.

As Bettina stroked her hair she said, "Go on, honey, go. I'll be right here if you need me."

When Bettina returned to Cady's hospital room, Brice and Mario were seated facing Cady in her hospital bed with their backs to the doorway and she could see that they were praying and she was relieved. She stayed in the doorway so that she would not disturb them.

Once they both said, "Amen" she heard Brice say softly, "I know you care a lot about June, but I need you to know that her life has changed. She is responsible for more than just herself. And as her husband and father to her children I'm asking that you not ask her to take any more of these types of risks."

Mario looked up at Brice and said, "I don't know

how much she's told you about us but I only stopped pursuing June because I realized that I wasn't what she needed. I couldn't really make her happy. You need to know that if I thought for a second I could, things would be much different. So while I respect your request, preacher or not, if you can't make her happy, if you slip up in the least way, I will definitely be right there to try again because I still love her and I always will."

Bettina quietly backed out of the doorway and walked down the hall. She felt as if a hole had been punctured in her heart. Neither Mario nor June had ever told her anything about a romance between them. She decided to push her feelings of betrayal down and wait until Cady and June were better before addressing this. She purposely stepped loudly back into the room so that Mario and Brice would know that she was there.

When Crystal pulled up in front of Pastor June's house. She saw her sitting on the porch with Billie. Crystal parked across the street watching Pastor June, she thought about that day when she allowed her then boyfriend, Raymond, to attack Toni. She was very ashamed of her cowardice. She regretted now more than ever never making amends with Toni. Whenever she saw Toni after that night, she just ignored her. She knew Toni was angry with her but she never told anybody what happened. The night it happened Crystal was just happy that it wasn't happening to her again.

Her attention came back to Pastor June when she could hear Rosie shouting,

"Look at me, Mommy. Look what I can do, Nana Billie."

"Wow, that's good, honey dew," Billie shouted back.

"I know it's only been two months but she's gotten so big," June said.

"Tell me about it. She a little sugar plum though. Junie, I got to tell you something important," Billie said.

"Okay, go ahead," June said as she continued smiling while she watched Rosie riding back and forth.

"Well, I'm -- hey, somebody's coming. Do you know that girl?" Billie asked.

"Yeah, that's Crystal, Mario's daughter. I hope everything's okay. She can't stand me. Something big must be going on for her to come to me," June said.

"I'm going to call Rosie in so you two can talk out here. I'll make us some lunch," Billie said.

"Okay, thanks," June said.

Crystal could feel herself shaking, she could not help it. She breathed in through her nose and exhaled through her mouth. She felt an irresistible urge to unload all her secrets onto Pastor June and she needed to do it today, right now.

"Hi, Crystal. Is Cady alright?" Pastor June asked as Billie and Rosie went into the house.

"Oh, yes. Well, she's the same, there's no change. Daddy and Bettina have been there every day."

"And you, are you okay?" June asked.

"Actually, no. Bettina said I could come and talk to you about what's bothering me. I know you're not well and I feel selfish but I have to talk to somebody," Crystal said as she began to let go and sob.

"Oh no, come on over here and sit down," June said.

Pastor June directed Crystal into the rocker and stroked her hair as she said, "It's okay darling, take your time you just start whenever you're ready."

After several minutes of crying Crystal slowly lifted her head away from Pastor June's chest. She looked up at Pastor June who was standing over her and then bowed her head. Crystal then slowly pulled back the long sleeve on her left arm revealing numerous cuts, many were healed over, and many were recent.

"Oh my God, Crystal, you've been cutting yourself. Some of them are real deep. Sweetheart, what's going on?" June asked.

"I went to Toni's funeral. I can't believe she's dead," Crystal said.

"Were you close?" June asked.

"Not really. We shared an incident that I'm ashamed of. I felt guilty when she died that's all," Crystal said.

Pastor June's experience in counseling taught her the benefits of being silent and patient, eventually the person seeking to unload will get to the heart of the matter.

"I know about you and my dad," Crystal said.

"I didn't know it was a secret," June said.

"Yeah, he's been keeping a lot of secrets. But I guess I have too. I've been really mean to you," Crystal said.

"I think I know why. You're angry at me because of my representation of God. You're really angry at God, but I was his tangible representation. Does that sound close?" June asked.

"That's part of it I guess, but I'm not ready to talk about that. I came here about something else," Crystal said.

"Okay. It has to do with your cutting? Based on the scars, it looks like you've been doing it for a while," June said.

"Yes, since high school. When I was in high school I had a boyfriend named Raymond. He was my first. You know what I mean?" Crystal asked.

Pastor June nodded her head as she sat back down and poured Crystal a glass of pineapple sweet tea.

"One day when he was over and my dad was out on a case, he and I were studying in my room. He was upset over something that happened that day at football practice. And he wanted to -- he wanted to -- but I was trying to study for an exam I had the next morning," Crystal paused to drink her tea.

And Pastor June said, "Take all the time you need."

Crystal continued talking slowly and softly, "When I wouldn't give him what he wanted he pinned me down on my bed and raped me. Nobody was home. Nobody could hear me screaming or crying. And he must have liked it that way because he continued to rape me for the next several weeks. Then one night when we came home from one of his football games, he walked me to the door but when he saw my dad and my grandparents having dinner at the table he pulled me to the side of the house. He attempted to rape me again. I didn't want to have sex on the side of the house. I kept pushing his hands away but he was so strong. He put his hand over my mouth so my dad wouldn't hear.

"I started to cry and then out of nowhere Toni came and pushed him away. She knocked him off balance. He fell on the ground and so I ran. I ran to the front of the house until I realized that Toni wasn't behind me. I went back to the side of the house and he was -- he was raping her. I just stood there. I couldn't move for several minutes.

Then I ran into the house, I just left her there. She came to help me and -- she was younger than me, she was younger than Cady. I should have -- I should have helped her."

"And what happened after that?"

"Well, the next time I was with him, I decided not to fight him. I didn't struggle, I didn't move. I just laid there perfectly still. It must have turned him off because he didn't want to be with me anymore."

"I meant what happened with Toni, honey," June said.

"Nothing. I told her not to say anything to anybody. After that, I couldn't look her in the face anymore. I reacted badly when I did. I did the same thing to her that I've been doing to you. I was so mean to her."

"And the cutting, when did that start?" Pastor June

"After that. I couldn't be close to another guy unless I was drunk. Usually the next day I felt so -- so powerless, it felt good to cut myself. I can't explain it," Crystal said.

"Have you ever talked to anyone about your cutting before?" June asked.

"No, you're the only one who knows," Crystal said between her tears.

"I'm going to make an appointment for you with a really good therapist. She will address your cutting issue because sweetheart you can't keep doing that. But I'd also like you to come and see me because I want you to know that although for all these years you've felt alone, you're not alone. I know you feel like nobody else could possibly understand what you've been through but God understands. I know you're angry at God but God didn't fail you, society did. Your heart is grieved because of what happened to you but I want you to know that God's heart is also grieved. He is grieved whenever somebody or something hurts one of His children," June said.

"I haven't been able to date anybody. All through college I made excuse after excuse not to get serious with anybody. I didn't date," Crystal said.

"Well often people who have been harmed like you were, live their lives with a victim's mentality because they yearn to have their hurt validated. To have their hurt acknowledged. I'm telling you right now that this was not all right. It was not your fault. He had no right to take advantage of your physical weakness and by doing that I can tell you that the devil really desired for him to steal your spiritual strength, which is God because His strength is perfected in our weakness."

"I feel better having told you," Crystal said softly.

Pastor June took both of Crystal's hands and said, "Let us pray, Lord God, we love you. We love that you comfort people with our arms. We pray that you will break this stronghold of shame, that you will restore her strength and confidence in who she is and whose she is. We ask that from this moment on, that she will allow herself to accept and feel your love. We thank you too, we thank you that you encouraged her to forsake her pride and feel comfortable to reach out, to speak out. We ask that you continue to build her up, Lord. We ask this in Jesus name, Amen."

Pastor June stood to embrace Crystal once again. While in their embrace, Pastor June made a mental note to contact Detective Wright to find out where exactly this Raymond was. They continued to embrace until they could feel Rosie joining in on their hug and saying, "I want to hug too, Mommy."

# 21

*"But now I have written to you not to keep company with anyone named a brother, who is sexually immoral, or **covet**ous, or an idolater, or a reviler, or a drunkard, or an extortioner—not even to eat with such a person."* ~1 Corinthians 5:11

That next Saturday afternoon, Joe Jr. and Lily sat waiting for Cowboy Joe and Wendy to get their grand kids settled and to join them at the kitchen table. Joe Jr. was overflowing with excitement. He and Sandy found an affordable office location and Lily was ready to decorate. He was anxious to tell his parents why they needed them to babysit for them on a Saturday morning.

Cowboy Joe came into the kitchen first. "I can't get over how big Wind Marie is getting, it's like she doubled in height since just last week."

"Yeah, they do tend to grow up, honey," Wendy said.

"Mom, Dad, we have some news to share with you," Joe Jr. said.

"Are we going to be grandparents again?" Wendy asked excitedly.

"No," both Joe Jr. and Lily said at the same time and then laughed together.

"I caught that case at the Public Defender's office, you know the triple homicide," Joe Jr. said.

"The one with Grimes' daughter?" Cowboy Joe asked.

"Yes, that's the one. Well, they wanted him to plea it out," Joe Jr. said.

"If that's what's best for that young man, I think he should. I mean we haven't exactly progressed so much as a society that you think he'd actually get a fair trial do you?" Wendy asked.

"I think he deserves the right to try. Without going into the merits of the case, I want you and Dad to know that Sandy, another person from the PD's office and I turned in our resignations last week. We're going to start our own practice. Lily and I are heading down to the new office right now to get started. The triple homicide is our first case and we're going to trial," Joe Jr. said proudly.

"Did you take any time at all to think about this, Son? I mean if you're sure, I'm happy for you but if you're going to trial in a triple homicide you're going to need a lot of seed money," Cowboy Joe said.

"Is that what was bothering you? You were unhappy at the PD's office?" Wendy said.

"Yes, Mom, it got really bad," Joe Jr. said.

"I haven't seen him this excited since the babies were born. I'm excited too. I'm the office manager," Lily said.

"Well who's going to watch the kids while you're managing?" Wendy asked.

"I'll only be there part time, that way Wind can get

socialized in daycare for a couple hours a day. You know I could use some productivity in my life too, Mom," Lily said.

"I understand that, Lily. I'll cut back on my hours at the Sunday Morning Café so if you need to stay longer on some days I can pick up the kids for you," Wendy said..

"That would be really great," Lily replied excitedly.

"All we care about, kids, is that you're happy," Wendy said.

"And that you don't have to borrow any money from us," Cowboy Joe said chuckling.

Lakesha was late. Jackson had been waiting almost fifteen minutes in the visitors area to see her and his son. It was all he had to look forward to after the many weeks he'd been in jail. Then he saw her shadow preceding her entrance coming up the hallway and his heart quickened. When he finally saw her, his breath was taken away. Her braided hair was piled high in a bump in the front and it flowed down freely with loose braids that covered her entire back down to the top of her waist. Her curvy frame made him yearn to reach through the partition, grab her and bring her close to him. She had on the dark pink lipstick that he liked and he could smell his favorite perfume penetrating the stench of the jail.

"Hey, Baby," Lakesha said.

Jackson smiled. "Where's little man?"

"Not ever brining my son to jail, sorry," Lakesha responded.

"Oh. I really wanted to see him."

"You will, when you get out."

"Yeah, one day," Jackson said softly.

"You don't know do you?" Lakesha asked.

207

"Know what?"

"Your momma, she came through. I just left Mr. Addelbury's office and --"

"Addelbury? She was supposed to be getting me a private lawyer. Oh my God why won't anybody listen to me? I can't go to court with no Public Defender, Baby," Jackson said frantically.

"Listen, baby, you don't understand. Mr. Addelbury left the PD's office. He started his own firm and you're his only case. He's going to give all his attention to you," Lakesha said.

"What? When was anybody going to tell me?" Jackson asked.

"He was on his way down here when I stopped in. Somebody in the PD's office told me where he was, all secret like. He told me your momma is financing it. I think if she think he can do it, he can. I mean I ain't never met her but if she as smart as you say, you know it's got to be a good thing," Lakesha said.

For the first time since he'd been locked up, Jackson began to feel hopeful. He spent the majority of his time daydreaming about a missed happy life with Lakesha. He couldn't believe all the times he mistreated her, cheated on her, made sure they spent their time together far away from anybody he knew. He wasn't ashamed of her but he knew his circle of family and friends wouldn't accept her. But she was the one who sent him care packages; she was the one who called him regularly. He hadn't heard from any of the socialites he openly dated while he's been in jail. He determined that he was going to make things right with Lakesha. He was done hiding her from his family and friends because none of them, not even his own parents visited or called while he was in jail. Now Jackson was aggravated by the plastic partition that separated him and Lakesha.

"I wish I could touch you. I wish I could hold you. You're all I can think about. I want you to know that I love you and I'm so glad that you're my lady, my only lady," Jackson said.

Lakesha smiled. "Me too."

After Lakesha left Joe Jr.'s new office a short plump white lady entered asking for him.

"I'm Mr. Addelbury, can I help you?" Joe Jr. said.

"Yeah, I'm Jimyia. You're father sent me over."

"He did? For what?" Joe Jr. asked.

"Ahh, he didn't tell you. I'm an investigator. He said you needed one for your case," Jimyia said.

"I could certainly use one but can't exactly pay one. We just literally opened today," Joe Jr. said.

"He already took care of the pay. I'm yours for the next two weeks, what do you need me to do?" Jimyia said.

"Oh wow. This is great isn't it Joe? We could use somebody to start running checks on the victims," Sandy said.

"Okay, give her the information. We don't have a lot on Mr. and Mrs. Jacobs. We have some account numbers on Cady and Jackson, there's not much else. But they both have large trust funds and we need to know who the executor of those trusts funds are or who else has access. There are some people that I'd prefer to interview myself but whatever you can find out would be a great help. Jimyia, if you'll try to find out more about the victims and our client that would be great. I'm going to see the lady Pastor June told me about," Joe Jr. said.

"Who is that?" Sandy asked.

"Somebody named Eartha -- Eartha Jones," Joe Jr. said.

"Mac. She goes by the name Mac. She's real good at what she does," Jimyia said.

"What exactly does she do?" Sandy asked.

"A little bit of everything," Jimyia said smiling as she took the files from Sandy and left through the front door.

Joe Jr. arrived at the coffee house in West Palm Beach's downtown City Place to meet with Mac with his briefcase in hand. All that was in his briefcase was a single notebook and several ink pens. It had been a while since he'd done an interview. Pastor June had given him some tips but he was a little afraid of not asking all the right questions. Pastor June arranged the meeting with Joe Jr. and Mac.

City Place was a shopper's Mecca with high end department stores fronting cobble stoned streets. The center attraction was the colored water fountain that changed colors according to the beats when the band played both day and night. Joe Jr. easily spotted Mac sitting outside the coffee house on the patio. She was easy to spot; she looked just as Pastor June described her.

"Ms. Mac?" Joe Jr. asked.

"Just Mac, please. Sit on down," Mac said.

"Mac, the prosecution has a lot of evidence against my client. I hope you have something that can discredit at least some of it," Joe Jr. said.

"I can tell you that your client has been set up and I can give you what you need to prove it," Mac said.

"Really? What do you have?" Joe Jr. asked.

"I usually charge a fee for this type of information, but Pastor June helped me out with something and I owe her. But just so we're clear, if you want anything after this, it will cost you," Mac said.

After speaking with Mac for over an hour Joe Jr. had a completely new perception of his case and he was happy about the trial beginning in three days. They spent the last several months with numerous preliminary hearings that seemed to all go in the prosecution's favor and Joe Jr. decided to focus on a defense that would force the prosecution prove his client's guilt. Now his goal wasn't simply to provide Jackson with a good defense but with the new information that Mac provided, Joe Jr. raised the goal to actually winning the case.

# 22

*"Not given to wine, not violent, not greedy for money, but gentle, not quarrelsome, not **covetous**"*~1 Timothy 3:3

After Crystal left, June and Billie began to prepare dinner. Mila had shown June how to cook one meal, paprika chicken. Billie was boiling water for the angel hair pasta; June was seasoning the chicken and Rosie was taking a bath.

"Junie, you know there's something not quite right about that girl," Billie said.

"Crystal? No, she's all right. She's really been going through," June said.

"I know but there's still something not quite right about her. Hey, remember I was trying to tell you something just before she came? There's some things I need you to know --"

"Ahh yeah, I think it's going to have to wait," June said.

"No, this can't wait, Junie. We need to have a talk about some things because --"

"Billie! I think my water just broke," June said.

"Oh Lord, that's part of what I was trying to tell you, the baby was gon come early," Billie said.

"Is he going to be all right? Oh my God, Billie, it's way too early," June said frantically.

"No, child, he's going to be fine. Go over there and sit down. I'm going to call the ambulance and your husband. It's good he's already at the hospital," Billie said.

"Please don't make a fuss, Billie, I can wait on Myrtle or Brice. Really, don't call the ambulance," June said.

"No, Junie, I'm calling the ambulance. He's coming early for a reason, and I don't want that preacher man of yours coming for me if something go wrong," Billie said.

For the first time in a long time June felt panicked. She began beating herself up for putting her pregnancy at risk in the first place. She wanted to be strong but she never felt so helpless before. Fainting at the crime scene, fighting with Brice and then Rosie's birth father dropping in, all took its toll and she became very frightened.

When Billie hung up with the 911 operator, she sat next to June on the couch and June practically collapsed in her arms. Billie stroked her hair and hummed until the paramedics came. June hated having the ambulance come to get her. She hated that the baby was coming early, and she hated that nobody was listening to her as she complained about it all.

After the medics transitioned her from the house into the ambulance, she could hear Brice talking to Billie on the phone. Billie insisted that she and Rosie ride in the ambulance with June, even though it was against the rules. When they reached the hospital, Billie took Rosie to the cafeteria while Brice stayed with June. In the emergency room, Dr. Khan concluded that June had begun dilating.

"It's happening too fast now to stop the delivery. The baby is viable Reverend Howard," Dr. Khan said.

"Are you sure? Is June going to be okay?" Brice asked.

"Well, it's early. Her blood pressure is elevated but we don't really have a choice, the baby is coming right now. So we're going to prepare her for delivery," Dr. Khan said.

June grabbed Brice's hand and said, "Brice, I'm sorry. I'm so sorry," she managed to say in between sobs.

"Sweetheart, you didn't do anything wrong. I promise you I'm not upset anymore. I love you. I realize now that means I have to love all of you, including the part of you that takes risks for the people you care about. I love you for that," Brice said.

Although June was comforted by Brice's words she was still struck with a fear unlike any she has ever known. She was plagued with the "what if's." What if something happened to the baby, what if something happened to her and Rosie lost another parent.

She grabbed Brice's hand and began praying, "Lord your word says that you did not give us a spirit of fear and if it doesn't come from you, I don't want it. We're calling in peace, we're calling in restoration, we're believing in your miraculous ability to heal, to make what is crooked straight and rough smooth. Hear our cry O' Lord and grant the desire of our hearts. Amen."

Six hours later, the reverends June Harris and Brice Howard were the proud new parents of a baby boy. Once June delivered their new son, Dr. Khan gave her a sedative so that she could sleep.

When she finally fell asleep Brice went down to the chapel and cried before the altar giving thanks to God for the survival of his family. The baby was premature but weighed in at five pounds which Dr. Khan said meant that if he had gone to full term he would have been a huge baby.

June was allowed to leave the hospital the next day but she wanted to stay in order to be near her new baby who was to remain in the hospital for observation. Dr. Khan said he was breathing on his own but that everything looked good and it would only be for a couple of days.

When June awakened later that day, she sat in a chair next to the isolette where her new baby slept. She watched him for hours. She couldn't believe that she had finally given birth or that from inside of her someone so beautiful was created. She continuously stroked the baby's head. Her new son was sort of a caramel color, she hoped that he would be the complexion of his father, the deepest richest brown, but he did have his father's green eyes.

Despite her repeated attempts to control her emotions, tears continued flowing from her eyes, especially as she thought about her Momma May. She was saddened by the fact that her Momma May would never know Rosie or her new little one. June was an only child. Momma May lived for the joy of mothering June. And though she did spoil June, she taught her that the truest gift she could ever have or give is to help others. Momma May passed away when June was still in the police academy. June couldn't help but think she missed so much, she missed her promotion to detective, her call into the ministry and now her children.

Looking at her new baby she felt as if she wanted to go out into the world and right every wrong so that he would grow up in a perfect world. She wanted him never to hurt, never to feel bad or sad.

Brice had fallen asleep in the chair next to her and when he awakened June said to him, "Brice, we didn't have a chance to discuss names yet. What are we going to name him?"

"I don't know, but I definitely don't want a junior," Brice said yawning.

"I know. If you say the name Joe at Cowboy Joe's house three different people would potentially come running," June said as they both chuckled.

"I want him to have his own name, something unique to him," Brice said as he stroked the new baby's cheek.

June's hospital room was jammed packed full of flowers from church members, other pastors in the area, and many of the local politicians. She and Brice each received their fair share of congratulatory gifts. Just as the nurse was removing the baby from the isolette Billie, Myrtle and Rosie came to visit with more flowers and balloons in hand.

"Oh, he's a beautiful baby. Gonna darken up some too," Billie said.

"How do you know that? Are you walking in your gift again?" Brice asked.

"No I can tell because of the darkened tips on his ears and the dark ridges on his fingers," Billie said followed by her deep raspy laugh.

"He has his father's green eyes," Myrtle said to no one in particular.

"I want to hold him, mommy," Rosie said.

"What's his name?" Myrtle asked.

"The Baby," June said as she looked at her husband and smiled.

"We're going to wait and see his personality and name him later," Brice said.

"We still have to put a nursery together, Brice," June said.

"No, we got that. Between Mila, me and Myrtle, we got the nursery covered, don't you worry about that. And we're going to go ahead as planned with the baby shower; the baby will just be an honored guest," Billie said.

June's smile widened when she saw Bettina coming through the doorway.

"Hi, Bettina," June said.

"Hi everybody. Let me see this new little guy," Bettina said as she stood in front of Brice who was now holding the baby.

"How's Cady doing?" June asked.

"The same," Bettina answered.

"I want to visit with her," June said.

The nurse was called and the request made for June to be able to go downstairs to see Cady. Billie accompanied Bettina as she wheeled Pastor June to Cady's room. As they traveled down the hall they passed many hospital employees that Pastor June knew but none of them seemed to recognize her. Pastor June soon realized that she was dressed in a hospital gown; and was without the clergy clothes that people had grown accustomed to seeing her in. And that pleased her because she believed it to mean that they first saw her as a representative of God and not of her own person.

When she entered the room she saw Mario sitting in the chair next to Cady.

"Hi, June. Congratulations," Mario said.

"Hi, Mario. How you holding up?" June asked.

"They want to move her to rehab because she's breathing on her own and there's nothing else they can do for her. We just have to wait for her to wake up," Mario said.

"Let them, she's gon wake up and be fine," Billie said.

Mario looked at Billie then back to June.

June smiled and said, "If she says so, I would believe it."

Then Mario turned back to face Cady because she had just squeezed his hand.

"Remember, Mario, they said that was reactionary and not a sign that she's awake," Bettina said

"I know, but I choose to see it as hope," Mario said.

By the end of the week the new baby and his new parents were settling in at home. The baby shower went as planned at St. Mark Church. The parking lot was filled to capacity as the church and community attended. June was adamant about not playing baby shower games.

She stated to Wendy, "I just want to eat!"

The Sunday Morning Café catered the shower and Wendy made sure that all of Pastor June's favorite foods were there. Wendy made oxtails, barbeque ribs, mac and cheese and a host of other delectable's that Pastor June had been denied throughout her pregnancy. She and her husband were well pleased with the turnout and they both felt very loved and appreciated.

By that week's end they began settling into a routine. Brice happily changed as many diapers as did June and Mila. Billie helped with the nightly feedings to allow June and Brice to be able to get a good night's sleep. June was anxious to get back to her church work. During her weeks of bed rest Brice had been filling in for her with the bible studies and administration of the church. He and Billie had been overseeing Sunday worship.

Pastor June sat at her office desk at St. Mark on this Monday morning making appointments so she could catch up with her counseling sessions. Then she planned to begin the outline for the next specialized bible study because she wanted to clear her mornings for the week so that she could attend Jackson's trial which had already began.

Myrtle suddenly appeared in her doorway with a young man. "Pastor, this young man is looking for you."

"Reverend June Harris?" the man asked.

"Yes?" Pastor June responded.

He entered into the office and handed Pastor June an envelope and asked her to sign something. As Pastor June opened the envelope Myrtle asked, "What is it?"

"It's a subpoena. The prosecution is calling me as a witness in Jackson's murder trial," June said.

"Well you were planning to be there anyway," Myrtle said.

"No, witnesses aren't allowed in the courtroom," Pastor June said and sighed. She felt stupid that she hadn't realized that she would be called to testify because she and Detective Grimes were the first ones at the scene.

# 23

*"They **covet** fields and take them by violence, Also houses, and seize them. So they oppress a man and his house, A man and his inheritance."* ~ Micah 2:2

Joe Jr. sat at the defense table awaiting the judge's appearance in the courtroom reflecting on the previous weeks when the prosecution continued to offer his client a variety of plea deals. He found it refreshing to finally have a client who was adamant about going to trial. Jackson was consistent and vehement about professing his innocence.

Joe Jr. looked very professional and handsome sitting at the defense table. He was a young man in his late twenties. His athletic physique was tall and slender but he was quite muscular and good looking in his new dark blue custom fitted suit, he wore a dark yellow and blue striped tie that contrasted beautifully against his dark complexion. He kept his hair really short and tapered. He also had a habit of clenching his jaw, which accentuated his chiseled facial bone structure. People always noticed him in a room.

Mr. Stills, the Assistant District Attorney, on the other hand was of a short and stocky stature, a white guy with sandy brown hair neatly trimmed. He wore a black suit with a black and grey striped tie. At first glance he looked competent and confident. He nodded at Joe Jr. as he took his seat at the prosecution's table. Joe Jr. thought he looked entirely too smug but then Joe Jr. could see that under the prosecutions table Mr. Mills continually tapped his foot nervously.

Jury selection had not gone the way that Joe Jr. had hoped but rather how he expected, leaving him with an all white fifteen member jury panel. Initially there were seven African American's in the jury pool but one by one the prosecutor successfully challenged them all and they were each excused from the jury.

Joe Jr. felt that Mr. Stills' opening statement was beyond typical, he thought it was stereotypical. He painted Jackson as another angry African American who got greedy or felt entitled. He accused Jackson of being solely responsible for the kidnapping and the murders. The prosecutor never mentioned Jackson's father or his success. Joe Jr. figured that the prosecutor didn't want Jackson seen as an exception to the stereotyping that plagued society and thus the jury panel.

In the courtroom seated in the gallery behind the defense table sat Lakesha. She had been there from day one of jury selection and every day since. On this morning she sat next to Jackson's mother, Nedra. His father, Jackson Bonnen II, had not attended any of Jackson's court proceedings beyond his initial arraignment. Also seated in the gallery behind the defense table in the courtroom was Cowboy Joe. He had come to see his son at work. This would be the first time he would see Joe Jr. in court beyond a short hearing. Also this morning seated in the gallery behind the prosecution's table sat Bettina as well as May Bell, Toni's mother. And seated with them were Detective Grimes and Crystal because they were each also called as witnesses for the prosecution.

Mr. Stills invoked Rule 615, which called for witnesses to be barred from the courtroom until after their testimonies were given if they weren't going to be recalled. So Detective Grimes, Crystal, Cowboy Joe, as well as Pastor June were all asked to leave the courtroom.

Pastor June was on call to appear as a witness for the State this morning. Supervising Elder Howard insisted on accompanying her. Billie and Mila were with the baby and Myrtle was in charge of Rosie. This morning Mario was the prosecution's first witness. And after he was sworn in the prosecutor asked,

"Detective Grimes, you failed to report the kidnapping of your youngest daughter. Can you tell the jury why?"

"Because I knew I would be excluded from working the case," Mario said.

"So nobody investigated your daughter's disappearance except yourself and your friend, a Ms. June Harris?"

"Yes," Mario said.

"And are you familiar at all with the defendant?"

"No. I've never seen him before that day," Mario said.

After several more factual questions and no questions from the defense, Detective Grimes was allowed to leave the witness stand.

"Your next witness, for the State?" the Judge asked.

"Your Honor, our next witness is June Harris," Mr. Stills said.

Pastor June walked up into the witness stand wearing a simple black pants suit with her clergy collar and plain black pumps with a three inch heel. Her hair resumed the standard style, a single braid that ended at her waist, the ends were held together with a pony tail holder that continued to bounce back and forth against her lower back as she walked.

"Do you swear to tell the truth, the whole truth and nothing but the truth, so help you God?" the Judge asked.

"Yes. So help me, God," June said.

"Counsel you may begin," the Judge said.

"Ms. Harris --"

Pastor June held up her hand and said, "Sir, I have a bachelor's degree in religion, a Masters degree in divinity and a PhD in practical theology. I was ordained by the Bishop of the largest African American Church in the world; please refer to me as the Reverend June Harris."

"Yes, I'm so sorry. Reverend Harris, you used to be a detective for the Sarasota Police Department is that right?" Mr. Stills asked.

"No, Sir," June said.

"No? What was your previous law enforcement employment?"

"I was employed as a detective in the Sarasota County Sherriff's Office, Sir."

"I see. And Detective Grimes was your partner?"

"That is correct."

"Now you sometimes consult for the Palm Beach County Sherriff's Office?"

"That is correct."

"And how did you learn about the kidnapping of Cady Grimes?"

"Her father, Detective Grimes."

"So you would admit to knowing that this was not an official investigation?"

Pastor June learned from her time with the Sarasota Sherriff's Office to be vague in answering questions on the stand and she also knew that the prosecution was trying to paint Detective Grimes as a rogue cop in order to clear the Sherriff's Office of any wrongdoing.

"Yes, I knew that he was acting on his own accord," June said.

"We learned from the police report that you were transported by ambulance to the hospital on the day of the murders," Mr. Stills said.

"Objection, is there a question, Your Honor?" Joe Jr. interrupted.

"Sustained. Ask a question Mr. Stills," the Judge said.

"Why were you taken to the hospital from the crime scene, Ms. -- Reverend Harris?" Mr. Stills asked.

"I was very pregnant and I fainted. It was discovered at the hospital that I had a condition called Toxemia."

"Okay. And can you describe to the jury what you observed when you first entered the boat where the crime occurred?"

"When I came on board, I saw nothing unusual for a vessel that size," June said.

"Seeing three bodies with gunshot wounds was

usual?" Mr. Stills said.

"Objection, prosecution is testifying. These are facts not yet in evidence," Joe Jr. said.

"Sustained. You have yet to establish a foundation for calling this boat the crime scene, counselor," the Judge said.

"Excuse me, Your Honor. Reverend Harris, why were you at the crime scene? I mean the boat in the first place?"

"Detective Grimes learned that the defendant owned a condo at that address and while in that residence we discovered the title to the boat," June said.

"And so you decided to do a search of the boat?"

"That is correct," Pastor June answered.

"What caused you to go on board?" Mr. Stills asked.

Pastor June knew what he wanted her to say but she also knew enough about the law to know how to avoid it. She was only obligated to answer his direct questions. Joe Jr. realized that although this was his first murder trial it appeared to him that it must have also been Mr. Stills as well. Joe Jr. surmised that the District Attorney assigned Mr. Stills the case to cut his teeth on. Everyone in the D.A.'s office assumed it was an open and shut case. Joe Jr. smiled to himself because he knew that it was not.

"While trying to identify which vessel belonged to the defendant we heard a series of gunshots," June said.

"Now, Reverend Harris, you stated that you were very pregnant and that you knew that Detective Grimes was conducting this investigation on his own, without any authorization from the Sherriff's Office. What made you take such a personal risk to help him?" Mr. Stills asked.

"Objection, Your Honor, relevance," Joe Jr. interrupted.

"What is the relevance, Mr. Stills?" the Judge asked.

"I'm trying to show that the witness's participation in this case was much more than a goodwill gesture on her part."

"Overruled. Go ahead," the Judge said.

"Do you need me to repeat the question?" Mr. Stills asked Pastor June.

"No. We were friends. Detective Grimes, his wife Bettina and his daughter, one of the victims, Cady Grimes had become very good friends with me and my family," June said.

"Isn't it a fact, Reverend Harris, that you and Detective Grimes were more than just friends?" Mr. Stills asked.

Pastor June looked first at her husband who nodded his head affirming for her to answer the question. Pastor June then immediately looked at Bettina. Pastor June had not realized until Crystal told her that Detective Grimes had kept their prior relationship a secret from his family. Pastor June hated secrets for this very reason; she knew that they always eventually came to light and that someone always got hurt.

"Yes," Pastor June responded still looking directly at Bettina.

"In fact, weren't you and Detective Grimes lovers at one point and time?" Mr. Stills asked.

Pastor June took several seconds before she would answer. She looked at Bettina with pleading and empathy in her eyes and then answered. "Yes."

"And isn't it a fact that you and Detective Grimes were engaged to be married?" Mr. Stills asked.

"Objection, Your Honor, again what's the relevance for this line of questioning?" Joe Jr. interrupted.

"Your Honor, I'm trying to establish the prior relationship between the only two people who discovered the crime scene," Mr. Stills said.

"What relevance is that?" the Judge asked.

"To demonstrate the degree to which this investigation was unauthorized, Your Honor," Mr. Stills said.

"Objection's overruled, but you're on a short leash, Mr. Stills. After this question is answered you need to move on. Answer the question Reverend," the Judge said.

Pastor June kept her gaze on Bettina. She hated that this is the way she would find out about her relationship with Mario. She couldn't understand why he didn't tell her. She and Bettina never discussed it, it just never came up. Pastor June was so far removed from her yesterday it honestly had not occurred to her that Bettina didn't know.

"That is correct, it was many years ago," Pastor June replied as she watched Bettina get up and leave the courtroom.

"Do you know the defendant?"

"Yes."

"And where do you know the defendant from?"

"He attended one of my church services and he joined me and my party for dinner afterwards," June said.

"And was the defendant dating the victim, Cady Grimes?" Mr. Stills asked.

"At that point, I was not aware that they were dating," June said.

"Was there a point in which you did learn that they were dating?"

"Yes."

"And when was that?" Mr. Stills asked.

"Later that summer," Pastor June replied.

Anyone watching Lakesha during the questioning would have never guessed that she was involved with Jackson at all. Her composure was stoic. She looked unmoved and unconcerned. Nedra, Jackson's mother however continued to silently cry as the prosecutor continued painting a picture of her son as a killer.

"Did you know that the defendant was in financial hardship?"

"I learned that during the investigation, yes," June said.

"The unauthorized investigation into the disappearance of Cady Grimes?"

"That is correct."

Mr. Stills continued this line of questioning for some time and then he gently led Pastor June into testifying about the crime scene and the placement of the bodies.

"After Jackson was taken into custody, I entered the room where the bodies were," June said.

"Now you were a police officer, you know about crime scene contamination. Why did you enter that room, Ma'am?" Mr. Stills asked.

"Because I am first and foremost a minister of God and I wanted to pray for God to receive their souls," June said.

"We have no further questions for this witness, Your Honor," Mr. Stills said.

"For the defense, Mr. Addelbury?" the Judge said.

"Thank you, Your Honor. Yes I have a few questions.

"Pastor June, when you arrived on scene, what did it appear to you had taken place?" Joe Jr. asked.

"I knew there had been gunshots because we heard them prior to entering. Once inside the boat or vessel the room where we were was empty of people," June said.

"At what point did you see the defendant at the scene?" Joe Jr. asked.

"When Detective Grimes asked him to disarm and exit the room," Pastor June responded.

"Now, Pastor June, did you automatically assume that my client was the person who shot those people?" Joe Jr. asked.

"No, Sir, I did not," Pastor June responded.

"Why not?" Joe Jr. asked.

"Objection, Your Honor," Mr. Stills said rising to his feet.

"On what grounds?" the Judge asked.

"Relevance. Ms. Harris was there in friendship. She was not acting as a police agent and she prayed for the victims. If she had an official capacity at all it was that of a minister, Your Honor," Mr. Stills said.

"Your Honor, Pastor June or the Reverend June Harris, can be classified as a crime scene expert. She was a decorated homicide detective, very experienced with crime scene analysis and she has testified in many cases prior to her departure from the force," Joe Jr. argued.

"I am familiar with Pastor June and her credentials in law enforcement. The court accepts her as a crime scene expert witness, unless the prosecution can present evidence to refute her expertise," the Judge said.

"Your Honor, Reverend Harris is our witness and we did not call her as an expert witness but rather as an eyewitness. We object to the reclassification," Mr. Stills said.

"Well, is she on your witness list, Mr. Addelbury?" the Judge asked.

"She is, Your Honor, and there is no classification. If one is needed, I move to have the defense's witness list amended to include the classification of expert witness in addition to eyewitness as it relates to this witness, Your Honor," Joe Jr. said.

"The State still objects, Your Honor," Mr. Stills said.

"Overruled. The witness shall be classified in the record as a crime scene and investigation expert. You may continue, counsel."

"Thank you, Your Honor.

"Pastor June, please give us your view of what happened based on what you saw, heard and experienced while on the crime scene." Joe Jr. asked.

"When the defendant was aware that we entered the premises he began to yell that he did not shoot anybody. And because he was in a different room I was unable to see his position versus the victim's positions, so I could not or would not make the assumption that he was the shooter," June said.

"What would you have done if you were officially investigating this crime, Pastor June?" Joe Jr. asked.

"I would have arrested the defendant but I also would have tested the defendant and everyone else for GSR, all those who was present during the gun shots," June said.

"To your knowledge, was this done?" Joe Jr. asked.

"To my knowledge it was not. Only the defendant was tested for GSR."

"And what is GSR an acronym for, Ma'am?"

"Gunshot residue."

"That's all I have for this witness, Your Honor," Joe Jr. said.

"Any redirect from the State?" the Judge asked.

"No, Your Honor. The State has no further questions for this witness."

"You may step down now, Pastor June. It was great seeing you and congratulations on your new baby. What's his name by the way?"

"We have yet to name him, Your Honor," Pastor June said while fighting the urge to roll her eyes, She was quickly growing tired of people asking for the baby's name.

"Your Honor, the rule having been invoked, we'd like to ask that Reverend Harris not be allowed to remain in the courtroom during the other witness testimony for the remainder of the trial."

"Well now counsel you just said you had no more questions for this witness. And if that's still the case I'm not going to bar her from these proceedings. You can't have it both ways," the Judge said.

"We would like to reserve the right to recall the witness, Your Honor," Mr. Stills said.

"Well you can reserve the right to recall her but

she has already testified and currently you have no other questions for her so whether you recall her or not, she will not be barred from observing at this point," the Judge said.

"Thank you, Your Honor," Mr. Stills said.

"Your next witness, counsel?"

"Our next witness is Dr. Joseph Addelbury, Senior."

The State called Cowboy Joe to the stand and he testified about the evidence that he informed Detective Grimes and Detective Wright about earlier. He did not however mention, because he was never asked, about his suspicions regarding the other bodies who were also injected and then killed. Mr. Stills asked Cowboy Joe to confirm whether or not the defendant, Jackson Bonnen III, had gunshot residue and Cowboy Joe confirmed that he did. Neither the defense nor the prosecutor had any objection to the current witness being the defense attorney's father.

"Your Honor, I tender the witness," Mr. Stills said.

"Cross examination from the defense?" the Judge asked.

"Yes, Your Honor, thank you.

"Mr. Addelbury, Senior. You said the defendant tested positive for GSR, correct?" Joe Jr. asked.

"Yes."

"And was the defendant the only one you tested for GSR in this case?"

"No."

"Who else did you test for GSR, Dr. Addelbury?"

"We tested Cady Grimes, Demetrius Daniels, and Toni Jacobs. We also tested Detective Grimes and Pastor

June."

"And what did your tests conclude?"

"We concluded that only one other person tested positive for GSR."

"And who was that person?"

"Demetrius Daniels."

"And where did the request to test the others for GSR originate?"

"From you, the attorney for the defendant."

Once Cowboy Joe was excused from the witness stand, the State spent the next couple of days calling a number of the police officers who analyzed and preserved the scene. Mr. Stills had them each identify the gun and pictures of the crime scene and entered it all into evidence. At the conclusion of the testimony of the last officer, the State called Crystal to the witness stand.

"Ms. Grimes, did you know the defendant or any of the victims?" Mr. Stills asked.

"Yes, Cady and Toni and the defendant," Crystal replied.

"How do you know them?"

"Cady is my younger sister. Toni is the daughter of May Bell, our former housekeeper. I know the defendant because I met him once when I ran into him and my sister on a date. I did not know the other victim though," Crystal said.

"So you can confirm that the defendant knew the victim Cady Grimes, your sister?"

"Yes."

"Now you said that the defendant and your sister were on a date. Do you know if their relationship was serious?"

"I don't know. I know that she seemed to like him but she never said anything to me specifically."

"No further questions for this witness, Your Honor."

"Cross examination, Defense?" the Judge asked.

"We have no questions of this witness at this time, Your Honor," Joe Jr. said.

"The State rests, Your Honor," Mr. Stills said.

"Ladies and gentlemen of the jury at this point the State has rested its case. We've gone a little beyond the dinner hour. We're going to adjourn at this time until tomorrow morning when the defense will put on its case. Remember your jury instructions; you are not to discuss this case with anyone. That includes your family members, coworkers, neighbors, anyone. You are not to read anything about the case. This case has gotten a fair share of press so don't watch any news stories about the case or read about it in the newspaper. If you do, I will be forced to sequester the jury panel and you will be away from your families for the remainder of the trail. Is that clear to everybody? To the jurors I mean," the Judge said.

Some of the people on the jury panel nodded their heads, and several answered.

Court was officially in recess. The attorneys and the people in the gallery were directed to stand while the jury panel left the courtroom for the day. Once the jury left the courtroom, Jackson glanced at Joe Jr. who spoke in the ear of the deputy waiting to escort Jackson back to the holding cell. Joe Jr. gave Jackson an approving nod.

Jackson then turned around to face Lakesha and his mother. His mother held her arms out but Jackson reached out instead to embrace Lakesha and they kissed for what seemed like an eternity to Nedra. Nedra now staring at Lakesha was not happy about her discovery of Jackson's relationship with what she considered to be a hoochie girl. Although they sat either directly next to each other or with one or two persons in between them from day one of the entire trial, without knowing who the other was to Jackson, Nedra now grimaced when she really noticed Lakesha for the first time. She looked Lakesha up and down and noticed that she was wearing a pair of jeans and a very tight T-Shirt with a plunging neck line. Her face showed a look of disgust as she read the word, 'Jackson' that was tattooed in cursive on the side of Lakesha's neck. Then she heard Jackson say to Lakesha as he cupped her face, looking directly into her eyes,

"I'm getting out of here, baby and when I do I want to marry you. You hear me? I want you to be my wife."

Lakesha smiled and to Jackson the whole room lit up.

Nedra's eyes widened as she watched the deputy pull Jackson away then he yelled back to his mother, "Give her my ring, Momma. Give her my ring."

Jackson was referring to a ring that had been given to him by his paternal grandmother. She said that it was for his future bride. The ring was being kept safely in a bank deposit box. Nedra had no intention of given Lakesha the thirty thousand dollar ring.

When she turned to leave, Joe Jr. put his hand on her shoulder, while standing next to Lakesha and said, "Let's talk out in the hall, there's something else you need to know."

When June and Brice got to the hallway she

immediately tried calling Bettina on her cell phone, but all she got was her voicemail. As she and Brice headed for the parking lot she saw Joe Jr. in the hall speaking with two ladies who she remembered seated in the gallery behind Jackson. Then suddenly Pastor June recognized the older woman and approached them saying,

"Neddie Gibson? Neddie is that you?"

"Hi, June. How have you been?" Nedra answered seemingly irritated.

"Wow, I didn't recognize you until just this minute," June said.

"You two know each other?" Joe Jr. asked.

"Yes, we grew up together in Belle Glade. We sang in the church choir together all through our childhood. It's so good to see you. Is this your daughter?" June asked.

"Hardly," Nedra said coldly.

"Excuse me, Pastor June this is Lakesha Dames. She's Jackson's girlfriend," Joe Jr. said.

"Oh, I'm so pleased to meet you. This is my husband, the Reverend Brice Howard," Pastor June said to everyone.

"My husband is not here but I haven't been Neddie Gibson for a long time, now I'm Nedra Bonnen, June."

"So you're Jackson's mother?" June asked.

"Yes I am. Forgive me, June, I'm a little thrown at the moment," Nedra said as she wiped under her eyes with a tissue.

"Pastor June is my pastor. It might help for the two of you to speak with her about the situation," Joe Jr. said to Nedra.

Nedra looked at June and then back to Joe Jr. and said, "Well, I guess it can't hurt. Is there somewhere more private where we could talk?"

Joe Jr. escorted Pastor June, Nedra, Lakesha and Elder Howard to a small conference room utilized by attorneys.

Pastor June began the conversation. "So Neddie is this your first time meeting Lakesha?"

"She saw me all week long. She just didn't know I was Jackson's girlfriend," Lakesha said.

"Now I'm told that she's not just his girlfriend but his baby momma," Nedra said sarcastically.

"I know we don't have a lot of time but typically I like to begin with prayer if you don't mind," June said.

After Pastor June prayed, Lakesha begin telling her and Nedra how she and Jackson met, how badly he behaved when their son was born and how much he changed for the better before he was arrested right up to his proposal today in court. Nedra was clearly moved finally hearing something positive about her son because she knew the path of destruction that Jackson had been on.

She looked a Pastor June and said, "I don't know what to say. I mean she's not exactly who I pictured my son marrying."

"Neddie, as parents we don't get to pick who our children love, but we are suppose to show them how to love. Then hopefully they'll learn to depend on God to lead them. I don't think I need to remind you that you came from very similar beginnings."

Nedra had forgotten that Pastor June was the one who found her after choir rehearsal one day in tears.

Nedra was pregnant while still in high school. Nedra left school shortly after that and appeared several weeks later as though nothing happened. Pastor June realized that she never found out what happened to Nedra's pregnancy.

"Well, June what do you expect me to do? Bring this girl and her baby home with me? I don't know her like that," Nedra said.

"I have a home. Don't nobody need to go to your house," Lakesha said defensively.

"No one is suggesting that, Nedra. But if you trust your son, you should at least get to know her and respect the fact that she is the mother of your grandson," June said.

Nedra and Lakesha parted ways agreeing to meet so that Jackie could finally meet his grandparents.

While Nedra walked alone to her car she contemplated the best possible way that she should relay all this new news to her husband. In that moment, she felt the loss of her own family, her parents, her sister, and brothers. She spent so much of her life trying to fit in with her elite friends that she consistently denied her family the pleasure of her company until finally they stopped inviting her to family functions altogether. Initially, she was happy about her family keeping their distance but now she wished she had them for support.

Driving home she reminisced. As far back as she could remember, apart from being poor, her childhood was quite good. She thought about the girl she used to be in high school, Neddie Gibson, the girl that Pastor June remembered before she became Nedra Bonnen. She thought about her pregnancy and how kind and comforting Pastor June had been when she discovered her crying in the back of the church. What Pastor June didn't know was that Nedra's mother had arranged for her to spend the next several weeks with her maternal aunt in Georgia where she had an abortion.

As the tears flowed down Nedra's cheek she decided that there was nothing that Jackson could ever do to cause her to turn her back on him, her only child. She still thought about the abortion all these years later. She decided that she could never confide this to Pastor June because she wanted to be remembered as the strong young lady she used to be and not the sad lonely lady she had become.

On the drive home Pastor June remembered Neddie in greater detail. She classified Neddie as a grass is greener type of girl. She was never satisfied with what she had. June decided that she would keep Nedra's family and their situation in prayer because she knew that Nedra's sudden discovery that she was the grandmother of an out-of-wedlock baby would be especially hard for her to accept with grace.

# 24

*"Woe to him who **covets** evil gain for his house, That he may set his nest on high, That he may be delivered from the power of disaster!"* ~ Habakkuk 2:9

The next morning, June arrived to the courthouse later than she expected. The parking lot was filled and there was a heightened alert in security so it took even longer than usual to make it through. When she finally made it to the courtroom and got seated she was relieved to learn that once the jury panel was seated the Judge needed to take a break so the proceedings had yet to begin. While she sat waiting for the Judge to return she could only think about how sleepy she was. Joe Jr. called her the night before asking if he could come over. He showed up on June's doorstep with his first witness for the defenses case, Eartha Jones.

"Eartha -- I mean Mac? What's going on Joe Jr.?" Pastor June asked when she answered the door.

Joe Jr. threw his hands up and said, "She says she has more information for my case but she will only speak with you about it."

Pastor June invited them inside. She left Rosie playing with Mac's dreadlocks in the family room while she packed Rosie's lunch in the kitchen for the next day so that she and Joe Jr. could speak privately.

"Joe Jr., I don't know how ethical it would be for me to speak to Mac for the defense, especially after being a witness for the prosecution. I mean this whole case smells strange to me I will admit but…"

"Look, Pastor you don't work for the Sherriff's Office, you consult for them. That means you are a free agent. Why can't you consult for my firm too?" Joe Jr. said.

"I never thought about that. Okay. I think that might work. Let me get Rosie settled and then we'll begin," June said.

During Joe Jr. and Mac's visit, Brice returned home after one of his quarterly conferences and June relayed to him what was going on.

"Can we barter the fees? In other words could you pay June whatever you would normally charge to represent us?" Brice said.

"Represent us? For what?" June asked.

"Kwame has filed for custody of Rosie, June," Brice said as he handed her the certified letter he received that morning.

"Of course, that is very doable," Joe Jr. said as June handed him the notice.

After Joe Jr. and Mac left, June and Brice spent most of the night discussing Rosie. They had each turned in for bed and from their respective sides of the king sized bed Brice insisted they purchase June said, "Brice, I don't think we should go to court and fight Kwame for custody."

"What? You can't be serious. You don't want to fight for our Rosie? Brice said.

"I love Rosie too, Brice. But you keep forgetting that I was adopted too," June said.

"What does that have to do with anything?" Brice asked.

"Why are you assuming that Kwame will be bad for Rosie or that because we can legally separate them that we have that right, spiritually?" June asked.

"I'm not following you but I don't like where you're going either," Brice said.

"Look, Momma May loved me more than anybody ever did in this world. She changed her entire life just so that she could raise me but I have always, even still to this day wondered about my birth parents. Even with Momma May being the best mother anybody could ever want, I still always felt disconnected or like something was missing. I spent a lot of time thinking about this in my life time and the truth is there is a spiritual connection in my life that was severed."

"And you turned out great because of it," Brice said.

"No, I turned out great despite it, there's a difference. I want what's best for Rosie. I want her to be whole, both physically and spiritually. Kwame may be taking this action because he feels like it's the only way he can stay connected with Rosie. What if he is willing to share her with us? I mean why does it have to be us or him? Why can't it be all of us?" June asked.

"You can't be serious? Remember I wasn't raised by my parents either. My grandmother raised me and I have never felt the way that you do," Brice said.

"Your maternal grandmother raised you, she gave birth to your mother. I had no physical or spiritual connection with Momma May. As I sit here today I'm telling you for my whole life I felt a disconnection, a certain kind of brokenness," June said.

"But even if your mother wanted to be in your life, which from what you told me she didn't, she died. How could anything have been different for you?" Brice said.

"Look, Brice, I'm not saying that I wasn't a bonafide orphan and I will have to live with the disconnection I've always felt for the rest of my life, but I do love Rosie just as Momma May loved me. I love her enough to not want her to have to live with that disconnection if she doesn't have to."

June was awakened from reminiscing about the previous night's discussions when the bailiff shouted, "All rise, court is now in session. The Honorable Judge Marvin Hardy presiding."

"Please be seated. Ladies and gentlemen of the jury, the State rested their case yesterday. This morning we're going to hear the defense's case. Mr. Addelbury, are you ready to proceed?" the Judge asked.

"Yes, Your Honor, the defense calls Eartha Jones to the stand."

June noticed as Mac walked down the aisle of the courtroom that it appeared as though she was gliding. She was tall, elegant and beautiful, even with all the tattoos and piercings on her face and arms and the multi colored shells in her hair, she was beautiful. After she was sworn in Joe Jr. began questioning her.

"Ms. Jones, do you know the defendant?"

"No, never seen him before in my life."

"The defendant owns a boat called the Richie Rich, are you familiar with that moniker?"

"Yes. I was hired by somebody who called themselves Richie Rich to do some background work."

"What kind of background work?"

"Financial."

"On who?"

"On the Grimes family."

"And what do you do for a living Ms. Jones?"

"Ms. Jones is my mother, please call me Mac."

"Sorry, Mac, what do you do for a living?"

"I gather information for people that they otherwise can't gather themselves or information they don't want anyone to know that they're looking for."

"Is what you do illegal?"

"Some of it is, yeah."

"And are you now on probation for this information gathering?"

"Yes, I am. Sometimes I didn't get permission."

"And so officially, you're on probation for hacking computers, is that right?"

"Yes."

"Okay, now Ms. Mac…"

"Just Mac, no Miss please."

"Okay, Mac, what can you tell us about the case that we're here about today?"

"Several months ago I received an email from an unknown person. This is usually how I'm contacted. This person asked that I trace the finances of the Grimes family."

"And you didn't know who sent you the email?"

Joe Jr. asked.

"Not at first, no."

"And at some point, did you find out who sent the email?"

"Yes. I traced the email back to an account. The email address for the account was Richie, no space, Rich, at mood dot com."

"Are you familiar with 'at mood dot com?"

"Yes it's a well known email company where you can get free email accounts."

"What happened after you received the email?"

"I replied and asked them to call a number to make arrangements for payment."

"And did you receive a call?"

"Yes, immediately. I gave the person an account number and told them that when the funds were confirmed I would do the work and email them back the results."

"And were the funds deposited?"

"Yes. And I emailed the party the information."

"Now Ms. -- I mean, Mac, was that the last communication with the person making the request that you received?"

"No it wasn't. A few days later there was another phone call."

"What was the nature of that call?"

"The person asked if I would be interested in a longer business arrangement."

"What kind of arrangement?"

"This person wanted me to hack into a bank and add fictitious funds to a specific account."

"Did this person want you to do anything else?"

"Yes. They also asked me to hack into that same bank account and pay off some debts."

"What kind of debts?"

"I was supposed to renew a property lease and pay off a boat loan and pay for the lease on a boat slip."

"Mac, if the funds you deposited were fictitious, isn't it just a matter of time before the bank would know about it?" Joe Jr. asked.

"It depends. If you convince the bank's system that the money was always there, it can take them a while especially if no one complains but yeah, eventually they would freeze the suspicious funds and investigate," Mac said.

"And was that all there was to this arrangement"

"No, this person also asked if I knew someone who could have somebody removed."

"Removed?"

"Killed."

"Objection, Your Honor. Are we just supposed to take her word for it that the defendant was set up?"

"You'll have your turn to question the witness, Mr. Stills. Overruled. Continue counselor."

"Now when you spoke to this person on the phone, did you recognize the voice?"

"No they used a voice changer each time."

"A voice changer? What is that?"

"It could be an app or a machine; it creates an audible overlay that causes the sound of your voice to sound differently than it normally would."

"Your Honor, I'd like permission to play two sets of recordings. The one that Detective Grimes discovered on his answering machine and the recording that Mac made of her own telephone conversations."

"Any objection from the State?" the Judge asked.

"No objection, Your Honor," Mr. Stills said.

Joe Jr. played the voice mail recording over the microphone for the courtroom to hear. Then he played the recording that Mac provided of her telephone conversation. Once the playbacks were complete, Joe Jr. asked,

"Mac, do you recognize this voice?"

"Yes and no. The voices may sound the same but the vernacular is different between the two recordings, so I don't believe that they are the same person."

"And for the record, Mac, can you tell this court and the jury how you are familiar with different vernaculars?"

"Yes, I was trained as a linguistic specialist in the Army."

"And as a linguistic specialist what were you trained to do?"

"We're trained to recognize syntax, vernacular, and most importantly sociolinguistics."

"Sociolinguistics? Can you explain to the court and the jury what that is?"

"Yes, it's learning the background of the speaker by the way that he or she speaks."

June could notice how impressed the jury seemed to be as did Joe Jr. The Judge still in disbelief interrupted.

"Ms. Mac, you said you were a trained linguistics specialist in the army?"

"Yes. For seven years."

"Impressive. Go ahead counselor. Sorry for the interruption," the Judge said.

"So now, Mac, what did you discover about the two voices, the one on Detective Grimes answering machine and the one in which you produced?"

"It was the same app but both communications were done by different people."

"And you could tell that by the words and phrases that each person used when they spoke?"

"Yes. When I heard the answering machine in your office last week it prompted me to want to lift out the voice changer on the recording that I had."

"So you recorded your conversations with the person who contacted you?"

"I always record my conversations, yes."

"And what did you discover?"

"The voice on Detective Grimes recording was deeper or of a lower decibel then the person I spoke with. In other words, the person calling Detective Grimes was obviously a male whereas when I stripped away the digital overlay of the voice changer app on my recording, I discovered that I had been in communication with a female."

Everyone in the courtroom was shocked to learn that a woman was a part of the kidnapping. Mr. Stills who had been quiet during most of Mac's testimony suddenly became very animated. "Objection, Your Honor, I object to this -- this speculation," Mr. Stills said.

"I bet you do," the Judge said.

"Your Honor, where is the proof that this is true? How do we even know that Ms. Mac or whatever is a linguistics specialist at all?" Mr. Stills asked.

"Well, counsel, I don't know what your copy of the defense witness list says but mine says she is a linguistics expert and you never contested it."

"Your Honor, in anticipation of the State's objection, the defense is prepared to provide documentation of Mac's army records," Joe Jr. said.

"Go ahead and enter the documents as evidence for the record but the objection's overruled. You may continue Mr. Addelbury," the Judge said.

Joe Jr. could see Mr. Stills and his co-counsel looking over the witness list. Joe Jr. smiled as he realized that the prosecution was so overconfident about this case that they didn't even bother to examine the witness list thoroughly, just as he had hoped they wouldn't.

"Mac, once you heard this person's voice, the woman's voice, was it a voice that you recognized?"

"No."

"And, although you never stripped the digital overlay on the voice mail recording made to Detective Grimes, did you recognize that voice?"

"I did. I recognized the sociolinguistics used by the person making the recording, yes."

"And who was it?"

"It was Two Touch or Demetrius Daniels."

"And how do you know Demetrius Daniels?"

"When the person I communicated with requested that someone be removed, I referred them -- I mean her to Two Touch or Demetrius Daniels."

"Why would you refer someone to Demetrius for such a request?"

"Two Touch and I go way back. He refers clients to me, I refer clients to him."

"So you knew Two Touch or Demetrius Daniels to be a hit man?"

"I knew Two Touch to be who you went to if you had a problem that the law could not resolve."

"I don't understand what you mean by that, Mac," Joe Jr. said.

"He didn't just go around killing people because someone paid him to. He was like a vigilante. He would get paid but he also would only take certain types of requests."

"Can you give us an example?"

"I could but at this point and time I will be asserting my Fifth Amendment right and so I decline to answer any further questions on the grounds that I might incriminate myself."

"Objection, Your Honor, this is very convenient! She can't take the fifth on parts of her testimony, Your Honor," Mr. Stills said.

"Well we're talking about different crimes, counsel. I believe that she can do that," the Judge said.

"I still object, Your Honor, and I move that her entire testimony be stricken from the record and that the jury be instructed to discount it in their deliberations."

"Let's take a brief recess while I consider the State's motion."

"Court is in recess," the Bailiff shouted.

June still stunned that Two Touch was actually a hit man. That was the information that Eartha would only share with her the night before. June convinced her that she had to testify about it this morning.

Joe Jr. was astonished that someone like Two Touch could be such a notorious hit man and for such a long time. He had the perfect cover of being disabled and though he'd never met him, everyone who described him to Joe Jr. described him as a meek introverted person.

Joe Jr. conferred with Sandy during the court's recess. "Wow, Joe, I can't believe this. The State is scared! We're winning this thing," Sandy said.

"I know but let's not celebrate just yet. I still don't know who the woman on the phone was and unless we find out, he may still be found guilty. I mean justice is still different for black men in this country. So unless we find somebody else they can blame they will blame the one they've got," Joe Jr. said.

"You know they're going to expect you to prove that Two Touch committed other murders. How are you going to prove that?"

"I'm going to recall my dad," Joe Jr. said.

"So you knew about this all along?" Sandy asked.

"No, I didn't. Pastor June mentioned it last night when Eartha or Mac confessed that she knew about it. Apparently my Dad told Detective Grimes about other similar murders to Toni's husbands, with the same M.O," Joe Jr. said.

"Court is back in session," the Bailiff shouted.

Once the Judge was seated he said, "Please be seated everyone. The initial line of questioning was about this specific crime and the witness testified as to her role in that crime and offered her expert testimony on the evidence. Once the questioning became about possible prior crimes she invoked her Fifth Amendment right. The objection is overruled and her testimony stays on the record and is allowed for consideration during the jury's deliberations. You may continue counselor."

"Your Honor, I have no more questions for this witness at this time but reserve the right to recall her later to utilize her linguistic expertise once some of my other witnesses have testified."

"Ms. Mac, the defense has asked that you remain available to be recalled. That means you need to wait outside until the conclusion of all the testimony. Do you understand?"

"Yes," Mac said and she left the courtroom.

# 25

*"O you who dwell by many waters, Abundant in treasures, Your end has come, The measure of your **covet**ousness."* ~Jeremiah 51:13

"Your next witness, Mr. Addelbury?" the Judge asked.

"Yes, Your Honor, we call the defendant, Mr. Jackson Bonnen III to the stand."

Joe Jr. spent a great deal of time trying to convince Jackson not to testify in his trial but, like so many defendants, Jackson thought if the jury heard from him, they would not believe that he could have committed such heinous crimes.

After Jackson was sworn in Joe Jr. asked, "Mr. Bonnen, how did you come to be aboard your vessel, the 'Richie Rich' on the day in question?"

"I got an email from the marina manager saying that they needed to change my boat slip."

"Why would that cause you to go to the boat?" Joe Jr. asked.

"Because I couldn't keep up with the payments. So the boat got repossessed several months before when my father cut me off. When I got the email, I called the marina to explain that there had been a mistake and I was told that not only had the debt been settled but that the boat was now mine free and clear."

"Was that all that you were told?" Joe Jr. asked.

"No. I was also told that my slip lease at the marina was paid for the rest of the year," Jackson said.

"And was this surprising to you, Mr. Bonnen?" Joe Jr. asked.

"Yes, because I had no money. I didn't pay off the boat or the marina. So I went to see what was going on," Jackson said.

"Did you have any idea how that could have happened?" Joe Jr. asked.

"The only way that could happen would be if my parents paid it but they didn't even know that I had the boat," Jackson said.

"Now, can you tell us what happened when you went aboard the boat?"

"I got on the boat and started looking around. When I reached for the door to the bedroom or whatever you call the living quarters, I heard people talking. When I put my ear to the door, I could hear Two Touch and Cady shouting. Then when I heard a gunshot, I opened the door and found Two Touch pointing a gun at Cady."

"And what did he say?"

"He didn't say anything. He turned the gun on me."

"And what did you do then?" Joe Jr. asked.

"I said, Two Touch what the hell are you doing?" Jackson said.

"Two Touch?"

"Demetrius Daniels, yes."

"Two Touch is a nickname?"

"Yeah, because he had some kind of condition that made him always touch everything twice."

"And you're testifying here today that even though you knew Demetrius or Two Touch, you had nothing to do with this crime?"

"Yes, I had nothing to do with this. Two Touch and I hung out sometimes, that's all."

"How did he know about your boat? Had he ever been there before?"

"Not to my knowledge. Two Touch was not the kind of person I would hang out with in public. I mean he was a nice enough guy and all but he was strange," Jackson said.

"Then what was the nature of your relationship?" Joe Jr. asked.

"We went to high school together. After we got out of school I would meet up with him from time to time to buy marijuana from him. Sometimes we got high together and that was it," Jackson said.

"Okay, Mr. Bonnen, let's go back to the day in question, when you saw Demetrius pointing the gun at you, what did you do next?"

"I grabbed the gun. We struggled and it went off several more times. The last time it got him and he fell down to the floor, dead."

"And then what happened?"

"I noticed that the two girls had been shot. I started to go and see about them but I heard Pastor June and Cady's dad yelling for me to come out of the room," Jackson said.

"So you didn't shoot Cady or Toni?"

"No I did not. I tried to take the gun away from Two Touch, that's all I did."

"And you maintain that you did not kidnap Cady Grimes or Toni Jacobs?"

"No I did not kidnap or kill anybody."

"Who do you believe kidnapped them?"

"I think Two Touch did this all the way."

"Why would you think that?"

"Well for several reasons. First of all, he was standing on my boat with a gun, and then shot somebody with that gun and also because he was broke and needed money. He was still living with his momma for God sake," Jackson said sarcastically.

"So are you saying that Two Touch was framing you for this crime?" Joe Jr. asked.

"Yes I am. He was always jealous of me, ever since high school," Jackson said.

"You heard the witness Mac testify that Two Touch was a hit man, did you know about that?

"I heard what she said but I never heard about that and the times I visited his momma's house I didn't see any evidence of that but then he was standing on my boat with those two girls shooting a gun, so I guess he fooled everybody."

"Your Honor, I have no more questions for the defendant," Joe Jr. said.

"For the State?" the Judge said.

"Mr. Bonnen, you expect for this jury to believe that you didn't know anything about those girls being on your boat?" Mr. Stills asked.

"I expect the jury to believe the truth and that's the truth," Jackson said looking directly at the jury.

"Let me see if I understand, the Richie Rich is your boat?" Mr. Stills asked.

"Yes."

"But you thought it had been repossessed by the bank?"

"Yes."

"And how did the marina know that you now all of a sudden owned the boat outright?"

"Because they have to see proof of ownership in order to rent the slip to me."

"Then how did that happen? I mean how did the marina learn that you paid the bank for the boat?"

"Objection," Joe Jr. said before Jackson could respond.

"The defendant has already stated that he did not pay off the bank loan off," Joe Jr. said.

"Let's play this straight counsel; it's confusing enough as it is," the Judge said.

"Yes, Your Honor," Mr. Stills said then continued, "Now, Mr. Bonner, if you didn't pay off the boat who did?"

"I don't know. I know what that lady just said on the stand but when I last checked my bank accounts it had a negative balance," Jackson said.

"It's funny you should say that because when we checked your account it showed that you have a two point five million dollar balance. And your bank account also reflects a payment to the bank for the boat as well as for the lease on your condo and the boat slip. How do you explain that, Mr. Bonnen?"

"I have no idea. That lady hacker said she messed with my bank account. Because believe me when I tell you that if I had known that I could have been staying in my condo, I certainly would have been there. I been staying with my fiancé in the projects, man, get real," Jackson said.

The people in the jury and the gallery began to laugh. The State continued asking Jackson questions about his finances and his relationship with his father. Joe Jr. noticed they were changing their strategy and now they were trying to prove that Jackson's father could have easily given him the funds to pay all of his outstanding debts.

"Call him in here if you don't believe me. My father cut me off months ago. My mother's sitting right over there you can ask her too," Jackson said.

"We'll get back to that later, Mr. Bonnen. Now let's talk about where you said you were. Lakesha Dames is your baby momma?" Mr. Stills asked.

"No, she is my fiancé and yes, the mother of my son," Jackson said.

"You said you were living with her all this time?" Mr. Stills asked.

"Yes."

"And now isn't it true Mr. Bonnen that Lakesha Dames lives in the housing projects?"

"Yeah, so?" Jackson said.

"Well doesn't it seem convenient that you were also dating Cady Grimes, whose father also has considerable wealth?"

"Yeah, I was dating her too but Cady didn't seem to know anything about her family's money."

"But you did, did you not, Sir?"

"Yes I knew."

"How did you learn about her father's wealth?"

"From Two Touch."

"Not because you or your girlfriend contacted Ms. Eartha Jones to do a financial trace on Cady's family?"

"No. All I needed was her grandparent's names and I did an internet search on them. I could see from all the high society stuff they were involved in that they were loaded."

"So you did do some research to find out if Cady's family had money?"

"I just said that, didn't I man?"

"Mr. Bonnen, now you've admitted that you have a fiancé, and that you were living with that fiancé in the housing projects. You also admitted that you were dating Cady Grimes at the same time. And you also said that Two Touch told you about Cady's family's wealth and you researched her family to double check. Yet you maintain that you, Lakesha Dames, and Two Touch, did not plan this crime together?"

"Objection, Your Honor, asked and answered."

"Sustained," the Judge said.

"Okay, Mr. Bonnen, if you were dating Cady Grimes and you were the one who was suddenly left in financial dire straits, how do you suppose that Two Touch or Demetrius could have pulled this whole thing off without your knowledge? You said yourself that he was broke didn't you?" Mr. Stills asked.

"I have no idea," Jackson said.

"Oh, so I guess we're just supposed to take your word for it, you know since you're such an honorable man and all."

"Objection, Your Honor!" Joe Jr. shouted.

"Sustained. Counselors approach now!" the Judge said.

Mr. Stills and Joe Jr. came to the Judge's bench and the Judge switched on the white noise so that their conversation could not be heard by the jury or the other people in the courtroom.

"Mr. Stills, you know very well I do not allow personal attacks in my courtroom. This is your only warning, Sir. You will find yourself in contempt of court if you say anything along the lines of a personal attack or a snippy remark that demeans this man or anybody else's character, is that understood?" the Judge said sharply.

"Yes, Your Honor, I'm sorry, Your Honor, it won't happen again," Mr. Stills said.

"See that it doesn't," the Judge said.

The attorneys each returned to their tables.

Mr. Stills said, "So, Mr. Bonnen, somebody, who you say was not you, paid for your condo, your boat and the marina, from a bank account with your name on it but that someone was not you?"

"That's what I'm saying."

"What motive would anybody else have for doing all of that?"

"I don't know! All I know is that it wasn't me!"

"Okay, Mr. Bonnen, let's say we take Ms. Jones word for it, that she paid your debts. She also said that the person who contacted her to do that was a woman. Could that woman have been Lakesha Dames?"

"No she would never do anything like that."

"So some mystery woman arranged to pay off all your debts, and then arrange to have your girlfriend, or the girl you were dating kidnapped?"

"Objection, Your Honor. Is there going to be a legitimate question?" Joe Jr. said.

"Strike that Your Honor, I withdraw the question. I'm finished with this witness, Judge."

"Any redirect, Mr. Addelbury?"

"Yes, Your Honor." Joe Jr. replied.

"Mr. Bonnen, tell the jury your purpose for dating Cady Grimes?"

Jackson looked down at the podium in front of him and said, "I'm not proud of it but when Two Touch told me about her, about how much money he thought her parents had, and after I confirmed that they did through the internet, I wanted to date her to see if I could -- at the most I thought we could maybe get married or something and I would use her for her money. At the least, I thought she could help me get my trust fund released."

"So you didn't care about her?" Joe Jr. asked.

"I didn't at first, but I didn't go through with it because I started to care about her. She is a good person, a really good person. We spent a lot of time together and she was always preaching to me about becoming a better person. On the morning I got arrested, I met her for breakfast. Even though I was living with Lakesha, I still tried to play Cady because I didn't have any money. When I went to the bathroom at the restaurant, I left my phone on the table. I guess Lakesha called me because her picture flashed on my phone and Cady saw it. When I got back to the table Cady asked me about her."

Jackson began remembering that morning at breakfast with Cady.

*"Who is Lakesha?" Cady asked.*

*"Well I guess I should tell you. I have a son. And she's the mother," Jackson said.*

*"Oh, do you have pictures of your son?" Cady asked.*

*"I guess so, yeah. Here's one."*

*"Wow, he looks every bit like you, Jackson. What's his name?" Cady asked.*

*"We call him Jackie." Jackson replied.*

*"Are you not together with the mother?"*

*Jackson shrugged his shoulders and said, "Off and on. She's not really my type if you know what I mean."*

*"Look, Jackson, love is precious. When you find it you should hold on to it. I can see your eyes soften as you speak about her. You love her don't you?" Cady asked.*

*"Yes, but my parents, you know, they would never accept her."*

While he was saying that to Cady he thought about his mother, Nedra. He realized in that instant that her family was full of Lakesha's. His mother came from humble beginnings and she made it all right. He relayed that to Cady and he remembered her saying,

*"I don't know many women who would love you under the conditions that you've put her under. You should be proud of your love for her and not hide it, go with your instincts, Jackson,"*

"Mr. Bonnen? Mr. Bonnen?" Joe Jr. said snapping Jackson back to the present.

"Oh, sorry. Cady was the whole reason I started trying to be a better person, a better father to my son, a better man for my lady, Lakesha. She helped me see the need to change my life. I wasn't the best father in the world but she spoke to me about repeating the mistakes I felt that my father made with me. She's the reason I decided to be with Lakesha, to really be with her because she was the one I truly loved."

"And how was she able to do that do you think?"

"She introduced me to God, plain and simple. She

helped me to understand God in a way that nobody else was ever able to do."

"And do you know how Two Touch knew Cady?"

"Yeah, he said he went to school with her and her sisters. I flunked out of that school by then and my parents sent me to a private school so I didn't know them, Cady, or her sisters I mean," Jackson said.

"Your Honor, I have no further questions for the defendant at this time," Joe Jr. said.

"Okay, Mr. Bonnen, you're excused from the witness stand. Mr. Addelbury, let's break for lunch and then we'll come back and you can call your next witness?"

When court recessed for lunch, June tried calling Bettina again. She could see Bettina walking down the hall but she apparently had her cell phone off. June followed her into the bathroom.

"How long are you going to keep ignoring me?" June asked once inside.

"I don't know what to say to you, June. I can't believe you never told me that you slept with my husband," Bettina said angrily.

"Look, Bettina that happened before I got saved, when I was still a cop. And it wasn't some trivial affair or a fling, we were engaged. He left me at the altar and for many years after that I was angry with Mario. But I didn't know he kept it from you, I told Brice about me and Mario right away; I assumed Mario told you too."

"Well he didn't. He didn't tell me a lot of things apparently and I am very upset with him, but you were my friend, I expected this information to come from you," Bettina said.

"Bettina, you've got to know that what Mario and

I had was years ago, it was long over by the time he moved here. We never even saw each other again until that case last year."

Bettina looked at June directly in the eyes and while tears formed in hers she said, "It might be over for you but it's not over for Mario. I overheard him telling your husband at the hospital essentially that if he thought you would take him back; he would leave me for you."

June couldn't believe that Mario would say such a thing, and to her own husband no less. She reached out for Bettina but Bettina pulled away.

"I'm going to need some time, June, please," and she left the bathroom.

June returned to her seat in the courtroom. She recognized that the situation with her, Bettina and Mario was one of those occasions where there was nothing that she could do. It would have to play itself out. Truths that had once been hidden now needed to be explained, and they weren't her secrets to tell. She turned to look at Brice seated next to her and she looked up into Brice's big hazel green eyes as they held one another's hands and then she leaned her head on his shoulder. She only sat up when the bailiff called court back into order. Then she remembered something and stood up to get Joe's attention.

"Your Honor, can the defense have a couple more minutes please?" asked Joe Jr.

"A couple is two minutes, counselor, that's all," the Judge said.

June made her way to the defense's table and whispered in Joe Jr.'s ear, "Who are you calling now?"

"I'm calling the condo manager, why?"

"You need to get Crystal back here."

"Why? What are you thinking?"

"Crystal testified that she didn't know Two Touch but they went to school together. Why would she lie about that?"

"I don't know but I don't want to find out on the stand, I'd rather know ahead of time, Pastor June," Joe Jr. said.

"Well then you need to get Eartha back on the stand and see if she knows Crystal at all," June said.

"Your Honor, the defense recalls Eartha Jones a.k.a Mac, to the stand."

After several seconds, the bailiff called Eartha's name in the hallway. People began looking around the courtroom for the witness but no one came forward. The bailiff entered the courtroom and threw his hands up at the judge gesturing "I don't know".

"Counsel, we're almost to the end of the day. We're going to break early. I suggest that you use this extra time to locate your witness. If she doesn't appear in this courtroom in the morning, I'm going to issue a warrant for her arrest. I gave her instructions not to leave this courthouse for the remainder of the testimonies," the Judge said to Joe Jr.

"Yes, Your Honor," Joe Jr. said as he began dialing on his cell phone.

At the same time June's phone began vibrating, the caller I.D. said, "Eartha."

"Eartha, where are you?" June asked.

# 26

*"'…nor thieves, nor **covet**ous, nor drunkards, nor revilers, nor extortioners will inherit the kingdom of God."* ~1 Corinthians 6:10

Within an hour Pastor June and Joe Jr. met Mac at a nearby playground. She was swinging on the swing set when Pastor June and Joe Jr. approached her.

"Why did you leave? The court is going to issue a warrant for your arrest if you're not in court tomorrow morning," Joe Jr. told her.

"Yeah well, I won't be there," Mac said.

"What spooked you so, Mac?" June asked.

"I saw that chick, the one who contacted me. She was in the hallway in the courthouse," Mac said.

"Who?" Pastor June asked looking at Joe Jr.

"The lady that ordered the hit on the Grimes girl was in the hallway with the cop at the courthouse, the Grimes girl father and as it turns out he's her father too."

"But I don't understand. Why do you think she is the same woman who contacted you?" Joe Jr. asked.

"Because it wasn't the first time she contacted me.

She contacted me months ago to arrange a different hit with Two Touch. But this time when she contacted me she disguised her voice with the voice changer app, the first time she didn't, so I didn't put it together right away. She doesn't know what I look like but see I don't just trace the emails, I trace the calls. I tracked her last call to me. It's in my best interest to know who my clients are. I never knew her name, still don't know it but that's one cold chick and she doesn't need to know who I am," Mac said.

"I still don't get how you know that these women are one in the same," Joe Jr. said.

"See, when she contacted me for the first hit, I made it my business to know who she was so I tracked her by her phone and went to where she was. I saw and heard her. She was talking on the phone with somebody at a bar downtown. And when I saw her in the hallway today, she called that cop, Dad. I never knew she was a cop's daughter. I never tried to get a background check on her or anything because she wasn't my client I just got a referral fee. But now she can tie me to Two Touch's stuff so I thought you should know about her before I took off.

As Mac handed Pastor June a box she said, "Tell my momma that I will be in touch directly with her. If she don't want to talk to me, tell her just to listen," and then Mac walked hurriedly away.

"Wait, Eartha, wait," Pastor June called behind her.

But as Mac walked away from Pastor June and Joe Jr., she threw up one hand and waved goodbye. Pastor June looked at Joe Jr. and she could see Joe Jr. thinking. Pastor June began looking through the papers in the box and then she began pacing, it was what she did when she needed to think things through. She picked up her cell phone and made a call to Detective Wright.

"Do you have that information on the Raymond Dover guy I asked you about?"

Pastor June listened to Detective Wright for several minutes then she suddenly turned to Joe Jr. and said, "You need to recall Crystal to the stand. You also need to pay a visit to May Bell tonight to see if Toni had a high school year book we could borrow."

That next morning Joe Jr. told the court that he contacted Mac the night before and decided that she couldn't add to his case and that he wanted to excuse her. The court reluctantly agreed not to file the warrant and excuse her.

"Do you have another witness, Mr. Addelbury?" the Judge asked.

"Yes, Your Honor. We would like to recall Dr. Addelbury."

Cowboy Joe took the stand.

"You are still under oath, Doctor. Go ahead counsel," the Judge said.

"Dr. Addelbury, when you autopsied the first victim found in this case, Dale Jacobs, did you find anything unusual?"

"Yes. An injection point wound."

"And did you run a tox screen on the body of Dale Jacobs to see what he was injected with?"

"Yes. The tox screen showed a high dosage of the drug ketamine."

"And what does this drug do?" Joe Jr. asked.

"In high doses it acts as a sedative."

"So a person will become unconscious?"

"If the dose is high enough, yes."

"Is that what killed Dale Jacobs?"

"No, Dale Jacobs died from a knife wound to the throat, his carotid artery was cut open, and he bled out."

"Now, Dr. Addelbury, the particular way that Dale Jacobs was killed, did it appear unique to you?" Joe Jr. asked.

"No. It was familiar to me because of the injection point on the neck. I had a body in my morgue last year with the same injection point combined with a knife wound. It's still an open case but the blood sample is too degraded at this point to run a tox screen for ketamine. Then one of my assistants pointed me to a newer case that was only a couple of weeks old. A man named Raymond Dover was found dead in his home. He had the same injection point and his throat was also slit across his carotid artery. Identical to the wounds found on Mr. Jacobs," Cowboy Joe testified.

"Is there anything else unique about these deaths, Doctor?" Joe Jr. asked.

"As a matter of fact, yes. All three victims were either stabbed or cut with a homemade knife blade. The mold that the blade was created in had a small distinct notch in it. That notch appeared in the wounds of all three victims."

"That's all I have for this witness, Your Honor," Joe Jr. said.

"Recross, Mr. Stills?"

"No, Your Honor."

"Your next witness, Mr. Addelbury?"

"Yes, Your Honor, the defense recalls Crystal Grimes."

Crystal came into the courtroom with a bewildered expression. This time Pastor June sat directly behind Joe Jr. in the gallery and watched Crystal as she approached the witness stand.

The Judge said, "You're still under oath, Ms. Grimes. You may proceed, Mr. Addelbury."

"Ms. Grimes, in your previous testimony you stated that you did not know Demetrius Daniels. But we've since had testimony that you and he went to the same high school at the same time. Do you recall attending high school with Demetrius Daniels, Ma'am?"

"No I do not. I didn't know him," Crystal said.

"If I were to show you a year book from your senior year of high school, where you and he are pictured together in the science club, would that refresh your memory?" Joe Jr. said.

"I guess it might," Crystal said as she shifted in her seat.

Joe Jr. then said, "Judge, may I approach the witness?"

"Yes."

Joe Jr. showed her the year book picture but Crystal's attention went to the opposite page which showed the drama club featuring a picture of Raymond Dover. Her facial expression changed drastically. June noticed it too and she knew why. Joe Jr. had deliberately chosen that page. When Joe Jr. returned to the table, June whispered something in his ear.

"Ms. Grimes, does looking at the year book refresh your memory?" Joe Jr. asked.

"Yes. Okay, I knew who he was. That doesn't mean I knew him, knew him. I mean we never had a conversation or anything. He was too weird and he had a crush on my little sister I believe," Crystal said.

"And if I were to show you telephone logs showing that your cell phone number called his cell phone number numerous times that began the weeks that led up to your sister's disappearance, would that refresh your memory regarding conversations with him?" Joe Jr. asked.

Crystal's face became angry. Her entire demeanor changed.

After several seconds, Joe Jr. asked, "Do you need me to repeat the question, Ma'am?"

"You can show me whatever you want. I don't recall ever speaking to him on the telephone."

Everyone in the courtroom was eager to see where Joe Jr.'s line of questioning was leading to. Mr. Stills' instinct told him that he should be objecting but he also wanted to know.

Joe Jr. continued, "You don't recall? Okay. Ms. Grimes, let me draw your attention back to the yearbook. Now, looking to the page opposite of the one where you're pictured, do you recognize the gentleman pictured there with the two girls?"

Crystal looked directly at Pastor June with a scowl on her face.

"Yes I know him, and he was hardly a gentle man," Crystal said.

"How do you know him?" Joe Jr. asked.

"He was my boyfriend for most of my senior year in high school," Crystal said harshly.

"Were you aware that he was also found dead several weeks ago, with the same injuries as Mr. Jacobs, the first victim Toni Jacob's husband?"

Crystal was silent.

After several seconds the Judge said, "Ma'am, you must answer the question."

"Yes. I was aware."

"And how did you become aware of that, Ms. Grimes?"

"Because I'm the one who arranged for him to be killed."

The courtroom erupted and the judge asked for a ten minute recess to clear the courtroom. Mr. Stills called for the police to arrest Crystal as soon as she finished her testimony. She had just confessed to arranging a murder, he didn't have a choice. Order was restored after everyone left the courtroom except for the jury, the attorneys, and the victim's families. Then Joe Jr. was asked to continue questioning the witness.

"Crystal, how did you arrange to have Raymond Dover killed?"

Crystal sat back in the witness chair, exhaled then said, "One day I went to a rape support group meeting, it was a while ago. I had never gone to one before so I sat in the back, I didn't want to share my testimony. To be honest I wasn't sober. And, I guess I must have looked really mad because after the meeting a lady approached me. She did share during the meeting. She talked about how she was raped and that she finally found freedom. After the meeting she gave me an email address and told me that she got her freedom with revenge. I sent an email right away. A lady answered back with a phone number with instructions to call and when I did, I asked her if she knew how I could have somebody taken care of.

"That lady told me somebody would call me back

by the next day. The person who called back was Demetrius. I knew immediately who he was because I used to pick on him in high school about his stuttering but he didn't know who I was. Anyway I told him that I needed somebody taken care of. But before he would take the job, he needed to know why. So I told him."

"And what was the reason you told Demetrius you wanted Raymond Dover killed?" Joe Jr. asked.

Crystal replied softly and slowly while staring off into space. "Because he ruined my life. Raymond Dover raped me multiple times all through my senior year in high school and I witnessed him raping another girl. Demetrius charged me six thousand dollars to kill him. For years I couldn't sleep without being drunk or high or taking several sleeping pills and whenever I did sleep I would have horrible nightmares. It was every cent that I had saved up but it was worth it," Crystal said while she smiled a little smile.

"And was Raymond Dover the only person you asked him to take care of, as you put it?" Joe Jr. asked.

"No," Crystal said now looking directly at Pastor June.

"Who else did you hire Demetrius to kill?" Joe Jr. asked.

"Me," Crystal said.

The jury began to gasp as did Pastor June and the state attorney.

"Why did you want him to kill you?" Joe Jr. asked.

"Because I didn't have the guts to do it myself, I tried several times. That fool was supposed to kidnap me and my sister. I found out that my father had more money than he could ever spend. I didn't have any more money.

Demetrius was supposed to get the ransom money for himself and then kill me and let Cady go but he is an idiot. Despite his genius SAT scores, he is an idiot. He botched the whole thing. It was so simple but then he got me and Toni confused. He actually confused me with the housekeeper's daughter. Idiot!"

"Did he know that it was you he was supposed to kill? I mean that you were the same one who put the contract out on yourself?" Joe Jr. asked.

"Of course not, I'm not an idiot! No, I told him that I or rather that Cady's sister set Cady up with this Richie Rich kid to help steal my dad's money because I knew from experience that Demetrius would only take the contract if he deemed it a worthy cause. That idiot thought he was some kind of superhero or something."

"Okay, Ms. Grimes, let's move to a different issue, you said earlier that you knew the defendant. Did you set this whole thing up to make my client look guilty?" Joe Jr. asked.

"Yes, I did," Crystal said proudly.

"Why? What had Mr. Bonnen ever done to you?" Joe Jr. asked.

"Oh I knew him or I knew his type. I knew when Cady introduced me to him what he was really after. He was so transparent and smug. He looked me up and down when Cady introduced him to me. She's not the sharpest tool in the box either. She actually thought he liked her goody two shoes act and all her Jesus talk."

"Did you mean for your sister Cady to be hurt?"

"No. She is my sister. I love her and even though she got on my nerves she was a truly good person. No, I wanted to scare her because I didn't plan to be here for her anymore and she needed to get sharper about men. He had strict instructions not to hurt her. I didn't know that he was beefing with the defendant over my sister. I didn't even know that they knew each other. Then Demetrius called me and said that Cady recognized him and he told me that he had to kill everybody."

"He told you he was going to kill both the girls?"

"Yeah and there was nothing I could do, he wasn't exactly asking my permission. There wasn't anything I could do," she said softly.

"And Ms. Grimes, you said that you hired Demetrius to kill you. Why did you want to die?" Joe Jr. asked.

After several minutes and several tears falling from Crystals face she said, "Because I'm already dying, I have the same disease that killed my mother. I don't want to die like she did. I remember her suffering for a long time and being in a lot of pain. I tried several times to do it myself but I never could follow through."

"If you are dying as you said, why kill Raymond Dover?"

"Once I was diagnosed, I knew that I had to do something about Raymond because I refused to leave this earth before he did, that simply could not happen."

"And as you sit here today, Ms. Grimes, do you regret anything that you've done?"

"Pastor June told me that what Raymond did to me wasn't my fault. She said it wasn't God's fault. It was a lot of people's fault. I put my dad through this because he didn't protect me. I put Cady through this because nothing bad has ever happened to her."

Then she looked directly at Pastor June and said,

"I gave you so much crap because I was angry. You thought I was angry at God but I was angry at you. If you and my dad had gone through with your original plans, you would have been my mother and I wouldn't be dying. It doesn't really make much sense when I say it out loud but that's why I was so angry with you. But to answer your question Mr. Addlebury, do I regret what I did? I regret what happened to Toni, but she was an acceptable loss as far as I'm concerned. No I don't regret much else. I only regret that it didn't work out the way I planned."

That night Cady opened her eyes for the first time since the shooting. She awoke to a dark room but for the flashing lights from the many machines that were monitoring her vitals. She tried to speak but she could barely move, but she could think. She tried hard to remember how she could have ended up in the hospital. Then her memory came flooding back. She thought about Toni throwing the voice box and then when the man -- who she now knew was Demetrius, came back through the door without the disguise, she remembered him saying,

*"You shouldn't have done that."*

*"Demetrius, what's going on? Why are you doing this?"* Cady asked.

*"You shouldn't have done that! Now I can't let you go. All you had to do was wait a little while longer."*

*"Why are you doing this?" Cady asked.*

*"Because somebody wants her dead and they're using you to get money from your dad. You weren't supposed to get hurt, Cady, but now that you know who I am, I can't afford to let you go. Don't you see that?"*

*"Yes, you can, Demetrius, you can. I won't tell anybody, you can let both of us go."*

*"No, I can't, she screwed that up. I would never have even taken this job if you would have considered loving me even a little bit but no, you wanted Jackson. He's a pumped up buffoon! All he wanted to do was use you. I loved you for real, Cady, I always have."*

*"I love you too, Demetrius, maybe not the way you wanted me to but I do love you. I don't love Jackson; Jackson is in love with somebody else."*

She remembered him just standing there looking at her without responding.

*"Please, Demetrius, what about all those talks we had about God and His love, how could you do this?" Cady asked.*

*"God? Are you kidding me right now?" he laughed. "I was playing you about that. I know more about the bible than you or that preacher lady put together. I spent most of my life between the hospital and my momma's house and the only constant thing I had was the bible my grandma made me take with me."*

*"Then I don't understand. You should know that God wouldn't want this," Cady said.*

*"I guess you could say that my heart is hardened to God, because I simply don't know the God you keep talking about. I can't be about Him, I have to be about me because nobody else is, nobody else ever was. All anybody ever did was use me. My momma used me as a live-in nanny. Jackson used me for free weed and you, you used me too. You were the closest thing to a real friend that I had and all I was to you was a target for your novice evangelism, another number to add to your Christian statistic. You should have given me a chance, but now it's too late."*

Cady remembered Demetrius pointing the gun at Toni and she immediately begin praying loudly,

*"The Lord is my Shepherd, I shall not want. You make me to lie down in green pastures, You lead me besides the still waters, You restore my soul. You lead me in the paths of righteousness for*

*Your name sake. Yea thou I walk through the valley of the shadow of death, I will fear no evil, for You are with me, Your rod and Your staff they comfort me --"*

She stopped praying when she heard the gunshot. Toni fell backwards and then he turned the gun on her but suddenly Demetrius fell forward and Jackson appeared in the room. They fought over the gun and then she heard another gunshot and that was the last thing she could remember.

Then she heard her father running into the hospital room saying, "Cady, Cady, you're awake."

Bettina grabbed her hand and then her hospital room was suddenly filled with people busying themselves all around her. But she could not speak, she could barely move. So she closed her eyes and went back to sleep.

# 27

*"For the commandments, "You shall not commit adultery," "You shall not murder," "You shall not steal," "You shall not bear false witness," "You shall not **covet**," and if there is any other commandment, are all summed up in this saying, namely, "You shall love your neighbor as yourself."* ~Romans 13:9

Two weeks later Joe Jr., June, Brice, Rosie, Billie and Kwame were seated in Judge Carter's chambers at the courthouse. They were given a special rescheduling date to have the final adoption hearing because of Pastor June's previous hospitalization.

Judge Carter said, "Now Rosie, do you understand what's going on?"

Rosie who was seated in Brice's lap responded, "Yeah -- I mean yes with an 'S'."

"Reverend Howard, Reverend Harris, and Mr. Stevens, you've all agreed to consent to an open adoption. Is everyone comfortable with the terms of the agreement of this open adoption?" Judge Carter asked.

They each replied, "Yes."

"So, Mr. Stevens, these terms are okay with you?" Judge Carter asked.

"Yes. I will be able to visit Rosie once a month and I get to visit her on major holidays and on her birthday," Kwame Stevens said.

"Well can you introduce me to your family, Rosie?" Judge Carter asked.

"That's my daddy with my first mommy, his name is Kamay. And this is my daddy with my new mommy, his name is Daddy. And that's my new mommy and that's my Nana Billie, and that is my baby brother," Rosie said. Then she whispered, "He doesn't have a name yet."

"And you understand what an open adoption means, Rosie?" Judge Carter asked.

Rosie got down from Brice's lap and went behind the Judge's desk and whispered in Judge Carter's ear,

"I'm going to get more birthday presents and Christmas presents too."

June was embarrassed because Rosie didn't lower her voice. Rosie went back to sit in Brice's lap.

"Well I think this is a beautiful thing and I wish you nothing but success with your new family, Rosie. This paper I'm holding says that your new name is now April Rose Howard. And I'm signing the petition for adoption right now."

Everybody clapped. June decided to give Rosie the name of April so she would be included in the month name trend of the women in her family, *April* Rose, Momma *May*, and *June* Marie, but they would still call her Rosie.

When everyone stood up, Brice and Kwame shook hands. June hugged Kwame first and then everyone else until she got to her husband. He reached down and pulled up her chin and kissed her fully on the lips. Then he said in her ear, "I know now that you were right about this and I thank you for sticking to what you believed would be best for Rosie. I love you so much."

"I love you too, babe," June said.

Because of Crystal's confession the prosecution dropped all the charges against Jackson. By that time the banks were alerted that Jackson's bank accounts had indeed been hacked, but the funds had already disappeared as had Jackson's real trust fund. Jackson was so happy to be freed he told his father he didn't need the trust fund money and that he would be more than willing to work for the rest of his life.

The weeks following Joe Jr.'s successful defense of Jackson, his practice blossomed with clients from all walks of life. He also ended up hiring two more attorneys who decided to leave the Public Defender's Office to practice law with him and Sandy.

Mario hired an attorney to represent Crystal for her criminal case but she fired him instantly, pled guilty, and remained incarcerated while awaiting sentencing. She asked not to have any contact with her father or any members of her family.

Mario had Cady transported to a rehabilitation center two hours away from Palm Beach County in Orlando, Florida where she began physical therapy because she had to learn how to walk and talk all over again. He and Bettina also relocated there to be near his family and to give their marriage a fresh new start.

Bettina stayed behind for a couple of days to ensure that all the furniture was taken care of by the movers. June parked in front of Bettina's home and watched the movers load the last of the boxes. She watched Bettina darting back and forth between the house and the moving truck and she was saddened about all that had happened between them. Mario attempted to contact June with numerous phone calls and texts but after June confirmed with her husband that Mario did confess his love for her to him, she ignored them all.

Bettina finally spotted her and waved for her to get out of the car.

"I'm glad I caught you before you left," June said.

"I am too," Bettina said.

"I'm so sorry about this whole thing, Bettina."

"It wasn't all on you, June, you were right. Mario should have told me the whole story."

"I just wanted to tell you before you left that you were a really good friend and I wish things had gone differently."

"I know. We're not going to be able to remain friends now are we?" Bettina said.

"No. The bible says, 'A fool has no delight in understanding, but in expressing his own heart' that's what Mario did. He had no business expressing his covetous heart to my husband. It was not an action that he meant to be fruitful but destructive. Mario is a coveter."

"What exactly is that anyway? I thought God wanted to grant the desires of our heart."

"Everybody remembers that part of the scripture but they fail to remember the beginning of it, the complete scripture says, "Delight yourself also in the Lord, and He shall grant you the desires of your heart," Mario's heart was not delighted by the Lord but rancid with covetousness. It's wanting something somebody else has, not something like somebody else has, the very thing that they have and whether Mario will ever admit it or not, he tried to break up my marriage. So, as far I'm concerned that means that I can no longer have him in my life. I think that would be the best and most respectful thing to do for you and Brice. I'm not blaming him entirely. Some of this is my fault because instead of making a life with Brice, I tried to fold him into the life I already had without making any changes or compromise."

"I understand, I truly never thought there would be a day that you weren't my good friend. But I made a vow to Mario before God and I need to give my marriage a chance, so I do understand but I'm going to miss our friendship greatly," Bettina said.

"Me too," June said.

"If you ever need me, I'll still be there for you," Bettina said through her tears.

"Me too," June said and they embraced and said a final goodbye.

June was left with that feeling she felt whenever she had to say goodbye to someone she cared about, a feeling of abandonment. It's what she had been trying to explain to Brice that she never wanted Rosie to feel. It's why it was hard for her to get close to anyone.

June had one more visitation to make on her way home. When she turned down Two Touch's street she waved hello to the twins who were riding their bikes in the circle of the cul de sac. She parked in Debra Walters driveway and prayed for strength before she got out of the car to knock on the door.

Mr. Walters opened the door. "Hi, Pastor June. Please come in. She's in the living room. The woman has not shed a single tear, but she won't move much either. She sits there all day and all night like she's expecting him to come walking back through the door. Now that's not normal is it?"

"I don't know, Brother Walters, she could still be in shock. People grieve in different ways but I'm glad you called." June said.

When Pastor June entered Debra's house there was a noticeable difference compared to any other visit, usually the house is immaculate, today it was a complete mess.

"How you holding up, Debra?" Pastor June asked softly as she sat down next to Debra.

Debra looked at Pastor June for a couple of minutes then said, "I was 15 when I was pregnant with Demetrius. I tried everything to end that pregnancy. I drank, I smoked, I ran into stuff on purpose. So when he was born with all those complications, I blamed myself. I decided that I didn't deserve anybody's help. So I worked really hard. I never been on welfare, never took food stamps, never been on housing. I wanted to be an example to him. For the next 15 years it was just me and him. How could I not know that he was a monster?"

"Debra, I wish I had something to tell you that could bring you some comfort but truly I don't. I was very fond of Demetrius, I was fooled too. I do know that the bible says we are either vessels of honor or dishonor. I think he was conflicted and confused spiritually but you are so strong, and you've been strong for so long. I want you to know that you really can let go now. God wants to carry all your burdens and renew you with His strength. Give them over to him one by one."

"How? I feel like I've been stabbed. When the police came and seized all that stuff he had in the shed out back; knives, guns, needles, and stuff I didn't recognize, I felt like my baby was stabbing me with each new thing I saw them pull out of there."

"Then start there. Tell the Lord just how you feel about all that you feel. He will listen and I assure you that he can lighten that load. You still have two little ones who need that strength restored."

Debra Walters then laid her head in Pastor June's lap and after several more minutes she finally begin letting go.

When June returned home she found Billie in the easy chair in the family room holding her new son. She and Brice still had not given the baby a name and time was quickly running out. If they didn't come up with some name soon the hospital would list him as Baby Boy Howard on the final birth certificate.

Rosie was playing with her Barbie dolls on the floor at Billie's feet. "Mommy, come and play with me and Nana Billie."

"I can't right now, sweetheart, I'm officiating a wedding in a little bit but I promise to play with you as soon as I come back, okay?" June said.

"So they're just going to get married without inviting anybody?" Billie asked.

"Yep. Jackson said they don't need anybody there," June said.

"What did you do, Junie? I know you're up to something," Billie said.

"Well I can't help it if I accidentally bumped into his parents," June said.

"Bumped into them where?" Billie asked.

"Uh, at the front door of their house," June said and they both laughed.

"Well, you tell that boy I'm praying for him and that sweet girl. She sho is sweet on him," Billie said.

"Yeah, they've been coming to marriage counseling and Sunday morning worship service pretty regular now. I'm very proud of how much Jackson has turned his life around," June said.

"He's working. A good man always provides for his family. Speaking of which, where yours at?" Billie asked.

"I don't know. He said he had something to get. You know, Brice, he's probably gone out and bought some kind of electric car or something," June said with a chuckle.

June ran upstairs and ran back down carrying her white robe and said, "Well, I'm heading to the church now. I'll see you guys when I get back."

Before she left she kissed Billie on the forehead, Rosie on the cheek and baby Howard on his nose.

When Pastor June arrived at St. Mark Church she was pleasantly surprised to see Nedra with her husband Jackson Bonnen the II.

"Where's the happy couple?" Pastor June asked.

"Jackson is in the bathroom and Lakesha is back in one of those rooms with her mother," Nedra said.

"I'm so glad you decided to come," Pastor June said.

"He's trying to be his own man, that's all I ever wanted. I will support him in doing that. Especially after all he just went through," Jackson Bonnen II said.

"Yeah and this little guy, is my world and I want him to have a happy home. I'll show Lakesha the ropes, she'll be all right won't she baby boy?" Nedra said to her grandson who was sitting on her hip.

Pastor June smiled. She smiled even wider when she saw Jackson appear at the entrance of the sanctuary in a black and white tuxedo.

"My, my, my you clean up well, Sir," June said.

Jackson smiled. He hugged his mother and extended his hand to shake his father's hand but his father pulled him close to him and they embraced instead. It was very moving for Nedra as well as Pastor June. Then they all turned their attention to Lakesha as she stood in the entrance way. She was simply stunning. Her hair was in an updo with a few braids falling freely down her back. There were little white flowers inserted into the braids that were on the top of her head. Her skin was flawless and her full lips were a beautiful shade of pink. Her dress was white and gathered in the front just below her hips and then flowed down to her ankles. Her dress also had a little train in the back. Jackson made a move to go towards her but Pastor June stopped him.

"Mr. Reynolds?" Pastor June said to her musician.

The musician began singing a Stevie Wonder song in acapella,

> *"Here we are, on earth, together, It's you and I,*
> *God has made us fall in love, it's true.*
> *I've really found someone like you.*
> *Well, in my mind, We can conquer the world.*
> *In love, you and I...*
> *'Cause in my mind You will stay here always.*
> *In love, you and I..."*

As the musician sang, Lakesha walked slowly down the aisle. Her mother was sobbing and trying to take pictures with her camera at the same time. When Lakesha was midway down the aisle, Jackson Bonnen II went to her and escorted her for the rest of the way to his son who was anxiously waiting by the altar. Lakesha reached out to take Jackson's hand once she reached him. Pastor June began the ceremony. When it got to the part of the ceremony for the vows, they decided to say their own.

"You are the love of my life. I will always be proud of that. You loved me when nobody else would and I will always love you for that. I love everything about you. I love that you're smart without throwing it in peoples face. I love that you are a good mother to my son and how you manage to take care of him and me. I love you, Lakesha, and I vow to love you for the rest of my life," Jackson said.

Then it was Lakesha's turn she said, "I love you too. I was willing to love you any way that you would let me. I love you because of all the things you don't know you are. I love you because even when you were mean, I could feel your heart was tender. I will always love you no matter what. I make that vow to you."

"You may exchange the rings at this time," June said.

Nedra handed Jackson the ring that his grandmother willed to him. It was huge and fit perfectly on Lakesha's small finger. Jackson Bonnen II handed Lakesha a wedding band too and she placed it on Jackson's finger.

"Now, Jackson, you may kiss your bride," Pastor June said.

They kissed a long passionate kiss and Pastor June and Nedra began blowing bubbles at them as they left the church and got into the waiting cab. They were headed to the airport for an all expense paid honeymoon in the Bahamas courtesy of Jackson's father.

Jackson Bonnen II confided in Pastor June that Jackson would be able to quit the car sales job he had because he had a job waiting for him at his accounting firm when he returned from his honeymoon. His wedding present was a new house that was close to him and Nedra so that they could be near their grandson.

Pastor June was pleased with how everything had turned out for Jackson and Lakesha. She smiled all the way home and listened to the oldie goldie radio station to further feed into her upbeat mood. When she arrived at the house she spotted her husband backing his suburban into the driveway. She rounded the back of the truck in time to see him rolling down a lavender striped spanking brand new motorcycle with the words, "Warrior Woman" in cursive written across the sides. Her hands immediately went to her face in surprise.

"Brice, you bought me a motorcycle? I thought you didn't want me on one of those things?" June said excitely.

"I know, I know. But look honey, we've been through a rough time in the last couple of months. First with you being on bed rest, than delivering the baby early, and the trial, I wanted to gift you with something that would make you happy. And I know that it's been particularly hard for you to share so much of yourself with so many people, me, Rosie and now the new baby and Billie. I know how important your independence is. So this way I thought you could go on long bike rides and commune with God and have some alone time. As long as you wear your safety gear, promise me please," Brice said as he handed her a matching helmet.

"I promise," June said while hugging him tightly.

"Well, are you going to give it a spin or what?" Brice asked.

"You better know it. Let me change my clothes and I'll be right out," June said and then entered the house.

Rosie ran to June in the foyer and said, "Yay, mommy's home. Are you ready to play with me and Nana Billie? She went to sleep but now maybe you can wake her up so we can play."

June looked into the family room from the foyer and she could see Billie sitting in the easy chair, holding the baby. She did look asleep but June knew that something was wrong because although the baby was in her arms, her head was slumped down instead of tilted backwards.

June dropped the motorcycle helmet and yelled, "Brice!!"

Brice ran into the house and was only steps behind June. When she made it to where Billie was seated in the chair she took the baby out of Billie's arm and handed him to Brice. She checked for Billie's pulse, but found none.

"Call 911, Brice, right now!" June yelled through her sobs.

She reached out and grabbed Billie and pulled her lifeless body to her chest and began yelling, "No God, not Billie. Please God don't take her from me now, please, Lord," June cried loudly and began speaking and sobbing incoherently.

When the ambulance came, the medics pronounced Billie dead on arrival or DOA. June was hysterically crying on her husband's shoulders. One of the medics who knew June from church gave her a sedative to calm her down. Brice called Myrtle and before he knew it, half of the St. Mark church was in his living room. By that time June had gone upstairs and was asleep.

"I am so sorry, Supervising Elder Howard. What else can we do?" Myrtle asked.

"Just be here for her, Myrtle. Right now she feels like Billie was all the family she had. That old girl tried to hang on but I could feel she wasn't long for the world. I just didn't have the heart to say anything to June. She was so busy with the trial and everything. I had hoped I was wrong," Brice said.

"Well, I'm not going anywhere. You take care of your Supervising Elder business and St. Mark and me will take care of our pastor, don't you worry about a thing," Myrtle said.

True to her word, over the next several days Myrtle, Mila and the Pastor's Aid Board from St. Mark church practically moved in with Pastor June and Supervising Elder Howard. They handled all the meals, all the telephone calls, Rosie and the baby. Flowers were arriving from everywhere. Everyone all over the state of Florida knew Billie or the Reverend Bella Grant. Flowers came from churches all over not only from June's district but from churches all over the state in and outside of their church denomination. Finally, Brice had to begin redirecting the flowers to the funeral home.

# 28

*"I have **covet**ed no one's silver or gold or apparel."* ~Acts 20:33

On the day of Billie's funeral, June finally started looking and feeling a little more normal. She had simply been distraught and was kept sedated for the first few days following Billie's death. This morning she came downstairs determined to make it to the funeral so she could formally say goodbye to her mother in ministry, her dearest friend.

As she sipped her coffee at the breakfast counter she asked Myrtle, "Where's the program for the funeral?"

"They're at the church, Pastor," Myrtle said.

"Who's preaching?" June asked.

"We put Supervising Elder Howard down to preach. We didn't think you would want to do it," Myrtle said.

"I'm preaching," she snapped as she glared at both Brice and Myrtle.

"That's fine, honey. We just didn't want to add to your grief, that's all," Brice said.

"I'm sorry, I just feel so betrayed," June said.

Brice went to embrace her and said, "I know

sweetheart, I know. This too shall pass, you'll see."

"The hurt doesn't go away, I'll just get used to it like with Momma May. I know I'm being selfish but I keep feeling like now I got nobody left." June said and began sobbing all over again.

Myrtle looked at Brice as if to say, *She's in no condition to preach this funeral.*

As Brice stroked June's hair he said to Myrtle, "It'll be all right. She will be all right."

Then he said to June, "You will always have me. Remember when I told you how God seems to know when to fill us? He may have taken Billie but now he's given you a brand new person to love."

"You're right, I know. I'm just really grieving. I'm sorry I keep snapping at you, Myrtle," June said.

"Listen, you'll always have me too, for what it's worth," Myrtle said.

"That's worth a lot, thanks," June said.

June had cried so much over those past few days that her eyes were so swollen she felt the need to wear sun glasses to the funeral. She dressed in her plainest black robe. And as she stood in the mirror braiding her hair, her thoughts again returned to Momma May and now Billie and an overwhelming feeling of loneliness overtook her. And Brice had to practically carry her to the car.

At Billie's funeral Pastor June, Supervising Elder Howard, Pastor Brown, and several other pastors from the district led the procession into the sanctuary. It is customary for each person to stop at the casket to view the body before taking their seats; this included the clergy as well. Supervising Elder Howard led the procession but he pulled Pastor June to his side to view Billie's body.

LEE M. SAPP

Pastor June stroked Billie's face, her heart ached as she imagined never hearing her loud raspy laugh again. She became overwhelmed and began sobbing heavily again. Supervising Elder Howard caught her and escorted her to the center seat in the pulpit. Reverend Danny suddenly appeared with a linen handkerchief for Pastor June.

Pastor June was oblivious to what was happening during the service. She noticed that the church was packed full of people downstairs as well as in the balcony. The members of St. Mark Church adored Billie not only because of what she meant to Pastor June but because she often shared her many gifts with them. Pastor June especially appreciated that Cowboy Joe, Wendy, Joe Jr., and Lily were in attendance as well.

The bishop was out of the country but he sent a resolution. There were several resolutions from a variety of organizations that Billie belonged to or was affiliated with, many were women's rights groups and of course one from Zephaniah Church.. Billie was the founder and pastor of Zephaniah Church in Arcadia, Florida for over twenty years. It was before the Zephaniah congregation that Pastor June preached her trial sermon. And they also put her through to the Annual Convention for ministry.

When Pastor June saw Billie's church's name printed on the program she remembered a conversation she had years ago with Billie concerning the odd name of her church. She recalled what Billie told her,

*"Zephaniah was a particularly political prophet. He actively opposed legislation that promoted a sinful society. That's how my church started; I thought it was a fitting name. It never occurred to me that nobody could pronounce it."*

Pastor June remembered Billie followed up that statement with her loud raspy laugh.

Members of Zephaniah traveled two hours all the way to West Palm Beach, Florida in their church bus in order to attend there founder's funeral. Billie's former church choir did two selections as well as the St. Mark's choir. There were almost a dozen of her peers there who spoke in reflection of the Rev. Bella Grant, describing who she was to them, how much she meant to them or a particular community. Pastor June thoroughly enjoyed hearing all the sentiments.

As it became close to the time for the eulogy, it occurred to her that she had not prepared a sermon at all. She knew that she didn't want to preach from the customary scriptures people usually preached at funerals. So Paul's words about finishing the race or Christ saying, "Well done my good, faithful servant" just would not do. Then she thought of a perfect scripture. When it was finally time for the eulogy everyone was on pins and needles because Pastor June continued to cry during much of the service.

She stood and went before the podium. She looked over the crowd, from left to right and then up into the balcony. She removed her sun glasses and put on her reading glasses. Then said simply, "Let us pray."

After she prayed she asked everyone to turn in their bibles to the book of Hebrews chapter 11 beginning at the 13th verse then she begin reading,

*"These all died in faith, not having received the promises, but having seen them afar off were assured of them, embraced them and confessed that they were strangers and pilgrims on the earth. For those who say such things declare plainly that they seek a homeland.*

*And truly if they had called to mind that country from which they had come out, they would have had opportunity to return, But now they desire a better, that is, a heavenly country. Therefore God is not ashamed to be called their God, for He has prepared a city for them.*

"The Reverend Bella Grant is in God's heavenly city. She's there surrounded by folks of good company. I can imagine her sitting at the table with Sojourner Truth, Jerena Lee, Lena Horne, and many other women who blazed the trail and paid their dues. Oh I'm sure there are plenty of men there as well."

Everyone laughed at that because everyone knew that Billie was a huge flirt and liked being in the company of good looking young men.

"She worked hard like other women who had gone on before her. She was every bit a hard worker as Martha was and still had the dedication to the worship of Christ that Mary had, Martha's sister. She was an evangelist and a preacher like the woman at the well and Mary Magdalene. I can hear her laughing her loud raspy laugh as she teases Eve about the state she left us women in. And I can see her embracing her best friend, my Momma May."

At this point Pastor June begin to cry again but quickly composed herself and continued.

"I can see her -- I can see her being compassionate to all the women who went on ahead of her because of a violent end. These women were her passion, her life's work.

"The scripture we read earlier really reminds me of my dear friend, Billie. She was never really quite comfortable here on earth. She lived her life knowing that this was her temporary home and still she made it bearable for so many. God means for us all to be like she was, to live each day as though it would be our last and most importantly, like it was the last day for us to help someone in need. We are to take what we need but give all we have and that's what Billie did. There will be a new hurt in our hearts because of the space that she used to fill with her bright smile and deep laughter. Where her counsel used to sooth our hurt or feed our hunger.

"But my tears are not for Billie, they are for me and for all of us who can feel the hole that she leaves in our lives but we also need to be rejoicing, amen, because she is finally at home. Yes, now she is finally at home. Home -- where they say the walls are made of pearl and the streets are paved with gold. Home -- where she is young and beautiful. Home -- where her body is at its best, no more aches and pains. No, no, my dear, dear friend is now at home with the Lord, in God's heavenly city. And so we have good reason to rejoice. Amen"

At that, Pastor June returned to her seat while everyone else stood to their feet shouting "Amen" and "Hallelujah!" When the shouting quieted down, Supervising Elder Howard stood up and gave the instructions for the committal and the repast. The Sunday Morning Café was closed to the public so that all of Billie's peers, the pastors, and clergy could dine together. Pastor June and Supervising Elder Howard made an appearance but they didn't stay. Pastor June wanted to return home to her children. Wendy stayed behind at the Sunday Morning Café to help serve the clergy who attended the repast.

Joe Jr. walked Cowboy Joe to his truck after they returned from the gravesite. "By the way, Dad, I forgot to thank you for Jimyia. She was a huge help."

"Who?" Cowboy Joe asked.

"Jimyia, the investigator you sent over," Joe Jr. said.

"Son, I don't know anybody named Jimyia," Cowboy Joe said.

"Really?" Joe Jr. asked.

"Are you sure she said I sent her?"

"I thought for sure she did," Joe Jr. said.

When June got home she told her husband to sit down because she wanted to wait on him for a change. She prepared a plate for him with the food that Wendy wrapped up at the church. They sat down with Rosie and had lunch, or linner as June called it when it was too late for lunch but still too early for dinner.

After their meal June sat down in the easy chair where Billie had drawn her last breath holding the baby. Brice sat on the couch next to her smiling at their son when Pastor June said,

"Brice, I want to name him after Billie. We can spell it, B I L L E E, instead of a 'Y', Billee Grant Howard. That way she'll always be around and we can remember her each time he laughs."

"I think that's a very suitable name, honey. Billee Grant Howard it is."

Once baby Billee had fallen asleep, June put him in the bassinct that was at her bedside. Brice and Rosie decided to take a nap as well. June took her braid a loose and dressed in blue jeans and t-shirt then grabbed her motorcycle helmet. She looked back at her husband before she left the room and he winked at her and she smiled back at him.

On her way downstairs her cell phone began vibrating. The caller I.D. said, "Unknown" and she answered. "Hello, this is Pastor June."

"When I called my momma, she hung up on me; she wouldn't give me a chance to talk," Mac said through her tears.

"Eartha? Where are you?"

"I'm far away. Please listen, I can't talk long. Tell my momma that her house is paid off so she don't have to worry about that anymore. And be sure to tell my family that they made me choose. Okay, tell them that their rejection made me choose."

"Eartha, please come back I'm sure we can work things out with your family, they love you, I know they do."

"It's too late now. Jimyia and I are starting over. We're making a new life," Mac said.

After several more seconds of silence Mac said,

"Please tell my family that I love them," and she hung up the phone.

June released a long sigh as she realized that Mac and whoever Jimyia was had in fact stolen the missing money from Jackson's case. She decided to include her on her list of prayer petitions for the day.

June put her helmet on, started her motorcycle's engine, and drove away. She felt so free feeling the wind blowing through her hair as she drove down a long winding country road not far from her house. Soon she entered an area of Loxahatchee where the land had not yet been totally cleared. There were acres and acres of wildflowers that caught her attention. Watching the flowers as she passed them by June again thought of her friend, her mother in ministry, Billie.

She decided to leave the road and drive right into

the middle of the field of wildflowers and park. She got off the bike and lay down on the ground amongst the wild flowers. There were purple, yellow, and red flowers. She thought of how Billie was so much like those wildflowers. They grew where ever they wanted, daring to be bright and bold. They had the audacity to spread their fragrance all around everywhere even though the world only viewed them as worthless weeds.

June decided that she would continue to meet with Billie in this field covered with bright wildflowers because as she closed her eyes and lifted her face to the sun, breathing in their loud fragrance, she could feel Billie's bright spirit dwelling there and her heart began to hurt just a little less.

Coming Soon: Book III Pastor June and the Witness: Billie's Story.

# ABOUT THE AUTHOR

The Reverend Lee M. Sapp was born and raised in Sarasota, Florida. She currently resides in Loxahatchee, Florida with her husband, Children and three Chihuahuas. Rev. Sapp has a bachelor's degree in Religion and is scheduled to complete a Masters of Divinity degree in May of 2014. She is a Certified Court Transcriber. An adoptive mother and an active adoption and children's rights advocate.

# THE COVETERS

Made in the USA
Charleston, SC
13 March 2014